AF797577

Riders of Glory

Also by Robert Vaughan

The Tenderfoot

On the Oregon Trail

Cold Revenge

Iron Horse

Outlaw Justice

Western Fiction Ten Pack

Orphan Cowboy

Slaughter at Rebel Ridge

Reckoning Day

Trail to Brimstone

Hidden Hero

Outpost in the Desert

The Hunt for Big Cat

The Founders Series

The Western Adventures of Cade McCall

Faraday Series

Lucas Cain Series

Chaney Brothers Westerns

Arrow and Saber Series

The Crocketts Series

Remington Series

...and many more

Riders of Glory

Robert Vaughan

WOLFPACK
PUBLISHING
— EST 2013 —

Riders of Glory
Paperback Edition
Copyright © 2025 by Robert Vaughan

Wolfpack Publishing
1707 E. Diana Street
Tampa, FL 33609

www.wolfpackpublishing.com

All rights reserved. No part of this book may be reproduced in any form or by any electronic or mechanical means, including information storage and retrieval systems, without express written permission from the publisher, except for the use of brief quotations in reviews. Any use of this publication to train generative artificial intelligence (AI) technologies is expressly prohibited.

This book is a work of fiction. References to historical events, real people, or real places are used fictitiously. Any similarity to real persons, living or dead, is purely coincidental and not intended by the author.

All brand names and product names used in this book are trademarks, registered trademarks, or trade names of their respective holders. Wolfpack Publishing is not associated with any product or vendor in this book.

Paperback ISBN 979-8-89567-147-4
eBook ISBN 979-8-89567-146-7
LCCN 2025930771

Riders of Glory

Prologue

Battle of Wounded Knee
December 29, 1890

The biting chill of the Dakota winter stung Captain Nelson Pickett's face as he surveyed the frozen camp at Wounded Knee Creek. The barren landscape stretched into an endless horizon, dusted with snow, and the steel-gray sky threatened more. His horse shifted beneath him, and he tightened his gloved hands on the reins, his breath visible in the icy air. Below, the scene weighed heavily on him—a tired, huddled mass of Lakota Sioux, women clutching children, some barely more than skin and bone, their hollow eyes fixed on the frozen ground. Chief Big Foot lay motionless on a crude litter, too sick to stand, his breath a rattling whisper.

Beside Nelson, Lieutenant Dan Calhoun adjusted his saddle, his face pale. The two had graduated in the same class at West Point, but this was Dan's first encounter with the harshness of the West's brutal campaigns. They exchanged a glance, both understanding the gravity of what was about to happen.

Colonel James Forsyth's voice barked orders from the ridge, carrying over the eerily quiet camp. Behind them, the Hotchkiss guns stood ready, their dark barrels pointed down like silent birds of prey. Nelson's troop was but one of many—nearly five hundred soldiers encircled the encampment, tension thick in the air.

"Prepare to disarm them!" Forsyth's voice echoed coldly.

Nelson shifted uneasily in his saddle. He had seen enough bloodshed to know when things were on the verge of spiraling out of control. The Lakota had surrendered—there was no fight left in them, only exhaustion and hunger. They had nothing, not even hope. But orders were orders.

"Dan," Nelson said, his voice low but firm, "tell the men—no one fires unless it's absolutely necessary."

Dan nodded quickly, riding down the line to relay the order. Nelson watched him go, a knot tightening in his chest. He respected Dan's instincts, but this was a test the lieutenant had never faced. Nelson feared it would be a day neither of them could forget.

The soldiers marched into the camp, moving among the ragged teepees, pulling out the men, their rough hands searching for weapons. The Lakota stood in stunned silence, more from weariness than defiance. And then, it happened—a single gunshot, piercing the stillness. No one knew its source. Maybe it was an Indian, maybe a jittery soldier—but its effect was instant.

Chaos.

The air erupted with the deafening roar of gunfire. The Hotchkiss guns spat shells indiscriminately into the camp, shredding canvas, flesh, and bone. Screams tore through the frigid air. Nelson's heart lurched as the violence swallowed everything in its path.

"Cease fire! Hold your fire!" Nelson's voice rang out, but it was drowned in the cacophony. Soldiers fired wildly, their faces frozen in shock or grim satisfaction, lost in the madness.

Dan appeared at his side, eyes wide in disbelief. "Sir, they're killing them! The women, the children—"

"I know," Nelson snapped, though his anger wasn't directed at Dan.

Nelson's gaze swept the camp. A group of women and children huddled in terror, caught in the crossfire. His decision came without thought. Spurring his horse, he charged toward them, his saber drawn, cutting through the chaos.

"Come with me!" he called to Dan, who followed without hesitation.

Bullets whizzed past, screams mingling with the thunder of gunfire. Nelson's troop, a disciplined unit in the middle of the madness, followed his lead. They reached the huddled group, dismounting quickly.

"Get them out! Now!" Nelson ordered, his voice sharp with urgency. His men moved swiftly, forming a protective cordon around the survivors, their bodies shielding the women and children as they led them out of the killing zone.

Nelson ran ahead, clearing the way. His breath came in ragged gasps, the cold biting into his lungs. All around him, the carnage continued—Lakota men fell where they stood, women wailed over lifeless bodies. The snow, once pure and white, was now stained red.

Finally, they reached the edge of the camp, out of the immediate danger. Nelson turned back, his chest heaving, his eyes scanning the battlefield. The massacre was nearly over. The Hotchkiss guns had fallen silent, and the sporadic crack of rifles had faded, leaving only the groans of the dying and the occasional shot as soldiers finished off the wounded.

Nelson's hands trembled as he sheathed his saber. Wiping his face, he realized his glove was smeared with blood. He hadn't noticed the cut on his cheek until now—but it didn't matter. Nothing about this day mattered except the lives that had been lost.

They had saved a few, but it wasn't enough.

Dan approached, his voice hollow. "They didn't stand a chance."

"No," Nelson replied, his tone hard and cold. "They didn't."

The Medal of Honor that would later be pinned to his chest was meaningless. It was a bitter token, a reminder of the innocents he hadn't saved.

Nelson mounted his horse and cast one last glance at the shattered camp. The wind carried the sobs of the few survivors who remained. His men waited in silence, their faces pale, their eyes downcast.

There were no words to offer. Nothing would undo the bloodshed.

The ride back to the fort felt endless, the cold biting deeper, the silence more oppressive.

No one would ever speak of the massacre again.

But Nelson would never forget.

One

Marty McGuire sat on a dark leather sofa in the outer office of the *New York Daily Banner*. The room was mostly empty, except for a small man hunched over a desk—a clerk stenographer with a green visor and wire-framed glasses, clicking away at his typewriter. Marty barely noticed him, her mind was elsewhere.

She'd heard that some businesses were beginning to hire women for these roles, but they were given a different title: typewriters. Women weren't considered skilled enough to be called clerks. But Marty wasn't here to be a clerk. She had her sights set on something far more significant than office work.

Her goal was to become a reporter for the *Banner*, the largest and most influential newspaper in the country. The odds were stacked against her—only 888 women were in the field compared to 21,000 men—but that didn't matter. She knew those odds made her task more difficult, but she had wanted to be a newspaper reporter for as long as she could remember, and she intended to do it, if not at the *Banner*, then at another paper.

As she waited, she looked around the office, taking in the large clock on the wall, the ornate umbrella stand, and the brass spittoons scattered about. The walls were decorated with front pages from the paper's history, marking significant moments with bold headlines and tight columns of text.

She noticed the evolution of the newspaper—the older issues had eight-column pages with five-and-a-half-point type, while the later editions had six-column pages and eight-point type. She supposed that change was inevitable, just like the change she intended to bring about in her own career.

Suddenly, a loud voice erupted from behind the frosted glass wall separating the reception area from the newsroom.

"You can't find out? What do you mean you can't find out?"

The voice belonged to Charles Talbot, the publisher, and it cut through the usual office noise like a knife. The place went quiet as Talbot's voice continued to boom.

"I am the publisher of the largest newspaper in New York! When I send a reporter to find out which commissioner is going to be indicted and why, I expect an answer!"

"But, Mr. Talbot," a quieter voice tried to reason, "I've tried every way I know to find out. Those grand jury transcripts are sealed tight. It's a closely guarded secret."

"By thunder, I pay you to find out those secrets, no matter how guarded!" Talbot barked. "Get on the telephone and call someone! What's the use of having these gadgets if no one uses them?"

Marty stood and walked over to the clerk's desk.

"Excuse me, sir," she said. "May I borrow a piece of paper and a pencil?"

"Yes, certainly," the clerk said as he handed them over.

Marty quickly scribbled a note to Talbot, her handwriting clear and direct. She folded the paper and handed it back to the clerk.

"Give this to Mr. Talbot, please."

The clerk hesitated, glancing at the frosted glass door. "Now's not a good time. He's a little upset."

"Exactly," Marty said. "It's the perfect time."

The clerk looked at her, then at the note, and finally nodded. He pushed through the door into the lion's den.

Marty moved to the window, watching the street below. The city was alive with activity, trolley cars clattering by, horse-drawn carriages navigating the busy roads, and crowds of people moving purposefully along the sidewalks. New York was a place where things happened, where people didn't wait for opportunities—they made them.

From behind the door, she heard Talbot's voice again, this time sharper, more focused.

"What's this?" Marty heard Talbot's voice say. "Where did you get this note?"

"I'm sorry, Mr. Talbot," the clerk stammered, "I tried to explain that you were too busy to…"

"Nonsense! I want to meet this man."

Marty turned as Talbot burst into the room, his presence filling the room. He was a short man with a large gut, a bald head, and bushy sideburns that made him look like a bulldog.

"I beg your pardon?" the clerk replied. "Where is who?"

"Who do you think I'm talking about?" Mr. Talbot glanced down at the note. "Marty McGuire."

"But Mr. Talbot," the clerk started, then he was interrupted by Marty.

"I am Marty McGuire," she said.

"You? You wrote this note?"

"That's right."

Talbot's eyes narrowed. "Listen, I don't have time for games. I run a newspaper with a circulation of over half a million, and that's daily. Now, what's this note all about?"

"It's about the information you want about the commissioner's indictment," Marty replied. "I can get it for you within two hours—if you hire me as a reporter."

Talbot snorted, tossing the note aside. "I don't have time for nonsense."

"Fine," Marty said, heading for the door. "I'll take it to the *Journal*."

Talbot paused. "Do you know which commissioner is about to be indicted?"

"Not yet, but I will know soon," Marty said. "And I'll give it to the *Journal* if you don't hire me."

"Why? Do you think Hearst will give you a job?"

"Probably not," she admitted, "but they'll get the story, and you won't."

Talbot studied her for a moment, then laughed—a short, barking laugh. "You've got guts, I'll give you that. Fine, bring me the story in two hours, and you've got a job. But you'll start at ten dollars a week as a typewriter."

"I want to be a reporter," Marty said, holding her ground, "and I want fifteen dollars a week."

Talbot stroked his sideburns, considering. "Reporter, twelve-fifty, and you do a column on women's news as well."

"Deal," Marty said, extending her hand.

Talbot shook it while a smile formed on his lips. Marty didn't smile back. She had two hours to prove herself, and she didn't intend to waste a single minute.

Marty McGuire made her way to the circuit clerk's office. She'd made a bold promise to Talbot out of sheer desperation, hoping it would get her the job. The truth was, she didn't have the first idea of how to get the information he wanted. Still, she was here now, and backing down wasn't an option.

As she entered the office, she found it crowded with half a dozen men, all wearing hats with press cards stuck in their headbands. They were hounding the clerk behind the counter.

"We have deadlines to meet," one of the reporters yelled, echoed by three others. "When are you going to give us the information?"

"I'm sorry, gentlemen," the frazzled clerk said. "The prosecutor has left specific instructions that no information be given out at this time."

"At this time? Then, pray tell, when will it be given?" another reporter demanded.

"I'm sorry, gentlemen, there's nothing I can do," the clerk repeated.

"Yeah, well, being sorry doesn't write our copy," one of the reporters muttered.

Marty felt a knot tighten in her stomach. If these experienced, hard-nosed reporters couldn't get anywhere, what chance did she have? She realized her enthusiasm had overridden her common sense. Now, she not only risked not getting the job, but she might also end up looking like a fool. And without anything to identify her as a reporter, she was in an even worse position.

"Yes, miss, can I help you?" the clerk asked, seizing the opportunity to escape the reporters' barrage.

"I'm a reporter," Marty said, the words sounding almost hollow to her own ears.

"Thank goodness they finally sent us a replacement," the clerk said, visibly relieved. "Did Judge Hawkins send you down? Well, no matter. Miss Johnson has taken ill, and we need to get the grand jury minutes certified."

"What? No, you don't—"

"Go on back there to the prosecutor's office," the clerk interrupted. "The transcription is already typed. All you have to do is compare the typed pages with the shorthand notes."

"Miss? Miss, I'm with the *Journal*," one of the reporters said. "When you're finished, could I get an interview?"

"And me as well?" another reporter chimed in.

The clerk stepped in between Marty and the eager reporters. "She has no authority to release information," he said firmly.

"Authority? Who cares?" one of the reporters replied. "She'll have all the information as soon as she reads those notes. That's all we need."

Suddenly, it clicked for Marty. The clerk had mistaken her for a court reporter, not a newspaper reporter, likely because there were so few female journalists. That mistake was her ticket to the very information she needed. But there was a risk. If she got caught accessing court documents unauthorized, she could be in serious trouble—contempt of court, maybe even jail time.

She hesitated for a moment, weighing her options.

"Please, miss, get on with it," the clerk urged.

That settled it. Marty nodded, a thin smile forming on her lips. "Very well. Where are the court notes?"

"In there," the clerk said, pointing to a door. "You won't be disturbed."

"Remember, miss, I asked for the interview first!" one of the reporters shouted as Marty walked through the door.

The room she entered was a legal library lined with books on all sides. A long oak table, surrounded by burgundy leather chairs, dominated the space. On the table lay a stack of typewritten pages and a stenographer's tablet. Marty sat down, grateful for her shorthand skills, and began comparing the notes. She was fully immersed in her work when the back door of the library opened, and a man stepped in.

He was tall, with blonde hair and blue eyes, wearing a military uniform. A crescent-shaped scar on his cheek caught the light as he raised a hand to his face, unconsciously rubbing it.

"Oh, uh, excuse me, miss," he said, his voice unexpectedly soft. "I didn't expect anyone to be in here. I'm Colonel Nelson Pickett, Tony's brother-in-law."

Marty looked up, her mind quickly assessing the situation. For now, she simply nodded and returned her attention to the documents in front of her.

"Tony?" Marty asked, trying to maintain her composure.

"The prosecutor," Colonel Pickett clarified. "This is his library."

"Oh, yes, of course," Marty replied, her voice steadying, though she could feel a flush creeping up her neck. This wasn't part of the plan. She had hoped to be in and out before anyone noticed, but now she was caught in a situation that was quickly spiraling out of control.

"We were going to talk in here and, oh, here he is now," Colonel Pickett said as another man entered the room.

"Ah, Nelson, there you are," the newcomer said, his eyes narrowing as he spotted Marty. He stopped just inside the door, sizing her up. "Is this a friend of yours?"

"No," Colonel Pickett responded, his brow furrowing. "She was in here when I arrived. I thought…"

"See here, miss, who are you?" the prosecutor demanded, his tone sharp and suspicious.

Before Marty could answer, the clerk who had sent her into the room appeared at the door.

"Clerk, do you know this lady?" the prosecutor asked, his gaze still fixed on Marty.

"Yes, sir," the clerk replied quickly. "She's the reporter Judge Hawkins sent down to certify the grand jury transcripts."

"But I just left Judge Hawkins's chambers," the prosecutor shot back, his voice laced with disbelief. "He apologized to me for not being able to send anyone down."

"Oh? I don't understand, sir," the clerk stammered, turning to Marty, clearly confused. "Miss, didn't you tell me you were the court reporter?"

"Uh, no," Marty said, trying to keep her voice

even. "I just told you I was a reporter. Actually, I'm a newspaper reporter, not a court reporter."

"What?" the prosecutor gasped. "You're a newspaper reporter, and you've been reading these documents?"

"I'm sorry if there's been a misunderstanding," Marty said, edging toward the door.

"Misunderstanding?" The clerk's voice rose in indignation. "A better word would be misrepresentation. Young lady, I'm going to press charges against you. You got in here under false pretenses."

"But I didn't," Marty shot back, standing her ground. "I never told you I was a court reporter. I told you I was a reporter. I never lied."

"She's quite correct," the prosecutor interjected, though his tone was anything but forgiving. "Young lady, I can't take action against you now, but know this—I don't take kindly to deceit. I'll be keeping an eye on you."

Marty nodded, swallowing her pride. "I'll be more careful from now on," she said, backing out of the room, her heart pounding but her expression cool.

The second she was out the door, Marty hurried to the trolley. The ride back to the *Banner* building was a blur, her mind racing. She had the story—against all odds, she'd pulled it off. But as the initial adrenaline faded, she couldn't shake the sting of the looks she'd received, the disapproval in their eyes. It was a hollow victory, tainted by the realization that she'd crossed a line.

She had what she needed to file her story, but the triumph she'd expected felt strangely empty. There was no time to dwell on it, though. If she wanted to work as a reporter, she had to do whatever it took to get the story.

"EXCELLENT WORK, MCGUIRE," Talbot said, a broad grin spreading across his face as he finished reading her story. "Pulitzer and Hearst will be kicking themselves when they see this in the *Banner*. You've earned yourself a job."

Marty felt a surge of satisfaction, a deep sense of accomplishment that washed away any lingering doubts about how she had secured the story. "You mean it?" she asked, her voice steady but tinged with excitement.

"Do I mean it? Of course I do. I gave you my word, didn't I?" Talbot said, his tone firm. "A newspaperman's word is everything. If it's no good, he's no good. I told you I'd hire you, and I stand by that."

"Thank you," Marty said. Without thinking, she reached out and gave Talbot a quick, genuine hug. "You won't regret this, Mr. Talbot. I'll prove you made the right choice."

Talbot cleared his throat, slightly taken aback by the embrace, and made a show of adjusting his jacket. "Well now, let's not make a habit of that, shall we? Not exactly standard office protocol," he said, though the twinkle in his eye revealed that he was more amused than bothered by her enthusiasm.

"I'm sorry," Marty said, stepping back with a sheepish smile. "I'm just really happy, that's all."

Talbot grumbled good-naturedly, "I'll let it slide this time. Now, are you ready to put in some extra hours if it means getting a story?"

"Absolutely," Marty replied, all business now.

"Good," Talbot said with a nod. "There's a ball tonight at the Crestview Country Club honoring the officers of the Lightning Cavalry. I want you to cover it." He scribbled the address on a piece of paper and handed it to her.

Marty took the paper, her mind already shifting gears to the assignment. "All right," she said, glancing at the address. Then, a thought struck her. "Mr. Talbot?"

"Yes?" he replied, raising an eyebrow.

"Is there going to be a war? Are we going to fight Spain over Cuba?"

Talbot chuckled, a sound that was both dismissive and knowing. "If we don't, Hearst is going to be sorely disappointed," he said. "He's invested a lot of ink into the *Maine* incident."

"Incident? You call it an incident? Two hundred and sixty Americans were killed when the *Maine* blew up," Marty said, her voice edged with indignation.

"So says Hearst," Talbot replied calmly.

"You disagree with the numbers?" Marty asked, narrowing her eyes.

"No, the numbers are likely accurate," Talbot conceded. "But I take issue with Hearst's claim that the Spanish were behind the explosion. That's the part that's up for debate. Regardless, it's a moot point now. The wheels are in motion, and a war with Spain seems inevitable." Talbot smiled knowingly. "When the war comes, the Lightning Cavalry will be among the first units sent into battle. That's why they're being honored tonight, and your coverage of the ball will be a good story, especially for our female audience."

Marty nodded, accepting the assignment but not

without a hint of reluctance. "I'll cover the ball, as we agreed. But I want you to know—I consider these women's stories a necessary sideline. I consider myself, first and foremost, a reporter."

Talbot chuckled, holding up her story about the indicted commissioner. "If this is any indication, you're going to be one hell of a reporter," he said with a grin. "Don't worry, McGuire. As long as you keep bringing me stories like this, I'll always make room for them. But remember, I'm counting on you for those women's stories too. Now, go find something suitable for a country club ball. You're going tonight."

"Yes, Mr. Talbot," Marty said, accepting the task with resolve. She wasn't thrilled about the social assignment, but she knew it was part of the job—and she intended to do it well.

Two

The Banner arranged a carriage for Marty, so she arrived at the ball in style. As her carriage rolled up under the portico, hired footmen were quick to assist her, helping her down and escorting her to the door.

The sounds of music, laughter, and lively conversation spilled out across the lawn, welcoming guests as they arrived. It was easy to get caught up in the joyous atmosphere, but Marty reminded herself that she wasn't there as a guest, she was there to work, to capture the essence of the evening for the readers of the *Banner*.

Inside, the ballroom was a riot of color and light, decked out with bunting, flags, and chandeliers that gleamed overhead. The American flag shared space with the regimental banners of the Lightning Cavalry and the bold colors of the Cuban revolutionary movement.

The room was alive with energy. It was full of women who floated about wearing butterfly-bright dresses and golden earbobs that sparkled as they moved. The men were equally striking in their crisp, bright uniforms, their boots polished to a mirror shine. Flowers were tucked behind ears, pinned to dresses, or slipped into the pockets of the officers, who carried themselves with the swagger of men yet untested by battle. The air was filled with the rattle of sabers, the jingle of spurs, and the hum of conversation as New York's high society gathered to celebrate the Lightning Cavalry and their recent call to duty by President McKinley.

Marty danced a few times before she began taking notes. She had a job to do, and the story wouldn't write itself. She jotted down descriptions of the debutantes' dresses and the officers' uniforms, making a point to check out the hors d'oeuvre table, where an elaborate swan-shaped ice sculpture caught her eye. Finally, she stepped into a darkened anteroom, away from the bright lights and swirling colors, to gather her thoughts.

As she stood there, squinting slightly to let the kaleidoscope of the ballroom settle in her mind, a voice cut through the quiet.

"Tell me, Miss McGuire, did you come here under false pretenses as well, or are you a legitimate guest at this affair?" a quiet but resonant voice asked.

Startled, Marty turned to see who had spoken. In the shadows sat an imposing figure, casually seated in a chair near the wall, as far removed from the party as he could get. It was Colonel Pickett.

"Colonel Pickett, good evening," Marty said when she had regained her composure. "I didn't expect to see you here."

"I might say the same of you," Pickett replied, his tone measured but laced with a hint of curiosity. "But

I've had experience with the press in the past and should know better than to underestimate their penchant for snooping."

"You...you make it sound so underhanded," Marty replied, feeling the need to defend her profession.

"Isn't it?" Pickett asked, his eyes narrowing slightly as he studied her.

"No, not at all. Journalism is quite an honorable profession, Colonel, and I'm proud to be a part of it."

Pickett chuckled, the sound deep and slightly cynical. "I must admit, I've never seen a reporter quite like you. Tell me, Miss McGuire, do you ever use your... charms to gain an advantage?"

The question hit Marty like a slap, and she felt a flush of anger rise in her cheeks. "I've never done so, and I think it's ungentlemanly of you to suggest it."

Pickett's expression softened, though his gaze remained sharp. "Forgive me, Miss McGuire," he said, offering a slight, mocking salute. "It's just that we met under circumstances that left me with a rather unflattering impression of your methods. Or do you deny that you used deception to access my brother-in-law's files?"

"I...I didn't intend to deceive," Marty replied, her voice firm. "An opportunity presented itself, and I took it. That's all."

Pickett suddenly laughed, a genuine, hearty sound that took Marty by surprise.

"Well put, Miss McGuire, well put. That's the very strategy we use in battle—seize any opportunity the enemy presents. In this case, Tony Watson, my brother-in-law, happens to be one of the biggest blowhards in New York."

"You speak of your brother-in-law in such a fashion?" Marty asked, surprised by his candor.

"Why not? Just because he married my sister doesn't mean I'm blind to his faults. But tell me, Miss McGuire, how long have you been following this… questionable career path?"

"Sir, I don't accept your harsh judgment of my profession," Marty said, her voice steady. "And as for how long? I…started today."

"Today?" Colonel Pickett raised an eyebrow, then laughed aloud, his amusement clear. "So, you're telling me this was your very first day as a journalist?"

"Yes," Marty replied. "And it all depended upon my getting the story about Commissioner Ford's indictment."

"So, when you outmaneuvered my brother-in-law, you weren't even officially a reporter yet?" Pickett asked, his tone both incredulous and impressed.

"No," Marty admitted quietly.

Pickett laughed again, the sound rich and full, until tears formed in the corners of his eyes. "Wonderful! Simply wonderful. You have my admiration, Miss McGuire, though I can't for the life of me understand why anyone would choose such a career. Now, would you care to dance?"

"No, not just yet," Marty said, shaking her head slightly. "I've danced enough for now. I'd much rather sit and talk for a few minutes."

Pickett nodded, his demeanor shifting from playful to serious. "Very well, Miss McGuire. Let's talk. I suspect there's more to you than meets the eye."

Colonel Pickett pulled out a chair for Marty. Once she was seated, he took the chair beside her, his presence commanding yet composed. Marty sized him up

—tall, strong, and probably around thirty. She, at twenty-one, was keenly aware of the age difference, though it didn't deter her curiosity.

"What would you like to talk about?" Colonel Pickett asked, his voice steady, with an edge of formality that came naturally to him.

Marty blurted out the first thing that came to mind, instantly regretting it. "Are you married?"

Pickett chuckled, a deep, resonant sound that seemed to lighten the mood. "No," he said, a hint of amusement in his eyes. "I've steered clear of marriage. It wouldn't be wise to have a wife living with me in the western forts."

"But I've read that many officers' wives do accompany them," Marty pressed, curious about his reasoning.

"When a man has a family, he worries about his family more than his career," Pickett replied.

"So, you're a career officer, not someone who was called up because of the situation in Cuba?" Marty asked, trying to steer the conversation into more neutral territory.

"Yes," Pickett confirmed. "I graduated from the academy ten years ago. I've been stationed out west ever since."

"And you've already made it to colonel? That's impressive."

Pickett smiled, though it was tempered with humility. "I must admit, until about a month ago, I was only a captain. The sudden expansion of the army meant rapid promotions for those with field experience. They needed cavalry officers who had seen action, so here I am."

"You must be proud," Marty said, sensing the complexity behind his words.

"Proud? Yes, I suppose so," Pickett replied, his voice carrying a weight that went beyond simple pride. "But leading these men into battle—it gives me pause. They're eager, but they've never faced the reality of war."

Marty frowned, confused. "Why the hesitation? I would think any man would be eager to fight for his country."

"Ah, yes, I had nearly forgotten. You are speaking with the voice of the newspapers now," Pickett said, a slight smirk playing at the corner of his mouth. "I've seen the headlines—*Blood on the Doorsteps*, *Hundreds of Americans Butchered by the Spanish*. And, of course, *Remember the* Maine! It's not quite as stirring as *Remember the Alamo*, but it serves its purpose. You know, it's the newspapers that are driving us toward this war."

"Don't you think the *Maine* should be avenged?" Marty asked, her voice firm with conviction.

"In what way?" Pickett countered. "There's a theory that coal dust caused the explosion. Such accidents are not uncommon, and if that's true, who do we attack? The coal miners in West Virginia?"

Marty was taken aback by the depth of Pickett's skepticism. Her mother was Cuban, and Marty had seen firsthand the brutality of Spanish rule. Her father's family in Illinois was filled with patriotic fervor, eager to see Spain punished. Colonel Pickett was the first person she'd met who questioned the rush to war. "I must confess, Colonel Pickett, it seems a little odd to hear a military man speak like this," she said.

"Why should it seem odd? We're the only ones who

should have an opinion on the matter," Pickett said, his voice growing harder. "These young officers, they're full of noble ideals. But I've heard the sound a bullet makes when it tears through flesh. I've seen men torn apart by cannon fire. I've heard the cries of the wounded and smelled the stench of death on the battlefield. There's nothing noble about it. I can't get worked up about the glory of war, no matter how righteous the cause."

Marty shivered involuntarily at the vividness of his words. "I suppose, when you put it that way, it does tend to lose its glamour," she admitted quietly.

Pickett turned his gaze from the shadows of the anteroom to the brightly lit ballroom, his hand absently rubbing the scar on his cheek. "There is no glamour in war," he said, his voice barely above a whisper. "Look at those young men out there. Fine officers, all of them. They think they're going to save Cuba from Spain. But they'll find a vast and unpleasant difference between maneuvering on a dance floor and maneuvering on a battlefield."

Marty followed his gaze, seeing the young officers in a new light. They were eager, confident, and utterly unaware of what lay ahead. And in that moment, she realized that Colonel Pickett wasn't just a soldier, he was a man who had been through hell and didn't relish the thought of leading others into it.

"Did you get that wound on the battlefield?" Marty asked, her eyes glancing briefly at the scar on Colonel Pickett's cheek.

"Yeah," Pickett replied, his tone matter-of-fact. "A Sioux war lance. The Spaniards won't be using such primitive weapons. A close encounter with them would likely leave a lot more than a scar."

Marty nodded, absorbing the weight of his words. "I've heard the name Pickett before," she said, trying to place it. "But I can't quite remember where."

Pickett chuckled, a deep, resonant sound. "My uncle was General Pickett—the one who led Pickett's Charge at Gettysburg."

"Was he a Southern general or Union?" Marty asked, realizing the significance of the name.

Pickett laughed again, a bit more heartily this time. "Southern," he said. "The fact that you didn't know might just mean the old wounds have about healed."

Pickett stood up, loosening his tunic as he did so. "Since you won't dance with me, how about a walk outside? I could use some air, and I hear this country club has one of the last formal gardens in the city."

Marty nodded. "I'd be honored," she said.

Taking his arm, they made their way through the back door and into the garden. The space was illuminated by strings of brightly colored paper lanterns, casting a soft glow over the manicured hedges and blooming flowers. In one corner, a fountain trickled water over a green mermaid statue, the sound blending with the distant hum of the party inside.

"I hear city real estate is too valuable now for luxuries like gardens," Pickett said, his voice carrying a touch of melancholy. "It's a shame to think places like this might not be around much longer."

"It's beautiful," Marty agreed, taking in the serene surroundings.

"Sure, but it doesn't hold a candle to the West," Pickett continued. "The deserts of Arizona and New Mexico, the Rocky Mountains in Colorado, the vast timberlands of California and Oregon—there's nothing like it."

"Are you from the West?" Marty asked, intrigued by the passion in his voice.

"No, I'm a New Yorker," Pickett replied. "That's why they gave me this command. And you? Are you from New York?"

"I'm from Litchfield, Illinois," Marty said. "My father works for the railroad."

"What brought you to New York?" Pickett asked, though he already knew the answer.

"I told you," Marty said, a hint of a smile tugging at her lips. "I wanted to be a—"

"Reporter, yes," Pickett interrupted, chuckling. "Well, whatever brought you here, I'm glad it did."

"You're glad?" Marty asked, surprised.

"Of course," Pickett said as they passed under the bough of a tree and stopped in the shadows. "If you weren't here, I'd be stuck back in there, miserable."

His words hung in the air between them, and for a moment, the noise of the party faded into the background. Marty found herself drawn to the colonel's presence—steady, grounded, and carrying the weight of experience that few men could match.

THE NEXT MORNING, Marty stood outside Talbot's office, her heart racing with anticipation. She knocked twice, firm but respectful.

"Mr. Talbot?" she called out.

Talbot, a grizzled man with years of ink stains on his fingers, looked up from his desk, his eyes narrowing before a grin tugged at the corners of his mouth. "Yes, what is it, girl?"

"I've finished the piece about the benefit ball. It's on Mr. Harrison's desk," Marty said, her voice steady.

"Good job," he grunted, not bothering to look away from his paperwork.

"Thank you," Marty replied, holding up another set of papers. "I also have this. I thought you might be interested."

Talbot glanced up, his curiosity piqued. "What is it?" He reached out, cigar wedged between his teeth, though unlit.

"Another story," Marty said, passing the sheets to him. "I managed to get an interview with Colonel Pickett last night."

Talbot's eyebrows shot up. "Colonel Pickett? The man who commands the Lightning Cavalry Regiment?"

"That's right. He's also a Medal of Honor recipient. I did some research this morning—he was decorated for his actions at Wounded Knee."

Talbot's expression shifted slightly, a mix of respect and intrigue. "Didn't know that," he muttered.

"I didn't either, until I dug into it," Marty added.

Talbot took the papers but placed them on his desk without reading them. "Good work, Miss McGuire," he said, more out of habit than genuine praise. "But Chambers handles our military pieces."

Marty frowned. "I wasn't aware."

"You're new. You'll learn," Talbot replied dismissively. "Now, how about you get down to the Brooklyn Bridge? There's a fella up there threatening to jump. If you're quick, you might catch the story before he does."

Marty nodded, pocketing her pad. "All right."

By the time Marty arrived at the bridge, hundreds of people were gathered below. Looking up, Marty saw him then, a tiny figure against the sky, standing there as calmly as if he were taking a stroll in the park. Marty weaved through the crowd, her senses sharp as she jotted down details, interviewing police officers and bystanders alike.

The situation resolved peacefully—a small victory that left her relieved. But back at the office, Talbot's reaction was far from what she expected.

"We can't use it," he said bluntly, pushing her latest story back across the desk.

Marty's face tightened. "But you didn't even read it."

"Don't need to. The man came down, didn't he?"

"Yes, but—"

"He wasn't pulled down, wrestled down, or saved by some heroic act?"

"No, sir," Marty admitted. "He came down on his own."

Talbot snorted. "That's not news, McGuire. News is what people talk about. If he'd jumped, we'd have a story. If he hadn't, it's just another day in the city. Do you have any idea how many people *didn't* jump off the Brooklyn Bridge today?"

Marty hesitated, then answered, "Nobody did."

"Exactly. You see, newspapers thrive on the unusual, not the mundane. A man not jumping isn't newsworthy."

Marty sighed, a bit of her earlier determination fading. "I understand."

Talbot leaned back, the chair creaking under his

weight. "Look, you're learning. But I'll give you this—you did good with the Pickett story. I'll run it."

Marty's eyes widened. "You will? What about Mr. Chambers?"

"He's off to Washington to get accredited by the War Department. When we head to Cuba, he's tagging along."

The thought of joining them made Marty's pulse quicken. "Mr. Talbot, do you think—"

"Don't even ask," Talbot cut in, his tone sharp. "There's no way I'm gonna send a woman to cover a war."

Marty swallowed her disappointment, masking it with a nod. "Understood, sir."

Talbot gave her a rare look of approval, a slight nod before turning back to his papers. "Keep at it, McGuire. There's a place for you here—if you can handle it."

Three

Marty had been with the newspaper for about two weeks when, one afternoon, she overheard a woman speaking Spanish from the front of the newsroom. The voice was familiar, a language Marty had known since childhood, and she got up from her desk, moving toward the commotion.

The speaker was a striking woman in her thirties, her attire and bearing signaling a background of privilege. Her accent was unmistakably Cuban, not European.

"Is there no one here who understands me?" the woman asked, her voice edged with desperation.

Marty scanned the faces of the men in the room, including Mr. Talbot, and it was clear none of them had a clue what she was saying.

"I understand," Marty said, speaking the language with an easy, comfortable command.

Talbot raised an eyebrow. "You understand this lingo?"

"Yes," Marty replied in English, then switched back to Spanish. "What seems to be the problem?"

The woman's relief was palpable. "Thank God, someone who can speak my language at last. It's terrifying to feel as if you've been struck dumb," she said with a slight smile. "I'm Francesca Alvarez Mendoza. My brother is Colonel Juan Alvarez, commander of the First Free Cuba Brigade." She held out an envelope. "My brother sent proof—photographs of Spanish atrocities against our people. Twelve young men, murdered and mutilated, their only crime being the distribution of pamphlets advocating free elections in Cuba."

Francesca handed Marty the photographs. Marty glanced at the first one and felt the blood drain from her face.

Francesca noticed. "It's difficult to look at them, I know. But the world must see, and the stories must be told if the American public is to learn the truth."

"What is it?" Talbot asked, his impatience growing. "What's she showing you?"

Marty handed him the packet without a word.

Talbot's eyes widened as he examined the photos. "This is incredible! Who are these people? What did she say?"

Marty quickly relayed Francesca's explanation.

"Fred!" Talbot barked, tossing the photos to another man. "Get art on these. I want cuts of these right away." He turned back to Marty, rolling his unlit cigar between his teeth. "How much does she want for these?"

"She doesn't want money," Marty said, shaking her head. "She just wants the truth out there, for people to know what's happening in Cuba."

Talbot nodded, a slight grin forming. "Tell her we'll run the photos and the story, but she's not to take any of this to Hearst or Pulitzer."

Marty translated, and Francesca nodded in agreement.

"I don't care which paper runs it," Francesca said, "as long as the public is informed. I'll honor Senor Talbot's request."

"Does she agree?" Talbot asked.

"Yes."

"Perfect," Talbot said. "Now, you interpret for her, and I'll get Johnny to write the story."

Marty bristled. "Why can't I write it?"

Talbot pulled the cigar from his mouth, staring her down. "You're a good writer, kid, no doubt about it. But I saw the way you reacted when you looked at those pictures. This story is going to need grit—blood, guts, all the ugly details. I'm not sure you've got the stomach for it."

"Mr. Talbot, if it needs to be gritty, I'll make it gritty. Just give me the chance."

Talbot studied her, then sighed. "All right. I'll give you a chance. Tell the lady you'll be doing the story."

Speaking in Spanish, Marty identified herself and explained that she would be writing the article.

Francesca smiled warmly. "Your employer must be quite progressive to allow a woman such responsibility."

"Would you be more comfortable with a man writing the story?" Marty asked, her tone neutral.

"No, no, not at all," Francesca said, gently touching Marty's arm. "I think it's wonderful to work with you. You speak our language so beautifully, and with a Cuban accent too. How is that?"

"My mother is Cuban," Marty replied. "I have many relatives there."

"How did she come to America?"

"My father is a railroad construction engineer. He went to Cuba to build a railroad, met my mother, and married her. Now they live in Illinois, but I've visited Cuba many times."

"Would you like to visit Cuba tomorrow night?" Francesca asked with a twinkle in her eye.

"Tomorrow night?" Marty chuckled. "What do you mean?"

Francesca joined in the laughter. "Not literally, of course. But the Free Cuba Legation is holding a dinner, a gathering that will feel like a night in Cuba. Food, drink, music—it'll be like being there. Would you like to join us?"

"I'd love to," Marty said, her interest piqued.

"What's all the chatter about?" Talbot cut in.

"She's invited me to a dinner at the Free Cuba Legation," Marty explained.

"What did you say?"

"I said I'd go."

"Good, good," Talbot said, his enthusiasm returning. "The closer you get to these people, the more exclusives we'll land. The other papers will be scrambling to keep up with us after this."

POSITIVE PROOF OF SPANISH ATROCITIES. The headline dominated the top of the paper the next morning, the woodcuts of the photographs giving the story even more impact. A notarized statement from a judge, a clergyman, and a college professor confirmed that they had seen the original photographs and that the woodcuts were accurate, unaltered depictions. This was crucial, especially since many papers had been accused of fabricating stories and images to boost their circulation.

Marty walked the fine line between delivering a hard-hitting story and avoiding sensationalism. The result was a front-page lead story that didn't pull any punches. That day, the *Banner*'s street sales were the highest in the paper's history.

FRANCESCA GREETED Marty with a firm handshake when she arrived at the legation that evening. Beside her stood her husband, Ricardo Mendoza, chief of the legation.

"My wife spoke highly of your command of our language," Ricardo said, nodding to Marty. "But none of us expected the power of your writing. I translated your article today so our non-English speakers could read it. It was outstanding."

"Thank you, Señor Mendoza," Marty replied, her expression steady.

"My wife and I have other guests to attend to, but please, let my secretary introduce you to the others."

Marty followed the young man Ricardo pointed out as his secretary. Before long, she found herself receiving nods of approval from those present. It wasn't just her story that drew attention, her sharp features and confident demeanor left an impression. After several minutes of polite conversation, Marty excused herself to get a drink. The room was warm, and she needed to clear her head.

As she waited for a servant to pour her a cup of punch, she felt a prickling sensation at the back of her neck. She turned and saw Colonel Nelson Pickett leaning casually against a wall.

Nelson strode over, took the cup from the servant, and handed it to her before grabbing one for himself.

"You're quite the center of attention tonight," he remarked.

"They're just glad to speak with someone who knows their language," Marty replied, brushing off the compliment.

"No, it's more than that. I respect that talent. My own linguistic skills don't go beyond French and a Sioux dialect."

"How's the training going?" Marty asked as they moved away from the punch table.

"Is that a journalist's question?"

"I am a journalist," Marty said, her tone firm. "So everything I see is material for my work."

"I figured that out when I read the profile you did on me. Didn't know you were planning to write about me, Miss McGuire."

Marty ran a hand through her hair, realizing she'd forgotten about that piece. "Were you offended by it?"

To her surprise, Nelson chuckled. "No. Actually, I found it flattering. Maybe a bit embarrassing, but not offensive."

"I'm glad to hear that," Marty said.

"I read your story today," Nelson said, taking a sip of his punch, his eyes steady on hers. "You're a damn good writer, Miss McGuire. What impressed me most was the solid evidence backing your story. Unlike some of the garbage Mr. Pulitzer and Mr. Hearst print. I take back what I said about journalists the other day. I was obviously wrong about some of you."

"Thank you, Colonel."

Another officer approached them then, offering a nod. "Evening, Nelson. I see you've found the most interesting person here, as usual." He extended his hand. "I'm Major Dan Calhoun, second-in-command."

"Marty McGuire."

Calhoun gave Marty a curious look before laughing. "You're Marty McGuire? I thought…" He chuckled. "Forgive me, Miss McGuire. I read your pieces on the colonel and also today's story. I assumed you were a man. You write like one."

"Oh? And how does a man write? Does he use different words?"

Calhoun cleared his throat, clearly embarrassed. "No, it's just—"

"Careful, Dan," Nelson interjected with a smirk. "She's sharper than both of us combined."

"I'm sure of that," Calhoun said, grinning.

An official from the legation interrupted them, asking Nelson to meet someone. Nelson excused himself from Marty and Dan's company.

"The colonel's taken with you," Dan remarked once Nelson was out of earshot.

"Oh? And what's that supposed to mean?"

Dan laughed. "I forgot, I'm dealing with someone who knows words. Let me put it this way—he's impressed."

"How can you tell? Until now, you didn't even know who I was."

"Not true, Miss McGuire. I knew you existed, just

not who you were. You were at the military ball the other night, weren't you?"

"Yes."

"And you and the colonel took a walk in the garden?"

Marty's eyes dropped to the floor. "He…he had no right to—"

"Relax, Miss McGuire," Dan said quickly, noticing her discomfort. "He didn't say a word out of turn. That's how I know how he feels. I saw you two heading to the garden, but from where I was, I couldn't see you. When I asked him later who the lady was, he got embarrassed and wouldn't even talk to Molly about it."

"Molly?"

"My wife," Dan said with a nod. "That also explains why he was so reticent to talk about the article you wrote."

"I hope I didn't embarrass him," Marty said.

"You did, but don't worry about it. He's self-conscious about his Medal of Honor. Doesn't feel he earned it, though anyone who was there that day knows he did."

"I know he earned it at the Battle of Wounded Knee," Marty said. "But I don't know the details."

Dan's expression darkened as he finished his drink and set the glass down. "It wasn't the Army's finest hour," he said quietly. "Chief Big Foot and a ragged band of less than three hundred Indians, including women and children, were camped at Wounded Knee Creek. It was late December, freezing cold. Big Foot was sick, and they'd surrendered. We had them surrounded with Hotchkiss guns and Gatlings. They were ordered to give up their weapons. When it seemed like they wouldn't, Colonel Forsyth ordered us to search the teepees. Somebody—don't know if it was an Indian or one of ours—started shooting. After that, all hell broke loose. The Hotchkiss guns opened up at point-blank, soldiers charged, and the Indians were cut down like wheat. Nelson ordered his men to hold fire, but he only commanded one troop. The rest kept shooting like it was a damn turkey shoot."

Dan fell silent, clearly reliving the horror of the event. Marty stayed quiet, letting him gather his thoughts.

"There was a group of women, kids, and old folks who had already surrendered, just standing there in the middle of it. Nelson ran into the camp, right through the gunfire, and led them out. They were about the only ones who made it."

"Why does Colonel Pickett feel he doesn't deserve the medal?"

"He feels guilty about the others, the ones who were killed."

"Why?"

"Miss McGuire, there's not a man jack of us who was there who doesn't feel guilty," Dan explained. "It was a massacre, plain and simple. I guess the thought that such a brutal massacre would result in a Medal of Honor, no matter how noble the reason, sort of sticks in Nelson's craw. He's a strange man that way. He's a good man, mind you, but he has his own code of honor, and he won't violate it."

A chime rang through the rooms, signaling that dinner was served. There were name cards at the dinner table, and Marty was a little disappointed to see that she would be sitting at the opposite end of the table from Colonel Pickett.

Major Calhoun's story lingered in her mind.

Colonel Pickett was clearly a warrior, but he was also a man of deep conviction. That knowledge increased her regard for him.

As Marty took her seat, she realized her dinner companion was none other than William Randolph Hearst. It seemed the seating planner had decided to group the press together. When Hearst was introduced to her, his surprise was evident.

"You?" he said, eyebrows raised. "You're Marty McGuire?"

"Yes."

"But surely, madam, you're not the author of those impressive stories I've seen in the *Banner*?"

"I work for Mr. Talbot, yes," Marty replied.

"How would you like to work for me?" Hearst offered without missing a beat.

Marty was caught off guard and let out a small laugh. "Two weeks ago, I wasn't sure any paper would hire me. Now I've got one job and another offer on the table. I'm flattered, Mr. Hearst, but I'm committed to Mr. Talbot."

"I'll double whatever Talbot's paying you," Hearst said, loud enough for others at the table to notice. Conversations around them paused, and all eyes turned to Marty.

"How can you make such an offer?" she asked, trying to keep her composure. "You don't even know what my salary is."

"I don't care what it is," Hearst replied. "Whatever he's paying, I'll double it."

The offer was translated into Spanish for the non-English speakers, and the room buzzed with renewed interest.

"What exactly would you have me do?" Marty asked, still processing the unexpected opportunity.

"The same thing you're doing for Talbot, of course."

"I'm also covering women's news for Mr. Talbot," Marty said, choosing her words carefully. "But I'd prefer to stick to straight news."

"And you should," Hearst agreed. "Someone with your talent shouldn't be wasted on tea parties. I want you writing hard-hitting pieces like today's, Maybe three a week, exposing the Spanish tyranny in Cuba."

Marty blinked, taken aback. "Are you saying you have that much documented evidence?"

"Documented evidence?" Hearst echoed, a smirk playing on his lips. "Someone with your gift doesn't need documented evidence. You'll write your stories from here." He tapped his temple. "And from here." He pointed to his chest. "Especially from here."

"I...I don't understand," Marty said, frowning.

"Allow me to interpret for you, Miss McGuire," Nelson said, speaking from the other end of the table and drawing everyone's attention. "I believe he is giving you carte blanche to create atrocities if you can't find any real ones."

Marty gasped. "You can't be serious, Mr. Hearst. I'm a journalist, not a novelist. If you want fiction, hire Mark Twain."

Hearst chuckled. "Believe me, I'd pay any price for Clemens to write my front-page stories, but he's not interested. You have the flair and ambition. I thought you'd be keen."

"Mr. Hearst," Marty said, her tone firm, "my stories are a bond with my readers. They expect the truth—or as close to it as I can get."

Hearst chuckled again, shaking his head. "My dear, I admire your sense of responsibility, but there's a difference between what's true and what's factual."

"What do you mean?" Marty asked, her confusion deepening.

"Take today's story. It's true, isn't it? An accurate reflection of Spanish treatment of Cubans?"

"Yes."

"Do you have evidence beyond what the Free Cuba Legation provided?"

"As a matter of fact, I do," Marty said. "My mother is Cuban. I've lived there, and while I haven't seen atrocities like these, I've witnessed Spanish oppression."

"Good, then it's a true story," Hearst said. "You also have photos and an eyewitness account, making it factual. Without that evidence, though, it would still be true, right?"

"Well…yes," Marty admitted reluctantly.

"Then I'm not asking anything more of you," Hearst said. "Just write stories like today's. True, even if not always factual. So, have I hired myself a new journalist?"

Marty shook her head. "I'm honored by the offer, Mr. Hearst, but I can't accept."

Hearst laughed. "Too bad. Come see me when the load gets too heavy."

"I beg your pardon? What load?"

"The halo of journalistic integrity, of course," Hearst said with a grin. "Now, could someone pass the salt?"

With that, the conversation was over, and the others at the table resumed their discussions. Nelson found himself talking to the wife of some bureaucrat, but his mind was elsewhere. His attention drifted back to Marty McGuire.

What an intriguing woman she was. She had guts, a sharp mind, and a strong sense of honor—qualities Nelson respected deeply. He'd never spent this much time thinking about any woman before. If he ever did get serious, it'd have to be with someone like her. But he wasn't planning on getting serious about anyone—not until his military career was over. Still, if he did, it would have to be with someone smart, independent, and with a code of honor as strong as his own. Someone like Marty McGuire.

Four

A few days after the Free Cuba Legation dinner, Mr. Talbot summoned Marty to his office. As Marty entered, Talbot didn't bother with pleasantries. He gestured to the chair across from his desk, and Marty sat down, facing him. Talbot leaned back in his chair, the unlit cigar hanging from the corner of his mouth like a permanent fixture.

"I just got a wire from Chambers," he said, his voice gruff. "He's tied up in Washington longer than expected."

Marty narrowed her eyes. "Is there an issue?"

"Not really," Talbot replied, his tone matter-of-fact. "Just bureaucratic red tape holding things up. But it leaves us with a slight problem."

Marty tilted her head slightly. "Oh? Is there something I can do to help?"

Talbot removed the cigar, leaning forward as he rested his elbows on the desk. He studied her, a calculating look in his eyes. "McGuire, I might be out of my mind, but how would you feel about going into the field with the Lightning Cavalry? They're gearing up for their final training exercise before shipping out."

Marty blinked, caught off guard. "Are you serious, Mr. Talbot? You would really let me do that?"

Talbot's expression didn't waver. "Do you want it?"

Marty didn't hesitate. "Absolutely. I'll handle it, no question."

A rare smile tugged at the corner of Talbot's mouth. "That's what I figured. You've nailed every assignment so far, and I don't expect this one to be any different. The only thing standing in your way is getting you permission to go."

. "Permission from who?"

"Colonel Pickett. You know him better than anyone else around here. Suppose I leave the clearance part up to you. Do you think you can get a pass from him?"

Marty's confidence didn't falter. "Yes, sir, I'm sure I can."

Talbot gave a curt nod. "Bring me the pass, and the assignment is yours."

Marty shot to her feet, her chair clattering to the floor behind her. She quickly righted it, brushing a stray lock of hair out of her face as she did.

"You won't regret this, Mr. Talbot. I'll deliver the best story you've ever seen."

Talbot chuckled, the sound low and rough. "McGuire, if only I could figure out how to get you more fired up about your work."

Marty stepped off the 23rd Street trolley at Broadway, pausing briefly to take in the chaotic energy of the city. For a girl from a small town in Illinois, such a dazzling display of advanced civilization was very exciting. The streets were packed with electric trolleys, horse-drawn omnibuses, and carriages, all jockeying for space. There were great, bustling crowds of people hurrying along the sidewalks and across the brick-paved streets: men in their derbies and women in feathered bonnets, all moving along under the watchful eyes of traffic policemen.

She was here on business—no time to get lost in the scenery. Marty was after a military pass that would let her join the Lightning Cavalry on maneuvers. Their headquarters was in the Fifth Avenue Hotel, a large white six-story building just up ahead. The hotel, like all the others along Broadway, was decked out in bright awnings, the kind that shielded both the streets and the windows from the sun.

She passed a series of signs on the buildings across the street—ads for everything from *Dr. Hall's Painless Dentistry* to a dubious *Elixir of Eternal Youth*. She'd heard that most of these were temporary businesses that were soon to be replaced by a new skyscraper they were already calling the Flatiron Building. She pushed through the crowd and into the Fifth Avenue Hotel.

The hotel lobby was as busy as the street outside. Marty didn't linger at the newsstand, though the papers caught her eye. April 22. The date was significant—America hadn't officially declared war on Spain yet, but things were moving quickly. The fleet was already on its way to blockade Cuba. There was also news about Admiral Dewey and the Pacific fleet in the Philippines, though Marty couldn't place those islands on a map if asked.

Her real target was the door guarded by two

uniformed soldiers. The sign above it read: *Headquarters, First New York Lightning Cavalry, Colonel Nelson A. Pickett, Commanding.* Marty squared her shoulders and headed straight for it. As she approached, the soldiers snapped to attention, their sudden movement catching her off guard for a moment.

"Can I go in?" Marty asked, nodding toward the door.

"Yes, ma'am," one soldier replied, his voice firm. "We're just required to come to attention for officers and civilians."

"And we're not supposed to talk to no one either," the second soldier grumbled, casting a sideways glance at his partner.

Marty gave them a quick, conspiratorial smile. "I won't tell anyone," she said, tapping her finger to her lips before pushing through the door without a second look.

Inside, the office was as busy as any place of business. Four desks lined the room, each manned by clerks hammering away at their typewriters. A large map dominated the wall, where a couple of sergeants and an officer stood, studying it intently. The officer, Major Dan Calhoun, glanced up as Marty entered, a broad smile spreading across his face.

"Miss McGuire, what a surprise," he said, stepping forward to greet her. "Major Dan Calhoun. We met at the Free Cuban Legation, if you recall."

"Of course, Major. How are you?"

"Doing well, thanks. What brings you here?"

"I'm here to see Colonel Pickett," she said, her tone direct.

Calhoun's smile faded slightly. "Ah, you just missed him. He's already headed out to the field."

"The training maneuver has started?" Marty asked, her brow furrowing.

"His part has, yeah," Calhoun replied. "He went out early to observe how the unit sets up in the field. He left me in temporary command. Anything I can do for you?"

"I hope so," Marty said, getting straight to the point. "My publisher, Mr. Talbot, has given me the assignment of writing about this training maneuver. I'm going along with you to observe and record everything, but I'll need a military pass to authorize my presence."

Calhoun hesitated, rubbing his chin as he considered her request. "I don't know, that's usually up to the commanding officer."

"But, didn't you just say you were now in command?"

"Temporarily, yes," Calhoun admitted.

"Then I only need a temporary pass," she countered.

Calhoun chuckled, shaking his head. "All right, Miss McGuire, you've convinced me. Let's just hope I don't wind up paying for this later."

"I'll stay out of everyone's way, you have my word," Marty assured him.

"Sergeant," Calhoun called out, turning to one of the men, "write up an authorization pass for Miss Marty McGuire. She's a journalist."

"Yes, sir," the sergeant replied, though he muttered, "Never heard of no female journalist before."

"You'll be hearing about this one," Calhoun said, a touch of admiration in his voice. "She's good."

"Thank you, Major," Marty said, appreciating the compliment.

Calhoun checked his pocket watch, snapping it shut with a decisive click. "Miss McGuire, my wife, Molly, is staying here at the hotel. We're about to have lunch in the restaurant, and I'd be honored if you'd join us. I've mentioned you to her, and I know she's eager to meet you."

"I'd be delighted," Marty replied without hesitation.

"Great," Calhoun said with a nod. "Let's go meet her, and you can pick up your pass after lunch."

Marty followed Dan out of the office, past the saluting guards, and across the lobby to the restaurant. Outside the entrance, a young woman sat on a wooden bench, looking up as they approached.

"Ah, here she is," Dan said. "Miss McGuire, this is my wife, Molly Calhoun. Molly, this is Marty McGuire, the reporter I mentioned."

Molly stood, offering a warm smile. "Marty, it's a pleasure. Dan's told me all about you."

"Nice to meet you, Mrs. Calhoun," Marty replied, keeping it formal.

"Molly, please," she insisted, laughing lightly. "And don't be modest—my brother has mentioned you more than once."

Marty raised an eyebrow, trying to hide her surprise. "I had no idea. Colonel Pickett is your brother?"

Molly nodded. "That he is."

Marty noticed the resemblance now—Molly shared the same sharp, blue eyes as her brother but softened into a more delicate beauty. The connection was clear.

"Shall we head in?" Dan suggested, cutting through the pleasantries as he gestured toward the restaurant.

During the meal, Dan leaned back in his chair, the mood relaxed but with an undercurrent of purpose. "I've authorized a pass for Marty," he said. "She'll be joining us in the field for the training exercise."

Molly chuckled. "I imagine Nelson will have a thing or two to say about that."

Dan smirked. "I'm counting on those family ties to keep him from busting me down to private."

Marty's curiosity got the better of her. "What's his issue with women?"

"It's not about dislike," Dan explained, his voice firm. "He's just convinced the military and women don't mix, especially for a career officer."

Marty leaned forward slightly. "And yet here you are, Major."

Dan met her gaze evenly. "I am. Nelson and I were classmates at West Point. He wasn't thrilled when I married his sister, but he came around."

Molly laughed softly, glancing at her husband. "He did try to talk us out of it."

Dan reached across the table, briefly taking Molly's hand. "But he couldn't," he said simply, his tone steady.

Marty watched the exchange, feeling a pang of something she couldn't quite place. Her life was full—she was a journalist for one of the biggest papers in New York, living out her ambitions. But watching Dan and Molly, she couldn't help but wonder if there was something missing.

Molly broke the silence. "Nelson's stubborn, but

one day, he'll meet someone who'll change his mind. Might even be someone like you, Marty."

Marty kept her response measured. "I'm just here to do my job."

Molly smiled, a knowing look in her eyes. "And you do it well. I've read your work—impressive stuff."

Dan interjected with a playful grin. "Next thing you know, you two will be marching with the suffragettes."

Molly shot him a look. "And why not? Women deserve the right to vote."

Marty nodded. "I agree."

Dan raised his hands in mock surrender. "Careful, ladies. Don't want to end up in jail for stirring the pot, and I'd hate to be locked up with you."

As lunch wrapped up, Dan pushed his plate aside and looked at Marty. "Your pass should be ready by now. Let's go get it."

Marty stood, offering a nod to Molly. "It was good to meet you. I hope we can talk again soon."

"I'm sure we will," Molly replied with a smile.

THE NEXT MORNING at six o'clock, Marty McGuire presented herself at Grand Central Station, gripping her small valise firmly in one hand. After paying the cabdriver, she dismissed him with a nod, barely registering the cluck of his tongue as he moved off to join the line of waiting cabs.

Moving swiftly through the main lobby, Marty pushed her way toward the massive, glass-roofed train shed. The station buzzed with activity, the air thick with the hiss of steam and the chugging rhythm of engines. Marty felt a surge of familiar energy. The sound of trains always brought a rush of memories—her father, the railroadman, and the countless hours spent around these iron beasts. If life had dealt her a different hand, maybe she would have been at the controls of one of these engines, her hands wrapped around the throttle instead of a pen.

As she navigated the maze of trains, her eyes caught a small sign identifying the troop train. With no hesitation, she headed down the line, her focus unyielding.

"Here, miss, I think you're headin' to the wrong train," a railroad official called out, his voice tinged with doubt.

Marty didn't break stride. She produced her military pass with a quick, practiced motion. "I'm assigned to the special journalists' car on the troop train," she stated, her tone leaving no room for argument. "This should clear up any confusion."

The official took the pass, his expression tightening as he read it. He handed it back with a grunt. "You're in the right place, all right. Just don't know why they'd send a woman on a job like this. But orders are orders."

Marty pocketed the pass and pressed on. She wasn't here to explain herself, she was here to work.

Reaching the first car behind the baggage compartment, she realized she had to walk the full length of the train to reach the journalists' car. She braced herself, not for the soldiers—who, despite a few lingering looks, let her pass without incident—but for the reception she knew awaited her among the reporters. When she finally reached the journalists' car, Dan Calhoun was there, his presence a buffer against the cold stares that greeted her. The men made it clear she wasn't welcome in their midst.

Five hours passed in an uncomfortable silence. Marty took a seat by the window, her eyes on the passing scenery, but her mind churning with thoughts. The men, content in their camaraderie, played cards, their laughter and banter filling the car. They ignored her as if she were a ghost—a specter in a place she didn't belong. Not that she wanted to join their game, but a word, even a curt acknowledgment, wouldn't have gone amiss. But none came, and she knew better than to expect it.

When the train finally reached its destination just before noon, the atmosphere shifted. Activity exploded as soldiers disembarked, unloading horses and forming into squadrons with practiced efficiency. The other reporters remained in their car, their card game more important than the scene unfolding outside.

Marty, however, was already on the move. She stepped off the train, finding a vantage point away from the commotion but close enough to observe the Lightning Cavalry as they assembled. She pulled out her pad and began to write, capturing the precision of the soldiers' movements, the energy in the air, and the unspoken tension that lingered between her and her so-called colleagues.

They could ignore her all they wanted, but Marty McGuire wasn't here to play their game. She was here to tell a story, and she wasn't about to let anyone, least of all a bunch of dismissive reporters, get in her way.

The Lightning Cavalry: A Symphony of Discipline and Valor

The Lightning Cavalry, much like a beehive in its

industrious fervor, is a living entity—a force that, when observed, becomes more than the mere sum of its parts. At first glance, one might be struck by what appears to be utter chaos. Horses gallop with seeming abandon, sabers catch and scatter sunlight, and the ground trembles beneath the rumble of caissons bearing the weight of formidable cannons. The air is thick with the shouts of sergeants, each commanding with a voice of authority, striving to impose order upon the tumult.

Yet, within moments, what was once a scene of confusion transforms with remarkable precision. The disorder gives way to disciplined unity as great blocks of horsemen and foot soldiers snap into formation. Each line stands perfectly aligned, a testament to military rigor and training, their banners—the guidons—snapping sharply in the breeze. These guidons, with their crimson and white pennants, held aloft on long staffs by their proud bearers, are more than mere markers, they are the symbols of the unit's honor. To each man, his unit's guidon is as cherished as the Stars and Stripes themselves, embodying the spirit and pride of the regiment.

A bugle's clarion call cut through the morning air, sharp and commanding. Four notes, precise and unmistakable, brought every soldier to attention. The regiment froze, guidons held high, as a mounted officer began a slow, deliberate approach toward the assembled men. Marty watched the scene unfold, her heart quickening as the officer drew nearer. This was Nelson Pickett, a man in his element—commanding nearly a thousand soldiers, each one a testament to his leadership.

Dan Calhoun wheeled his horse around, saluting smartly as he reached Pickett. Even from her vantage point on the hill, Marty could hear Dan's voice, clear and strong.

"Sir! The regiment is formed!"

Nelson returned the salute, then he and Dan rode to the far end of the formation and started a slow parade of the line, coming toward the end nearest Marty. Marty watched them, trying to capture the excitement she was feeling so she could convey some of it in writing to her readers.

When Nelson's gaze finally landed on her, his reaction was not what she had expected. For a brief moment, she saw something that resembled joy—a flicker of warmth that softened his rigid demeanor. But that expression was short-lived, because a frown of disapproval suddenly came across his face. He turned away, his posture stiffening as he rode back to the head of the formation, leaving her with a cold, sinking feeling in the pit of her stomach.

At the head of the regiment, Nelson exchanged salutes with Dan once more before the commands were given. The soldiers broke formation with shouts and cheers, dispersing to their bivouac areas, while Marty stood alone, trying to make sense of the colonel's reaction.

As the other reporters finally emerged from the train, grumbling about the discomforts of tent life, Marty remained lost in thought. She barely noticed the sergeant approaching until he spoke.

"Miss McGuire, the colonel asked if you would visit with him, ma'am."

"Yes, certainly," Marty replied, her voice steady despite the unease she felt.

The sergeant dismounted and led his horse, a gesture of respect, as he guided her to a nearby tent.

Once inside, Nelson dismissed the sergeant with a curt nod, leaving them alone.

Marty forced a smile, determined to break the tension.

"I guess you are surprised to see me," she said lightly.

"Surprised is not quite the word, Miss McGuire," Nelson replied, his voice as cold as iron. "Shocked would be more accurate. What are you doing here?"

His anger was palpable, and it caught Marty off guard. She had expected some resistance, but not this raw, simmering fury.

"I'm doing the same thing the other journalists are doing," she said, trying to match his tone with calm defiance. "I'm covering a story."

"Not this story," Nelson snapped. "I'm sending you back."

Marty bristled at his tone, her own anger rising to meet his. "You have no right to send me back. I have authorization to be here."

"Authorization from my executive officer," Nelson shot back. "I am countermanding that decision."

Marty narrowed her eyes, her voice laced with sarcasm. "You're countermanding an action he took while you left him in command? That must do wonders for the men's confidence in their officers."

Nelson's eyes flashed with irritation. "What?"

"I said—"

"Never mind," he interrupted, running a hand through his hair in frustration. The action was uncharacteristic, revealing a man at war with himself. He knew she was right, but admitting it went against every instinct ingrained in him.

"You are right," Nelson conceded after a long

pause, his voice losing some of its edge. "If I countermand his order now, it would undermine the principles of military command and discipline."

He stared at her, his gaze hard, but the conflict was there, just beneath the surface. He was torn between his duty and his feelings—feelings he had no right to acknowledge.

"Very well, Miss McGuire," he finally said, his voice steady but strained. "You win. You may stay."

"Thank you," Marty replied, her tone softer now, sensing the weight of his decision.

"But mind you," Nelson added, his voice firm once more, "stay out of harm's way. A military field is no place for a woman. I'm only thankful this is a practice maneuver and not a battlefield."

Marty smiled, her confidence returning.

"You won't regret this, Colonel. I promise I'll be no trouble at all."

NELSON SAT BEHIND THE TABLE, his gaze fixed on the tent flap where Marty had just exited. He knew he had overreacted to her presence, but there was something about her that set him on edge. It wasn't just her stubborn determination or the fact that she had a knack for challenging him at every turn—there was something more, something that gnawed at him in a way he couldn't quite shake.

He had known plenty of women, each with their own charms, and he had learned long ago to keep his distance, to never let anyone get too close. It was a rule he lived by, one that had served him well over the years. But with Marty, that rule felt suddenly fragile, like it was being tested in ways he wasn't prepared for.

She was attractive, sure, but he'd crossed paths with women just as pretty, maybe even prettier. She was sharp, but intelligence wasn't exactly a rarity in his experience. And her independence? Admirable, if often frustrating. Yet, there was something else—something he couldn't quite define—that set her apart.

Nelson shook his head, a wry smile tugging at the corner of his mouth. Maybe it was the scent she left behind, a mix of jasmine and something earthy, something real. But it wasn't just that. It was her presence, the way she held herself, the way she looked at him with those eyes that seemed to see right through his defenses.

He couldn't let himself get distracted, not now. He had a job to do, and letting his guard down wasn't an option. Marty McGuire was a complication he didn't need—an intriguing, maddening complication—but one that he'd have to keep at arm's length. He couldn't afford to let her or anyone else pull him off course.

Five

Major Calhoun had detailed a couple of men to pitch an officer's tent for Marty. The tent was just big enough for a cot and a writing table, with a keg of water nearby. It wasn't luxurious, but it was enough to get the job done. Thanks to Calhoun's practicality and the soldiers' efficiency, Marty's stay in the field was tolerable.

Marty was still excluded from the *club* of journalists who were covering the maneuver. To be honest about it, though, she didn't miss their company. The other reporters were a noisy bunch, always grumbling about the food, the weather, or the discomforts of camp life. Despite having tents similar to hers, they never stopped complaining. When they weren't griping, they were gambling or drinking. Marty often wondered when they found time to write anything worth reading.

She filed her own stories every day, sending them back to New York on the returning train. Marty wasn't sure if she was covering the right topics—military strategy, training progress, or Colonel Pickett's tactical ideas—but she didn't worry too much about it. Instead, she focused on capturing the atmosphere of a large army maneuvering in the field.

One night, about a week into the exercises, Marty sat, leaning back against a stone fence near her tent. The valley below was dotted with campfires, the smoke mingling with the scent of wildflowers. Behind her, untouched by the presence of the army, the sounds of crickets and frogs filled the night air. Fireflies blinked across the valley, their lights flickering like distant stars fallen from the sky.

From a nearby campfire, the soft strains of a song carried through the air, the soldiers' voices harmonizing with the night:

The years creep slowly by, Lorena,
The snow is on the grass again.
The sun's low down the sky, Lorena,
And frost gleams where the flowers have been.

As Marty listened, she noticed a figure approaching her tent. When the shadowy figure got closer, she recognized the silhouette of Colonel Pickett.

"Miss McGuire?" Pickett called softly into her tent, his voice carrying a note of authority even in the quiet. "Marty?"

His use of her first name caught her off guard, but she pushed the thought aside. "I'm over here," she called.

Pickett turned, spotting her by the fence, and walked over. In the week she'd been there, this was the first time he'd spoken to her directly. She wondered what had changed. Then she suddenly grew frightened that he was about to send her back.

"Oh, no," she said aloud.

"What is it?" Nelson asked. He was beside her now.

"You're not here to send me back to the city, are you?" she asked, a hint of tension in her voice.

To her surprise, Pickett chuckled, a rare sound from the stoic officer. "No, Miss McGuire, you're not getting rid of us that easily. May I sit?"

"Certainly," Marty replied. She was still curious as to why he was there. Why, after a week of avoiding her, had he decided to come see her?

Pickett settled down next to her. "How's the setup? You comfortable?"

"I'm managing," Marty said, keeping it brief. She didn't see the point in complaining.

Pickett smirked. "You might want to share your secret with the other reporters. They've been hounding me endlessly about the so-called hardships they're enduring."

Marty shrugged. "We don't really talk. I doubt they even realize I'm here."

"Oh, they know," Pickett said, his tone dry. "Your stories have made sure of that."

"I haven't had much to write about," Marty admitted. "I've asked to join the troops during their exercises, but no one's given me an answer. I've had to make do with what I can observe."

"Those *observations* have turned into some damn fine writing. Did you know some of the men are carrying clippings of your stories around? Like they were poetry."

"No, I didn't know that," Marty said, surprised.

"In the quiet of the night, deep in their souls, each man can hear the distant rattle of musketry, and he must ask himself if he can measure up to the test," Pickett quoted, his voice steady and reflective.

"You've been reading my work," Marty said, her tone more neutral than before.

Pickett nodded. From the campfire, the soldiers' song continued:

We loved each other then, Lorena,
More than we ever dared to tell.
And what we might have been, Lorena,
Had but our loving prospered well.

"That song," Marty said, turning her attention back to the music. "What is it?"

"'Lorena,'" Pickett replied. "It was popular with Confederate soldiers during the war."

"Do you have veterans from the Civil War in your ranks?"

"Several," Pickett said. "A few old sergeants, though one was just a drummer boy back then. A good song never dies, and *Lorena* is a good song."

"It's a sad song."

"Most of the best ones are," Pickett agreed.

"Some of the best are love songs," Marty pointed out.

"And those are the saddest of all," Pickett said, his voice flat and unyielding.

Marty studied his profile, shadowed by the moonlight. "Do you really believe that?"

"Yes."

"Why?"

"Because it makes a man, a man like me, painfully aware of what can never be."

"I see," Marty said, though she wasn't sure she did.

"Is that why you believe there's no place for wives in the military?"

"Yes."

"Have you ever read *Tenting on the Plains*?"

"No, I can't say that I have."

"It's by Elizabeth Custer, General Custer's wife."

"You see where Custer is now, don't you?"

"You're not saying he got himself killed because he was married, are you?"

"No," Pickett said, a slight edge to his voice. "Just making a comment."

"General Grant was married, so was George Washington. They managed all right. Maybe you've got a personal reason for not wanting to marry, but don't use the military as your excuse."

Pickett laughed, a genuine sound this time. "Miss McGuire, the way you're defending marriage, someone might think you're applying for the job."

"I am not," Marty shot back, her voice sharp enough to cut. She felt her cheeks heat up, and she was grateful for the darkness that hid her reaction. Why was she defending marriage so vigorously, anyway?

"I apologize," Pickett said, his tone sincere. "That was out of line."

Marty let out a small laugh, relieved the tension had eased. "All right, you're forgiven."

Pickett stood, brushing the dirt from his trousers. "I've got a long day tomorrow, so I'll be heading back. And if I stay out here much longer in the moonlight with a beautiful woman, I might do something I'll regret."

He started to walk away but then paused, turning back to her. "Miss McGuire, Dan mentioned you can ride. Is that true?"

"Yes," Marty said. "I can."

"Are you any good?"

"I'm better than good," she said, not bothering to hide her confidence.

"You'll get to prove it tomorrow," Pickett said. "If you're up for it, you can ride with me during the exercise."

"Really?" Marty asked, her excitement breaking through.

"Really," Pickett said, his tone still even. "Just don't be late. We leave at six."

"I'll be ready," Marty promised.

DAN CALHOUN ARRANGED for a horse for Marty early the next morning. One of the soldiers delivered the animal to her tent shortly before six o'clock.

"Miss, you might want to take this canteen," the soldier advised. "It gets mighty dry out there."

"Thanks," Marty said as she began filling the canteen at the water keg. "And thanks for the horse."

"You won't have any trouble with him. Dandy's a good, reliable horse."

Marty finished filling the canteen and hooked it onto the saddle pommel. She patted the horse's nose. "Hello, Dandy. I'm sure we'll get along just fine. The only problem I've had so far is with these ridiculous clothes. This riding skirt is a joke. Too bad women can't wear pants like men."

The soldier chuckled, the idea clearly amusing him. "Imagine that, women wearin' pants."

"It would be a lot more practical," Marty replied. She swung up into the saddle just as the bugle call for

Boots and Saddles sounded, making her worry that the regiment might leave without her. "Where's the colonel?" she asked.

"He's over in that field," the soldier said, pointing to the other side of the stone fence that had been Marty's backrest the night before. "There's a gap in the fence about half a mile down.

"I can't be late on my first day," Marty muttered, pressing her knees against the horse's sides and urging him forward toward the stone fence.

"Here, miss, be careful!" the soldier called after her, but Marty was already focused on the stone fence.

Dandy was indeed a good horse, responding eagerly to her command. Marty bent low over his withers, feeling the rush of wind in her face and the familiar thrill of a good ride. She and Dandy moved as one, his hooves drumming a steady rhythm on the ground. As they neared the fence, Marty gave the slightest nudge, and Dandy soared over the stone wall as if it were nothing at all.

What she hadn't told Nelson—or anyone else—was that she'd competed in county fair steeplechases as a girl. This fence was no challenge for her.

A sergeant rode out to meet her as she landed on the other side.

"Miss McGuire, the colonel sends his regards and asks if you'd like to ride with him."

"Thank you, Sergeant. I'd be delighted."

The regiment was already moving out when Marty reached Nelson's side. He sat tall on his horse, watching the men file past and returning the salutes of each unit commander.

"Quite impressive," Nelson remarked. "You said

you were good on a horse. I didn't realize how good. Where'd you learn to ride like that?"

"From my mother," Marty replied.

Nelson raised an eyebrow. "Your mother?"

"Yes. The Spanish and Cubans value their women's skills on horseback. They even hold national equestrian contests for women. Twenty-seven years ago, my mother won that event."

"It's a shame we don't have such contests here," Nelson said. "You'd do well."

"Maybe someday they'll have athletic contests for women too," Marty said. "I've read there's a movement to include women in future Olympic Games."

Nelson laughed. "You'd like that, wouldn't you?"

"I would. I suppose you're the kind of man who'd oppose it?" Marty challenged.

"No," Nelson said, rubbing the scar on his cheek as he smiled at her. "I'm not opposed to it. Truth be told, I'm not against women getting the vote either, but I'd rather not go around broadcasting such radical views."

"Why, Colonel, are you afraid?" Marty asked, arching an eyebrow.

"You might say that," Nelson admitted, a hint of seriousness in his tone. "Come on, A Troop should be in position by now. Let's go check on them."

Nelson kicked his horse into a gallop, and Marty followed suit. Whether he rode this way all the time or was showing off for her, she wasn't sure, but they leaped fences, splashed through streams, and tore down shaded roads at breakneck speed. It was exhilarating.

They were challenged by an advance sentry as they approached the troop.

"Halt! Who goes there?"

"Colonel Pickett and a friend," Nelson replied.

"Advance and be recognized," the sentry responded.

As they drew closer, the sentry examined them closely. Marty caught a flicker of something in the soldier's eyes, as if he suspected she was more than just the colonel's *friend*, but he remained professional.

"The colonel and his friend may pass," the sentry said, snapping to attention.

"Good work, soldier," Nelson said, then led Marty into the defensive position A Troop had established.

Nelson inspected the troop meticulously, moving a few men to different positions and discussing ominous terms like *fields of fire* and *killing zones*. Marty took it all in, fascinated by the precision and cold efficiency of military planning.

They were checking on their third troop when the sky darkened rapidly, and a thunderstorm erupted. Lightning slashed across the sky, illuminating the landscape in jagged, brilliant flashes. Thunder crashed overhead, rolling through the hills like cannon fire. The rain followed, pouring down in sheets, drenching them within seconds.

"Over there!" Nelson shouted, his voice barely audible over the storm. "That house—we can take shelter!"

Marty spurred Dandy forward, staying close to Nelson as the rain brought the visibility to near zero. They reached a small overhang on one side of the house, where they tied their horses. Nelson took her hand and pulled her quickly through the downpour to the shelter of the small, weather-beaten house.

"Don't you think you should knock?" Marty asked as Nelson pushed the door open without hesitation.

"No need," Nelson replied. "This house belongs to Mr. Fielding Sinclair. He offered it to me as headquarters during the exercise, but I thought it better to stay in the field with the men."

"Did he move out?"

"He comes here occasionally, but he has a place in Middletown, too," Nelson explained.

The storm raged outside, the sound of rain hammering on the roof nearly drowning out their conversation. Nelson took a moment to secure the door and check the windows, ensuring they were as protected as possible.

Just as they settled into the dim interior, they heard the sound of horses approaching, followed by the muffled voices of men.

"There are their horses, they must be inside," one voice said, followed by a sharp knock on the door.

"Colonel! Colonel, are you in there?"

Nelson moved to the door, opening it to reveal a drenched soldier.

"Colonel, we just got the news we've been waitin' for! Congress has declared war on Spain. Orders are to return to the city immediately and then prepare to ship out to Cuba. We'll be in action by next week!"

"Does Major Calhoun know?"

"Yes, sir, he sent us to find you and Miss McGuire."

"We got caught in the storm," Nelson said briskly. "Get word to all unit commanders to break off their exercises and return to the bivouac area. I want everything packed and ready to move. Have Calhoun recall the train—we're heading back tonight."

"Yes, sir! Don't worry, sir, we'll give them Spaniards

hell. They've never faced anything like the Lightning Cavalry."

Nelson nodded, his expression unreadable. "We'll do our duty."

As the soldier hurried away, Nelson turned to Marty, his voice lowering. "Did you hear?"

Marty nodded, her voice steady despite the weight of the news. "Yes, I heard."

Nelson looked out at the storm, the relentless downpour reflecting the tension in the air. "Get ready. It's going to be a long night and an even longer journey ahead."

Six

When Marty returned to the newspaper office the next day, she found a pile of letters all over her desk.

"What is this?" she asked Talbot, her voice carrying a note of impatience.

Talbot leaned back in his chair, a smirk tugging at the corners of his mouth. "Letters from your many admirers, Marty. Looks like you've got yourself quite the following. Readers really like your articles."

Marty raised an eyebrow. "Really?"

"Yeah, and there's one official-looking envelope from the Embassy of the Republic of Cuba. That might interest you."

"The Republic of Cuba?" Marty echoed, her curiosity piqued.

"Yep. The US just recognized them. The Free Cuba Legation you visited in New York is now their consulate, and guess what? You're an honorary citizen of their new nation."

Marty blinked in surprise. "I am?"

"Seems Senor Mendoza pulled some strings for you," Talbot said, eyeing her with a mix of amusement and admiration.

Marty allowed herself a small, satisfied smile. "Well, that's something. My mother will be proud. It's a shame I can't go there now."

Talbot shifted in his seat, his expression growing serious. "About that…I've been meaning to talk to you."

Marty's demeanor hardened. "What's the problem?"

Talbot let out a deep breath. "It's Mr. Chambers. He jumped ship—took an offer from Hearst. Stabbed me in the back."

Marty crossed her arms. "Chambers? Your military writer?"

"Ex-military writer," Talbot corrected, bitterness edging his voice. "He resigned two days ago."

Marty's eyes narrowed. "Watch out for Hearst. He tried to recruit me too. He's poaching from the *Banner*."

"Yeah, well, that's the game," Talbot said, the faintest trace of a grin returning. "But it got me thinking… How would you like to be my new military writer?"

Marty's pulse quickened, but she kept her voice steady. "Me? Are you serious, Mr. Talbot?"

"As serious as a heart attack," Talbot replied. "You've proven you can get the story and write it damn well. You want the job, it's yours—comes with a two-and-a-half-dollar raise, naturally."

Marty arched an eyebrow. "What was Chambers making?"

"That's different. He's a man," Talbot said, his tone almost dismissive.

Marty didn't flinch. "Uh-huh. And he's a man who sold you out. What was he making?"

"Twenty-five a week," Talbot muttered. "Plus bonuses, depending on column inches."

Marty leaned forward. "I'll take twenty, plus the same bonuses."

Talbot rubbed his forehead, studying her. After a long pause, he relented. "Fine. But keep it quiet. If word gets out I'm paying a woman that much, I'll have a mob at my door."

"Not a soul will hear it from me," Marty promised. "What about my accreditation?"

Talbot allowed himself a grin. "Lucky for us, the accreditation belongs to the *Banner*, not Chambers. So, if he's not using it, you can."

Marty nodded, considering the logistics. "How do I get there?"

"The original plan was to send you to Key West by train, but the ships leaving from there are packed. No accommodations for a woman, they say. So, I pulled a favor with General Shafter. You'll sail aboard the *Conqueror*, Commodore Vanderbilt's private ship. It's transporting the Lightning Cavalry to Cuba."

"The Lightning Cavalry?" Marty echoed.

"Yeah. You should be right at home, considering you've already spent a week with them in the field."

Marty hesitated, then spoke cautiously. "Although…"

Talbot's eyes narrowed. "Although what?"

"It's just… I hope Colonel Pickett doesn't find out and try to stop me."

Talbot gave her a puzzled look. "What's the deal with Pickett? You've always written well of him."

"It's not that," Marty said, choosing her words carefully. "He just might not appreciate having a woman tagging along."

Talbot shrugged. "Your orders come from General Shafter, not Pickett. He'll have to live with it. Now, get to your apartment and start packing. You sail tomorrow."

As Talbot turned to leave, Marty impulsively reached out and planted a quick kiss on his cheek. He jumped, nearly dropping his unlit cigar.

"Hey," he said, trying to sound gruff. "None of that."

"Just wanted to thank you," Marty replied with a grin.

Before Talbot could retort, a clerk called out from the front of the room. "Marty, there's a call for you."

Marty sighed, leaving her desk and walking over to the clerk's station to use the phone.

"Hello?" she answered, hearing static on the line.

"Marty?" The voice on the other end was faint but unmistakable. "Marty McGuire?"

"Yes, this is Marty McGuire."

"Ah, good," the woman said. "This is Molly Calhoun, Dan's wife. We met last week."

Marty recognized the name. "Molly, of course. How are you?"

"Fine. I've been reading your articles. They were wonderful. They made me feel like I was right there with you."

"Thank you, Molly. I appreciate that."

"You know the boys are leaving tomorrow?"

"Yes, I'm aware."

"That's why I'm calling," Molly said. "Dan, Nelson, and I are having a farewell dinner tonight. We'd like you to join us."

"Nelson will be there?"

"Yes," Molly confirmed.

Marty hesitated. "Does he know you're inviting me?"

Molly chuckled. "He does. In fact, it was his idea. He thought you might be more likely to accept if I extended the invitation. Will you come?"

Marty's mind raced, but she finally answered. "All right. Where and when?"

"Fifth Avenue Hotel, around seven?"

"I'll be there."

"Good," Molly said. "Nelson will appreciate it, and I'm looking forward to seeing you again, too."

Marty hung up the phone, a small smile playing on her lips. *So, it was Nelson's idea*, she thought. *Maybe there's more to this than I realized.*

THE DINING ROOM of the Fifth Avenue Hotel had been taken over entirely by the Lightning Cavalry. Flags, streamers, and banners like *Good Luck, Lightning Cavalry!* and *Remember the Maine!* adorned the walls. The soldiers were dressed in their sharp ceremonial blue uniforms, a stark contrast to the gritty, battle-worn men Marty had seen during their recent exercises. A few soldiers introduced their wives to her, their faces serious beneath the polite smiles.

One of the wives leaned in as she shook Marty's hand. "I'll admit, I was jealous when I heard a woman was out there with my Benji while I had to stay home.

But your stories were so wonderful that I was glad you were there. It made the waiting easier."

Marty nodded, a hint of respect in her reply. "How nice of you to say that."

There were several more introductions and many more comments such as the one made by the first woman, until, finally, Marty made her way to the front table, where Molly, Dan, and Nelson were seated. As she approached, Dan and Nelson rose, with Nelson pulling out a chair for her.

"You've certainly made an impression on my men—and their wives," Nelson remarked.

"And on their commander," Molly chimed in, a teasing edge to her voice. "Why don't you admit it, Nelson?"

Nelson hesitated, then gave a slight nod. "I'll admit, I wasn't keen on having you in the field. But your stories…they did a lot for morale, both here and back home."

Marty met his gaze, weighing her words. "I'm glad you think so, because…" She almost mentioned her assignment to Cuba but stopped herself. Despite his change of heart, she doubted Nelson would be thrilled about her joining them on the battlefield. And given his influence, he might even persuade General Shafter to pull her authorization.

Nelson watched her closely. "Because what?"

"Because it's more meaningful coming from someone who wasn't exactly on my side at first," Marty said, sidestepping the truth.

Nelson leaned back slightly. "I was never against you, Marty—not personally."

Marty's eyes narrowed slightly. "You could've fooled me."

Before Nelson could respond, a voice boomed through a megaphone. "Ladies and gentlemen! The orchestra will play its first waltz. Please remain seated for this honor, reserved for our colonel and his lady!"

The room erupted in applause, and all eyes turned to the head table. Nelson turned to Marty with a grin. "Looks like you've been volunteered as my lady for the night. Would you care to dance?"

Marty stood and offered her hand. "Why not?"

Nelson was an excellent dancer, leading with the kind of confidence that mirrored his command in the field. As they moved together, Marty felt the strength in his grip, the disciplined control in his movements. For the duration of the waltz, she let herself fall into the rhythm, almost forgetting the hundreds of eyes on them. It wasn't until the waltz finished and the others applauded that she recalled they were giving a performance.

They danced two more numbers before returning to the table for dinner.

"Eat up, Dan," Nelson said with a grin. "This is the last decent meal we'll have for a while."

Molly's forced smile faltered slightly. "You promised we wouldn't think about tomorrow."

Dan reached over, touching her cheek. "Come on now, none of that."

Molly managed a weak smile. "I'll be all right. It's just… I'm going to miss you."

Nelson turned to Marty. "And you, Miss McGuire? Are you going to miss us?"

Marty shot back a wry smile. "After all your talk about women being a distraction, you're asking if I'll miss you?"

Molly laughed, easing the tension. "She's got you there, Nelson."

Nelson coughed, trying to cover his embarrassment. "It was just a figure of speech."

Dan leaned forward. "You will come see us off, right? We're leaving at six in the morning."

Marty kept her expression neutral. "Six is early. You'll be busy, and I wouldn't want to get in the way."

She wasn't lying entirely—she did plan to be there, just not in the way they expected. It was better if Nelson didn't have time to try and stop her from boarding.

"Oh," Dan said, sounding a bit disappointed. "I suppose you're right."

Molly nudged him. "Don't put her on the spot, Dan. She probably has better things to do than stand on a pier at dawn."

Marty glanced at Nelson, but his face gave nothing away.

After dinner, Marty and Molly excused themselves to the ladies' room.

"I think Nelson's a little disappointed you won't be there tomorrow," Molly said as they walked.

"I couldn't tell by looking at him," Marty said.

Molly chuckled. "You didn't know where to look. Whenever he reacts to something, he gets tiny strawberries in each cheek. When we were kids together, I could always tell what he was thinking by looking for the strawberries."

Marty raised an eyebrow. "And were they there?"

Molly nodded. "Almost as big as tomatoes. But don't let on I told you. He'd hate that."

"Your secret's safe with me."

Molly grew more serious. "It's probably smart not

to show up tomorrow. It might make him realize how much he actually cares."

Marty stopped and faced her. "I will be there tomorrow."

Molly looked confused. "I thought you said—"

"I won't be there to see them off. I'm going, too."

Molly's eyes widened. "What? Does Nelson know?"

Marty's expression tightened. "No, and I need you to keep it that way."

Molly hesitated. "Are you sure you know what you're doing? This isn't a game, Marty. It's dangerous —you could be killed."

"I'm not afraid," Marty said. "Please, Molly, don't say anything about it. I told you because I wanted you to know, to understand why I wouldn't be waving goodbye tomorrow."

Molly studied her for a moment, then nodded. "All right, I won't say anything. But I have my own reasons. Your stories from the field made me feel like I was there with Dan. If your reports from Cuba do the same, it might make the wait a little easier."

"Thanks, Molly. I appreciate it."

MARTY BOARDED the *Conqueror* at five o'clock sharp the next morning. The *Conqueror*, a six-thousand-ton steam vessel, was usually assigned to the Atlantic route as a passenger ship. She had been loaned to New York's militia unit, the Lightning Cavalry. It wasn't a government assignment—if it had been, the ship would likely have ended up in the Florida fleet—but rather a stroke of good luck for the Lightning Cavalry.

General Shafter, commanding the American Expeditionary Force, was down in Tampa, scrambling to load twenty-five thousand men, along with their horses and gear, onto a mismatched fleet. The situation there was a mess—men and animals crammed into the stifling holds of ships, some still powered by paddle wheels, others so outdated they'd have to be towed to Cuba. Malaria was already making the rounds.

The crew running the *Conqueror* was its normal crew, and when they took a look at Marty's authorization, no one challenged it. She was shown to a cabin with a private bath—a concession to her gender, no doubt. Once settled, she found a spot on deck where she could keep an eye on the loading of men and equipment without drawing attention to herself.

Crowds began gathering on the pier even before six o'clock, and by six, there were hundreds of spectators present. A band struck up some martial tunes, but the real sound came from the distant rumble of a thousand horses moving in unison.

"Here they come!" someone shouted.

"Hurrah for the Lightning Cavalry! Hurrah for Colonel Pickett!"

From her vantage point on deck, Marty had a clear view as the cavalry wheeled their horses off West 51st and down to the 90th Pier. The crowd's cheers echoed over the water, and she could see Nelson in the lead, smiling and waving as the men quickly and efficiently loaded onto the ship.

By eight o'clock, the whistles started blowing, and stewards moved through the docks, herding the last of the civilians ashore. Marty had positioned herself in a small canvas chair between two large ventilator horns—massive scoops designed to funnel fresh air below deck. From there, she could observe the action without being noticed.

Tugboats arrived, securing their lines and slowly *walking* the ship out of its berth. The band's music was soon drowned out by the ship's horn, the shouts of the men, and the rumble of the engines. Marty watched as the shore receded, the figures on the dock shrinking to mere dots as the *Conqueror* powered its way toward the Statue of Liberty.

As they passed the statue, the men's rowdy behavior quieted. Marty couldn't help but be struck by the immense size of the monument. Though only twelve years old, it had already become an enduring symbol of America, as iconic as the Liberty Bell or the Capitol itself—a beacon for those leaving and a welcome sight for those returning.

She wondered how many of the men on board were seeing it for the last time. She shivered and put the thought out of her mind.

Seven

For the first three days at sea, Marty McGuire began to question her decision. The ship hadn't hit any storms, but the constant rolling and pitching in the heavy swells left her fighting off waves of seasickness. As long as she stayed in bed, she could stave off the nausea, but once she stood up, it would overtake her.

There was a residual advantage to her bout with *mal de mer*, even though it was uncomfortable. She was able to stay out of the way of everyone, and thus, her presence on board the ship was still unknown to Nelson.

By the evening of the third day, the sea had finally calmed, and Marty started feeling more like herself. After a long bath and a change into fresh clothes, she ventured out of her cabin. She felt almost invigorated, an especially pleasant feeling since she had begun to think she would never feel good again.

The ship had seemed enormous while docked in New York, a towering giant of steel and wood stretching the length of a city block. But now, in the middle of the ocean with nothing but horizon in every direction, it felt small—vulnerable, even. They were heading south, the setting sun off the starboard side made that clear enough. Marty smiled to herself. *Starboard*—she'd finally gotten the terminology down.

As the sun dipped lower, its fiery reflection stretched across the water, casting the ship in a warm glow. The sky ignited with colors, the kind that made you stop and just take it all in. Marty watched until the last bit of sun vanished beneath the horizon.

"It's something, isn't it?" a voice cut through her thoughts. Marty turned to see Dan Calhoun leaning casually against a stanchion.

"Dan," she said, a bit startled. "How long have you been there?"

"Long enough to see you enjoying the sunset," Dan replied. "I didn't want to interrupt."

She brushed a stray lock of hair behind her ear. "It was beautiful," she admitted, then smiled. "Are you surprised to see me?"

"No, not really," Dan said with a shrug.

"Not really?"

"Molly told me you were coming," he said, holding up a hand to forestall any concern. "Don't worry, she didn't tell Nelson, and neither have I. Your secret's still safe. But I was beginning to think you might stay holed up in that cabin the whole trip."

"I've been a little under the weather," Marty said.

Dan chuckled. "You're not alone. Half our men have been wrestling with the same thing."

"You?"

"Not me. I've sailed plenty of times. Nelson's been fine too, but I know it can knock the wind out of you.

It's hard to think about it, but the best thing to do is eat."

"You're right. For the first three days, I couldn't even think about food," Marty said with a laugh. "I must confess that I'm hungry now, but I have no idea where to find the dining area—or if it's even still open."

Dan grinned. "Officers eat in the wardroom mess. They'll be serving until four bells."

"Four bells?"

"Eight o'clock. Come on, I'll show you."

Marty followed Dan along the deck to a metal door he referred to as a hatch. He turned the levers, opened it, and motioned for her to step inside. Marty carefully stepped over the high sill and found herself in a space that was quite different from the deck. Outside, the deck was of gray, weathered wood. This floor could have been the floor of a fine home, for it was a rich, glossy brown. The floor branched out into a hallway. Dan led the way until they stepped through another door.

"This is the wardroom," Dan said as they entered a large room dominated by an impressive table set with china, crystal, and silver. A few young men in crisp white uniforms stood ready to serve.

As Marty was about to sit down, more officers entered the room. Nelson Pickett among them. He stopped short when he saw her.

"What the—? How did you get here?"

"She came aboard last night," Dan said with a grin, earning a round of chuckles from the others.

"I got here the same way you did," Marty said. "I walked up the gangplank."

"Are you a stowaway?" Nelson asked, disbelief evident in his voice.

"No," Marty replied calmly. "I have authorization from General Shafter to be aboard. I'm going to Cuba as a war correspondent."

"You what?" Nelson's voice was thick with incredulity.

"You heard me."

"Oh, I heard you all right," Nelson said, his eyes narrowing. "I just don't believe it."

"I can show you my authorization if you'd like," Marty offered.

"It's authentic, Colonel," one of the ship's officers interjected. "I saw it myself when she boarded. I assumed you knew of her, or I would have said something sooner."

"Oh, I know her," Nelson said, his voice hard. "I just didn't think she'd have the audacity to stab me in the back like this."

"Stab you in the back?" Marty echoed, her eyes narrowing. "What are you talking about?"

"You know damn well what I'm talking about," Nelson snapped. "You know my stance on women in combat zones, and yet here you are, undermining me."

"Colonel Pickett," Marty said, her voice steady, "I wasn't aware that this war was being fought because of us or our personal feelings. I thought it was being fought for a much nobler cause."

"Oh, yes, I'd nearly forgotten," Nelson said, his tone dripping with sarcasm. "It's about the noble cause of journalism. Steward!"

"Yes, sir," the steward responded promptly.

"Serve the lady in her cabin."

"What? You have no right to banish me to my cabin!" Marty's voice was sharp. "I have General Shafter's permission to be here."

"You have General Shafter's permission to accompany us to Cuba," Nelson said coldly. "But as the commanding officer of the Lightning Cavalry, I'm responsible for security. My officers and I will be discussing military tactics at this table, and I won't risk any of it making its way into your stories."

"You…you know I wouldn't do that!" Marty's voice cracked with frustration.

"Regardless, I'm not taking any chances," Nelson said firmly. "You'll take your meals in your cabin for the duration of the voyage."

Marty's eyes welled with tears of anger and humiliation. She glanced around the room, but the other officers avoided her gaze, their loyalty to the chain of command binding them to silence.

"Come along, Marty," Dan said gently, placing a hand on her shoulder. "I'll escort you back to your cabin…"

She bit back her retort, knowing Dan wasn't the enemy here. "Thank you," she managed, swallowing her pride as she let Dan lead her out.

It was dark now, and as they walked along the deck, the only light came from dim lamps placed low to avoid detection by any Spanish warships. The reduced lighting was a reminder that, out here, speed was their only defense.

"You shouldn't be too hard on him," Dan said after a stretch of silence.

"Oh? And why not? He humiliated me in front of all those men, he refuses to deal with me fairly, and you think I should go easy on him?" Marty's voice was edged with frustration.

"You scare him."

"I scare him?"

"Yes. He's never had to face anything like this before. Never had to contend with the feelings you stir in him."

"Well, he's doing a fine job of handling it," Marty said dryly.

"You have to understand, Marty, Nelson's used to being in control. He's a natural leader—graduated top of our class at West Point. He's led men in the toughest situations out West, making decisions with no one to answer to but himself. Now he's a full colonel at thirty, leading a regiment into battle. He can handle all that. But when it comes to his own feelings, it's a different story. He's not as in control as he wants to be."

"Dan, are you trying to tell me Nelson has feelings for me?" Marty asked, a mix of skepticism and surprise in her voice.

"Yes," Dan said simply. "I know it, Molly knows it, and even though he won't admit it, Nelson knows it too. The real question is, what do you feel about him?"

Marty stopped as they reached her cabin door. She ran a hand through her hair, trying to process what Dan was saying. "Oh, Dan, I don't know," she said, her voice quieter now. "I have the same reasons Nelson does for not wanting to fall in love. I have a career that excites me, and now I have a chance to do something no woman's ever done before—cover a war from the battlefield. There are a hundred reasons not to get involved with a man, and a dozen more why it shouldn't be Nelson Pickett."

"Do you love him?" Dan pressed, his tone firm.

"God help me, yes," Marty admitted, almost reluctantly. "But I'm afraid all that's going to come from it is hurt. I wish…"

"You wish what?"

"I wish I'd never met him."

Dan laughed, a deep, genuine sound.

"That's not funny," Marty said, a bit hurt by his reaction.

"It is, actually," Dan said, still chuckling. "Because just last night, Nelson said the same thing about you."

"Last night? He was talking about me?"

"He was. We were having coffee in the wardroom, just the two of us. He mentioned that he missed you—said he's never missed any woman before, but he's missing you. Then he said it would have been better if he'd never met you at all. So you see, Marty, you're not alone in this. Nelson's right there with you, feeling the same way."

Marty shook her head, still trying to wrap her mind around it. "Dan, you and Molly are in love. I've never dealt with anything like this. Tell me, is it supposed to be this painful?"

Dan smiled, a knowing look in his eyes. "In the beginning, yeah. The uncertainty, the doubts—that's part of it."

"Then why do people write poems and songs about it like it's some grand thing? Who'd want to feel this kind of hurt?"

Dan's smile grew. "Because once the hard part's over, when all that's left is the good, there's nothing on earth that compares to it. That's when you realize it was worth every bit of the pain, and then some."

"Do you think Nelson and I will ever get there?" Marty asked, her voice a little softer.

"That's something only time will tell," Dan said. "You'll just have to wait and see. Now, let me go hurry up the steward. I know you're hungry."

"Thanks," Marty said, opening the door to her cabin. She paused before going in. "Dan?"

"Yeah?" His voice came from the shadows, a few steps away now.

"Molly's a lucky woman to have you," she said.

Dan chuckled. "You can tell her that for me sometime. I'm not sure she knows what she's got."

"I'll make sure she knows," Marty promised.

DINNER in the wardroom was tense and quiet. The usual banter was absent, replaced by the sound of utensils against plates as the officers ate quickly and left with muttered excuses. Soon, Nelson was the only one left at the table.

Nelson sat there, staring at his untouched food. The stewards were still on duty, efficiently clearing away the plates and replacing them with fresh settings, but Nelson's plate remained, mostly full. He had barely eaten, though his coffee cup was empty.

"More coffee, Colonel?" one of the stewards offered.

"I'll get it," Nelson replied, getting up to refill his cup from the large pot on the small stove. Instead of returning to the table, he settled on a leather sofa along the wall. The room was lined with paintings of famous ships—the *Mayflower*, the *Constitution*, and the *Olympia*, Dewey's flagship in the Pacific. These were ships that carried the weight of history, and Nelson found a strange comfort in their silent presence.

"Is the colonel finished with his dinner?" the chief steward asked.

"Yes," Nelson said with a dismissive wave, signaling for the food to be cleared away. He sipped his coffee, lost in thought, until Dan entered the room. Dan poured himself a cup and settled into a leather chair near Nelson. The stewards, sensing the need for privacy, quietly exited, leaving the two men alone.

"I don't know why I did that," Nelson finally said, breaking the silence. He leaned his head back, letting out a long sigh. "It was like someone else was speaking."

"Nelson, whatever's eating at you, don't take it out on Marty. She's just doing her job, same as the rest of us," Dan said, his voice steady.

"I know, but you don't understand what's going on in my head."

Dan chuckled. "You think we're all blind? It's clear as day, Nelson. You're in love with her."

Nelson looked at Dan, surprised. "Does it show that much?"

"Of course it does."

"It's not fair," Nelson muttered.

"Not fair? To who?" Dan asked, eyebrows raised.

"To Marty," Nelson admitted. "I have no right to ask her to love me. I'm a career soldier, Dan. I'll spend my life in places like this, and she can't always come with me."

"You don't think she's tough enough? Military wives face that reality every day. Maybe our time together is short, but that just makes it all the more valuable."

"It's not just that," Nelson continued. "It's not fair to the men I command. They deserve my full attention. If I'm distracted by thoughts of a woman, they could suffer for it."

"Let me ask you this—have you been thinking about her for the past few days?" Dan asked, cutting to the heart of the matter.

"Well, yes, but—"

"But nothing," Dan interrupted. "Fighting against it is only making it worse. Trust me, I know. When I think of Molly, it gets me through the rough patches. But you're tearing yourself up inside because you're trying to deny what you feel. The men will suffer more if you're not at your best, and you weren't tonight."

Nelson sighed. "Maybe you're right."

"Of course I'm right. Go to Marty's cabin. Apologize."

"No, that'll just make things worse," Nelson said, shaking his head.

"It's the right thing to do," Dan insisted.

"I…I need to think about it."

Dan stood, placing his cup on the counter. "You think on it, but let me tell you as a friend—if you let this woman slip away, you'll regret it for the rest of your life."

Nelson watched Dan leave, the room falling into silence. Alone now, he walked over and turned off the lights, leaving the room in near darkness, illuminated only by the faint yellow glow from the passageway outside. He sat back down on the leather sofa, his thoughts inevitably drifting back to Marty. Every moment they'd spent together replayed in his mind.

He stood up, knowing he couldn't sit there all night brooding. With all the coffee he'd consumed, sleep was out of the question. He decided to visit the troop holds, see how his men were handling the voyage.

Nelson followed the dim lights to the ladder and climbed down to the lower deck. As he stepped into the troop compartment, one of the soldiers noticed him and called the men to attention.

"As you were, men," Nelson said, waving them off. He looked around, seeing the men scattered across the compartment—some writing letters, others playing cards, and a few gathered around a young private with a guitar. Nelson walked over to the group.

"Does Jake here really know how to play that thing?" he asked.

The men were surprised he knew the private's name. Nelson didn't know every soldier in his regiment —it was too large for that—but he had a knack for remembering names and faces when he overheard them. It made an impression.

"Yes, sir, Colonel. He plays as sweet as any angel," one of the men replied.

"Well, listen closely, Simmons. With the life you've led, you might not hear angels playing anytime soon."

The men laughed, easing the tension.

"Some of us might be hearing angels before this is all over," another soldier said, bringing a sobering silence to the group.

"What do you think, Colonel?" Jake asked. "Are some of us gonna get killed?"

"We're going to war," Nelson replied. "People get killed in wars. But you're well-trained and well-led. If you do what you're supposed to, your chances are no worse than getting thrown off a horse."

"There ain't a horse born that can throw me," one of the men boasted, lifting the mood again.

"Got a song you'd like to hear, Colonel?"

"How about *When Johnny Comes Marching Home*?

Always a good one to lift the spirits—picture us parading down Fifth Avenue with the ladies cheering us on."

"All right, men, let's give it a go," Jake said, strumming the first chords as the others joined in singing.

Nelson continued through the compartment, exchanging a few words here and there, looking at photographs some of the men showed him, all while the song played on behind him, each *hurrah* echoing with renewed vigor. When he finished, he headed back to the ladder.

"Good night, Colonel!" someone called out.

"We're gonna give 'em hell, sir!" another added.

As Nelson climbed to the next compartment, he could still hear the men singing, their voices strong and confident. In the next room, he found an argument in full swing.

"I'm telling you, I saw her. Clear as day."

"You're seeing things. She ain't on this boat."

"This here's a ship, and I'm saying I saw her!"

"Ten-hut!"

"As you were, men," Nelson said as the soldiers snapped to attention, then relaxed.

"Colonel, maybe you can settle this for us," one of the soldiers said. "This knucklehead says he saw Miss McGuire on this boat."

"It's a ship, and I did see her," the other soldier insisted.

"You didn't."

"He might've seen her," Nelson said, cutting off the argument. "Miss McGuire is on board."

"She is?" The disbelief was evident.

"Yes."

"Well, I'll be damned. She's gonna be writin' about us in Cuba like she did during trainin'?"

"That's her plan," Nelson confirmed.

"Well, how about that? My folks will get a kick out of that."

"You don't mind her being with us?" Nelson asked, a bit surprised by the reaction.

"Mind? Heck no, Colonel. First off, with her writing, maybe my folks won't be houndin' me for letters so much. And second, well," the soldier hesitated, looking a little embarrassed. "Truth is, Colonel, if there's a woman around, I'll be damned if I'm gonna turn tail. Might get scared, but I ain't showin' it if she's watching."

"Me too, Colonel," another man chimed in.

"Same here!" added a third.

Nelson smiled. "You won't have to worry about that. I know you men well enough to say you'll do just fine when the time comes."

"Colonel, if you think I won't be scared, you're givin' me too much credit. I'm scared already."

"Courage isn't about not being afraid," Nelson said, his voice firm. "It's about doing your duty even when you are afraid. And I know you've got that in you, Paul. All of you do."

"Yes, sir," Paul said, clearly proud the colonel knew his name. "I won't let you down."

"We're the Lightning Cavalry," Nelson said, his voice carrying a note of pride. "Years from now, when you're telling your grandkids about this war, you'll be glad to say you were part of this regiment."

"Hip, hip!" someone shouted.

"Hooray!"

"Hip, hip!"

"Hooray!"

"Hip, hip!"

"Hooray!"

Nelson waved to the men, then climbed back to the upper deck. He'd connected with his men, left them motivated and confident. So why couldn't he manage the same with Marty McGuire?

Eight

Marty stood at the stern, gripping the rail, her eyes on the dark sea. The wake churned behind the ship, stretching far into the distance. The moon hung low on the horizon, casting a cold glow, while stars flickered faintly overhead. The sea, once blue by day, had turned a deep shade of violet, with only a few white caps breaking the surface.

The steady hum of the engines and the rhythmic roll of the ship no longer bothered her. She was over her seasickness once and for all. Now, she believed she could actually enjoy the voyage, though she would have been able to enjoy it much more had Nelson not acted as he had at dinner.

Six bells rang in the night, which meant it was eleven o'clock. Marty hadn't realized how late it was. No wonder she no longer heard the sound of music or laughter coming up from the troop holds.

"Marty?" A low voice broke through the silence.

She tensed. She knew that voice too well. Nelson. She gripped the rail harder, her jaw tightening.

"Marty, I need to talk to you."

"Please," Marty said quietly. "You've made your feelings quite evident. I really don't wish to hear them expressed again."

"But that's just it, I haven't," Nelson said as he stepped up beside her, leaning on the rail. "May I join you for a while?"

"You already have."

They stood in silence, the ocean stretching ahead of them, before Nelson spoke again.

"When I was a kid, I made a sling, like David's in the Bible. I was good at it, too. One summer, I spotted a couple of doves on my grandmother's farm. I decided I wanted one for dinner." His voice was steady, but the story had weight. "It took a few tries, but I got one. I felt proud of myself—until I saw the other dove. It stayed there, watching, for the rest of the summer. Birds, you know, mate for life. And I'd taken one of them out, just for a meal."

He paused, his gaze fixed on the sea. "I swore I'd never cause that kind of pain again. I don't want anyone getting close enough to feel that kind of loss if something happens to me."

"Life doesn't work that way," Marty said, keeping her voice even. "You've got people who care about you whether you want them to or not. Molly? Dan? And me?"

He turned his head slightly but didn't meet her eyes. "I don't want to hurt you, Marty."

"You don't get to pick and choose," she said. "That's the way it is. You can't avoid it."

Nelson didn't say anything, just looked at her, his face unreadable. For a second, his hand brushed against her cheek, almost hesitant, and he met her gaze. "I wish I could explain what I'm feeling."

"Maybe you don't have to." Marty stepped closer, her tone direct.

Nelson stiffened, clearly conflicted. "Marty, this isn't—"

She cut him off, leaning in. "Am I bothering you?" There was no teasing in her voice, just quiet resolve.

Nelson's hand hovered by his side, as if caught between pulling her close and stepping back. His jaw tightened, the conflict clear, but the moment passed quickly. He pulled her in, the kiss hard and fast, no hesitation left.

Marty smiled as she sat up and started preparing for breakfast. Nelson had said they'd meet, and she took a little extra time to make sure she looked presentable. Not that it mattered—her striking looks weren't something she didn't think much about. She finished up and headed to the officers' wardroom.

Stepping through the door, her smile faded. The room was empty. She glanced at the clock: five minutes past eight. She was sure Nelson had said eight.

A steward entered the room. "Ma'am, would you like breakfast now?"

"Uh, yes," Marty replied, sitting down as the steward poured her coffee. "Where is everyone?"

"At their stations, ma'am," the steward said.

"Their stations?"

"Captain ordered all hands to battle stations at four this morning."

"Battle stations?" Marty asked just as Nelson walked in. He was dressed differently than before, in a tan canvas uniform and boots, with a pistol strapped to his side.

"Nelson, what's going on? Why are you dressed like that?"

He sat beside her. "This is a new field uniform for combat. Cooler, waterproof. Not much to look at, but it gets the job done."

"Coffee, sir?" the steward asked.

"Please," Nelson said.

"Why are they at battle stations?" Marty pressed.

"At four this morning, the watch spotted two Spanish warships tailing us," Nelson said, casually sipping his coffee.

Marty's eyes widened. "What?"

"Nothing to worry about," Nelson said calmly. "This ship's fast. We'll outrun them before nightfall. But until then, the men are on alert."

"That's why you weren't here at eight."

Nelson nodded. "I had to check on the men. They're on edge, stuck below deck. Not easy for them."

"No, I suppose not," Marty said.

Nelson leaned in slightly. "Marty, I could use your help."

"Of course."

"Would you come down with me and talk to the men?"

Marty blinked, surprised. "You want me to go below deck?"

"It's hot and uncomfortable. But it would mean something to them."

"I'll go," she said without hesitation. "I've been wanting to see them, but I didn't think you'd allow it."

Nelson smiled faintly. "Up until now, I probably wouldn't have. But I think they could use a boost."

She stood as the steward brought her breakfast. "Let's go."

"Easy there," Nelson said, chuckling. "You've got time to eat."

Marty ate quickly, barely tasting anything, then stood up again. "Now can we go?"

"All right," Nelson said.

Out on deck, Nelson pointed to the horizon. Marty saw two columns of smoke rising in the distance, though the ships were still out of sight.

"How does the captain know they're Spanish?"

"They fired at us earlier," Nelson said.

"You're kidding," Marty said. "I missed my first battle?"

Nelson laughed. "You didn't miss much, and I'd rather that be the last one you ever get near."

They reached the hatch to the troop holds, and Nelson paused. "Wait here. It's hot down there, and a lot of the men have stripped down to stay cool."

Marty waited while Nelson went below. When he returned, he nodded. "All right, you can come down now."

Marty followed him down the metal stairs, stepping into the stifling heat of the hold. The air was thick, and she felt the weight of it immediately. She scanned the room, catching the eyes of the soldiers, all packed into the tight, sweltering space.

"I told you I seen her," one soldier said. "Didn't I tell you?"

"Hello, Miss McGuire," a nearby sergeant called out. "You remember me? I brought you the horse out in the field."

"Of course I remember," Marty said. "Give my regards to Emma when you write her, won't you?"

"Yes, ma'am," the sergeant said, grinning.

"Miss McGuire, are you going to write about us?" one of the soldiers shouted.

"That's why I'm here," she replied.

"You won't write about anyone else, will you? Just us?"

"You'll give me plenty of action to write about, I'm sure," Marty said with a smile.

"That's right," another soldier chimed in. "We won't let you down."

"I'm gonna show her," one of the men said.

"Don't. It's embarrassing," another soldier muttered.

"It ain't embarrassing. It's good, and I'm gonna show it."

Marty looked over at the men, one of whom shoved a piece of paper toward her. It was a drawing.

"What do you think of this, Miss McGuire?"

Marty looked at the paper and raised her eyebrows. It was a near-perfect likeness of her.

"Who did this?"

"Eddie Stone here," the soldier said, pointing at his friend. "He's always drawing something."

Marty studied the sketch. "Mr. Stone, this is excellent."

"I could've done better," Eddie said, looking down. "Had to do it from memory. You're never still long enough."

"That makes it even more impressive," Marty said. An idea came to her. "Mr. Stone, would you mind if I sent some of your drawings to the paper while we're in Cuba? We'll pay you for them."

"Whooee, Eddie! You're gonna be famous like Miss McGuire!"

"As famous maybe," another soldier said, "but not as pretty."

That drew a laugh from everyone, including Nelson.

Later that day, after visiting the holds and talking to nearly all the men, Marty wrote her first dispatch, based on those visits.

Life in the Troop Hold of the Lightning Cavalry

By Marty McGuire, Special Correspondent

The men of the Lightning Cavalry, those gallant riders bound for battle, find their rest in a place known as the troop hold. *This hold, a great square chamber dimly illuminated by electric lamps with yellowed glass, is far from the comforts of home but serves as their refuge in these turbulent times.*

Along the four walls of this room, and on poles set through its middle, are beds stacked high—some as many as eight or nine in a row. The soldiers who occupy the highest bunks must scale their way up, using the lower berths as stepping stones to their nightly perch.

In the center of this hold, a roped-off space is reserved for their rucksacks, yet it also becomes a gathering spot. It is here, away from the confines of the beds, that the men assemble to exchange stories, sing, and write letters home. Though their talk often begins with bravado, filled with tales of what they will do to the Spanish, it soon shifts to more personal matters—their loved ones, wives, sweethearts, and children, left behind in the quiet towns they protect.

In these quiet moments, beneath the shadow of war,

one sees not only soldiers but husbands, fathers, and sons—men whose hearts, though steeled for the battle to come, still yearn for those far away.

By late evening, they had outdistanced the two Spanish warships completely, their plumes of smoke long gone on the horizon. In the wardroom, a sense of relief set in, and though liquor wasn't permitted aboard, the ship's orchestra was pressed into duty. The dining table was moved aside, and a makeshift dance was organized.

Marty, the sole woman present, found herself at the center of attention. The officers took turns dancing with her, their order determined by lot, each man eager for his chance.

As Dan took his place, he shot her a grin. "Do I detect a certain sparkle in Nelson's eye? Or am I seeing things?"

"I hope you do," Marty said, keeping her tone light. "And I hope I'm not imagining it myself."

Dan raised an eyebrow. "So, you and the colonel have reached some kind of understanding?"

Marty gave a small nod. "We have, Dan."

"That's good to hear." His grin widened as they moved through the steps, their conversation clipped by the pace of the dance and the eyes of the other officers watching them. Over the previous several weeks, Dan had come to be like a brother to her, and though they had to keep things brief, she wasn't about to not tell him how she felt.

The dance wound down around eleven, by which point Marty had danced with every officer present—twice over, in some cases. Nelson, however, had stayed back, allowing the others their turn. He didn't mind.

But he did step in as her escort back to her cabin, claiming that as his privilege.

As they walked along the deck, he glanced at her. "Tired?"

Marty chuckled, rolling her shoulders. "I've never been this popular at a dance before, that's for sure. A night to remember."

"You did good tonight," Nelson said, his voice steady. "Not just here. The men appreciated your time earlier today. Morale's high because of you."

"I'm glad to hear that," she said, suppressing a yawn.

He stopped at her cabin door, then turned her toward him, catching her gaze for a moment before leaning in and giving her a firm but brief kiss. "Good night, Miss McGuire."

"Good night, Colonel," she replied as she stepped inside, closing the door quietly behind her.

Nine

Marty had never seen anything like Tampa Bay. It was as if all the excitement of the war was swirling around like a hurricane, and Tampa Bay was the hurricane's eye. As soon as they arrived, she wasted no time in filing a story, capturing her first impressions with the detail that would make her readers feel as though they had stepped right into the heart of the action.

Tampa Bay: The Staging Ground for War

By Marty McGuire, Special Correspondent

The first thing that strikes the eye is the explosion of color. Signal flags of red and yellow flutter from the halyards of the ships, their white hulls gleaming in the sun, polished brass fixtures shining like mirrors. And then there is the vast expanse of blue—the water below and the sky above—seemingly endless and undisturbed except by the wakes of boats and ships crisscrossing the bay on their various duties.

The surface of the bay is alive with motion. Every craft, from the smallest launch to the largest warship, leaves a foamy white trail in its wake as it navigates between tasks. Captains, perched on their bridges, communicate through flashing signals or by the precise movements of signalmen, whose flags speak in a language understood only by those trained to decode them —a language of action and command.

On shore, thousands of soldiers, prepared for the coming campaign, drill relentlessly. The steady beat of drums and the rhythm of their marching feet echo across the water, a constant reminder that this peaceful bay is soon to be a gateway to war.

Among the many vessels docked here is one familiar to those aboard the Lightning Cavalry, similar to the ship that carried them from New York. But it is the battleship Oregon *that truly dominates the scene. Having completed an extraordinary journey from Bremerton, Washington, around Cape Horn, and up through the treacherous South Atlantic in a mere 68 days, the* Oregon *is the talk of every sailor in Tampa Bay. Her arrival is spoken of in tones of reverence.*

The Oregon *is a marvel of modern engineering, a fortress of steel and iron bristling with weaponry. Massive cannons, as long as trees, sit atop her decks, and her hull is studded with ports for even more guns of immense power. It is this warship, along with her formidable sisters, that will lead the charge when the invasion fleet sets sail for Cuba, ensuring the seas are clear of any enemy that dares oppose the might of the United States Military.*

After Marty filed her story, she learned that the

Lightning Cavalry would be leaving the ship for a brief period. The soldiers were being given a chance to stretch their legs and conduct some final drills before they embarked for Cuba. It meant she and Nelson would be separated for a while, but with all the activity around Tampa Bay, there seemed to be plenty of things to occupy Marty's time.

A few nights later, Admiral Sampson, commander of the invasion fleet, hosted a dinner for the war correspondents. By now, Marty's work had gained attention, and when she arrived, she was admitted without hesitation.

"I've read some of your stuff," one of the reporters said as she stepped in. "Pretty impressive."

He extended his hand. "Richard Harding Davis," he introduced himself, and Marty was caught off guard by the compliment. Davis was one of the most well-known journalists in the country. His approval signaled a shift, and the other reporters—many of whom had snubbed her back in New York—began to acknowledge her, though with some reluctance.

"I'm not sure how you did it," one of them said.

"How I did what?" Marty asked, her tone sharp but curious.

"Found anything interesting to write about during that field exercise. I remember it being nothing but cold mornings, blistering afternoons, and long stretches of boredom. Yet back in New York, all anyone could talk about was how exciting your stories were."

Marty smiled, but there was an edge to it. "Well, it was my first time covering something like that. I suppose it's all in how you look at things."

The reporter shifted his feet awkwardly, glancing at the floor. "Listen, about New York… I wanted to apologize for how we treated you. We weren't exactly gentlemen."

"I wasn't asking to be treated like a lady," Marty replied firmly. "Then or now. I'm here to do a job, just like you."

The reporter looked taken aback, but before he could respond, Davis chimed in with a laugh. "She's not just doing the job, she's doing it better than most of us."

That broke the tension, and soon enough, the rest of the reporters began introducing themselves. By the end of the evening, Marty had earned their respect—something more valuable to her than the initial snubs had been.

Before the dinner concluded, a young naval officer approached Marty with an invitation from Admiral Sampson. She followed him to a smaller room off the dining area, where the admiral stood and greeted her with a smile.

"Thank you for joining me," the admiral said, motioning to a chair. "What can I get you to drink?"

"A glass of white wine, please."

"Excellent. I'll have the same. The admiral made a slight motion with his hand, and his aide left quickly to get the drinks.

"It's a lovely gathering tonight," Marty said. "I thank you for including me with the other journalists."

Sampson chuckled. "You really don't know, do you?"

"Know what?"

"You're not just any journalist now, Miss McGuire. Your stories have been picked up by papers all over the country. You're making quite the name for yourself."

Marty blinked, momentarily caught off guard. "I…I didn't realize."

"And that's part of why I wanted to speak with you," Sampson continued. "Tomorrow morning, I'm leading an attack squadron to Matanzas. We're going to engage any Spanish ships we find and target the fortifications there. How would you like to come along?"

Marty straightened. "You're serious?"

"Absolutely. I think the navy could benefit from your way with words."

Marty felt the excitement rise in her chest. "How long will we be there?"

"Not long. Why do you ask?

"My primary task is to write about the Lightning Cavalry. They are New York's own, so to speak, and I do write for a New York paper."

"Not to worry, Miss McGuire. We'll leave in the morning, be off Cuba by dawn, handle what we need to, and be back here before the Lightning Cavalry returns to the ship. They won't miss you."

Marty nodded. "In that case, Admiral, I'd be honored to join you."

THE SQUADRON MOVED OUT EARLY the next morning, and Marty took her place on the bridge of the battleship *Oregon*. From there, she had a clear view of the entire fleet as they advanced. The ships sailed in two columns—the battleships to the left, the cruisers to the right—cutting through the water, leaving massive wakes in their path. Darting between them were the smaller, faster torpedo boats, skipping across the waves like corks in a storm.

For Marty, the scene was exciting. She had spent almost two weeks aboard the *Conqueror*, but this was different—here she was on the bridge, in the thick of things, watching the captain issue commands to the helmsman, shouting orders down the speaking tube to the engine room. She was also in the perfect position to watch the gun crews as they prepared the monstrous weapons for firing and the other sailors as they prepared the ship for battle.

The fleet steamed steadily through the day, slowing only during the night before resuming full speed the next morning. Suddenly, Marty spotted a streak of light arching up from the horizon ahead.

"What was that?" she asked.

"A signal rocket," Admiral Sampson replied, standing at the helm. "The Spaniards have spotted us. Captain Bradley, signal the fleet to form a line of battle."

"Aye, aye, sir," Bradley answered, and a signalman began wigwagging orders to the rest of the fleet. Marty watched as the ships maneuvered into a long, battle-ready line just as the green outline of Cuba appeared on the horizon.

Moments later, a series of flashes lit up the shore.

"Admiral, the fort's opened fire," Captain Bradley reported.

"Let them," the admiral replied, calm as ever.

A line of geysers erupted in the water, but they fell far short of the fleet.

"They're off by a mile," Sampson said with a slight smile.

"They'll need to elevate by at least ten degrees," Bradley replied with a cool nod.

The Spanish guns were firing at them, yet the admiral and the captain were talking about it as if it were just a routine task. Indeed, they were calmly discussing what the Spanish could do to correct their error and thus succeed in their attempt.

"Captain, lookout reports the Spanish fleet," someone called.

"Where?" Bradley asked.

"To starboard, sir."

Marty rushed to the right side of the bridge and looked across the water. A dozen Spanish ships were fast approaching.

"Engage the ships," Sampson ordered. "Alter course to meet them."

"Aye, aye, sir. Mr. Crane, take the stadimeter to the foremast."

Crane grabbed a device from a felt-lined box and hurried out, climbing the mast to take his position.

"What's a stadimeter?" Marty asked.

"It's a device to measure the distance to the target," Captain Bradley explained, just as an enemy shell hit the water so close to the ship that a wall of seawater splashed up onto the bridge, drenching everyone—including Marty.

Sampson wiped his face. "Captain, fire one salvo toward the fort. Reload and prepare for action against the Spanish fleet."

"Aye, sir!" Bradley barked the order to the gun crews, and Marty hurried to watch as they sprang into action. The gunnery team worked with precision, shouting commands over the roar of the engines.

"Set fuse, point detonating!" the gun captain yelled.

"Fuse, point detonating, set!"

"Load explosive shell!"

Two men hoisted a heavy shell and placed it on the track, and a third man rammed it home with a long rod.

"Shell loaded!"

"Load charge, two bags!"

Linen bags of powder followed the shell, the breechblock slammed shut, and the barrel was cranked to the proper elevation.

"Charge loaded! Range, one-five-double-O yards!"

"Number one turret, ready for firing!" the gun captain shouted as the other turrets reported their readiness in turn.

"Miss McGuire, I suggest you cover your ears," Admiral Sampson said calmly.

Then to Captain Bradley, "Fire at your discretion."

Bradley nodded, and the command was passed down. A moment later, the entire ship shuddered as all guns roared to life. The noise was like nothing Marty had ever heard, an ear-splitting blast that left a thick cloud of smoke lingering around the ship. Through the haze, she saw explosions ripple across the shore as the shells hit their mark. One by one, the other ships in the fleet fired, the thunder of their guns echoing across the water. As the smoke cleared, Marty could see fires burning on the shore, columns of black smoke rising into the sky.

The men cheered as the enemy fortifications crumbled, the first volley a clear success.

The fleet steamed at full speed, leaving the smoldering fort behind as they closed in on the Spanish warships. The Spaniards had already formed their battle line, and one of the officers handed Marty his binoculars for a closer look.

"Notice they're cleared for action," the officer said, "and they've got *engage the enemy* signals flying from their halyards."

Through the lenses, Marty saw figures moving hurriedly aboard the Spanish ships, prepping for battle much like the American crews had moments earlier. She watched as a group of them cheered, but then her gaze landed on one sailor, isolated from the others, vomiting over the side of the deck. Fear? The sight unsettled her, and she lowered the binoculars.

"What did you see?" the officer asked.

"The men," Marty replied quietly.

He nodded. "It's different when you realize they're just like us. This stops being a show and turns into something very real."

"Miss McGuire, step away from the glass," Captain Bradley called.

She did so just in time—at that moment, a Spanish shell burst a hundred feet above them, showering the bridge with shrapnel. Glass exploded from the window where Marty had been standing, shards flying everywhere. One piece struck the helmsman, cutting his arm, but he remained at his post, barely flinching.

"You may return fire when ready, Captain," Admiral Sampson said, his voice steady.

The *Oregon* and the other American ships responded in kind, their guns roaring to life. Marty felt the deck vibrate with every salvo. The deafening noise made her ears ring, but a sailor handed her cotton puffs to stuff in her ears, providing some relief from the relentless barrage.

The American fleet executed a precise back-and-forth movement in front of the Spanish line, firing repeatedly, pausing only when the smoke became too thick to see. Marty watched in awe as the ships moved methodically, their firing pattern almost like some carefully rehearsed show. Through the haze, she could track the shells as they arced toward the Spanish fleet—black streaks followed by flashes of fire as they found their marks. Within minutes, four Spanish ships were burning fiercely, thick smoke rising from their decks.

Marty glanced down at the American sailors below. She was surprised to see how calm and orderly they were. They were handling the guns and ammunition with a mechanical precision that belied the fact that they were in a life-and-death struggle.

Every time the *Oregon* fired a broadside, the ship shook violently, forcing Marty to grip the railing to keep her balance.

"Captain, the engineering officer reports the temperature in the engine room is over 130 degrees. Some men are passing out," reported a crewman with a set of telephone earphones.

"Tell the engineering officer to rotate his men," Bradley replied. "Send a third up for ten minutes, then rotate them back."

"Aye, aye, sir."

One hundred and thirty degrees! Marty's heart went out to those men who were having to spend this battle in the engine room, battened down without ventilation, baking in the heat of the furnaces and engine boilers, working hard from the physical exertion of shoveling coal. She hurried to the opposite side of the bridge and saw ten of them tumble out onto the deck. They were naked except for shores and drawers, and they were covered in sweat and soot. They lay near exhaustion, breathing hard, showing no concern or interest whatever in the battle that was still going on.

As the battle wore on, Marty could discern the admiral's plan. The American fleet was moving in a large oval formation, steaming past the Spanish ships at a steady six knots before circling back to re-engage. Each pass brought them closer to the enemy, the *Oregon* leading the charge. By the time they were within close range, Marty could see the Spanish sailors with her naked eye. It was obvious that they were suffering far more than the Americans. Every Spanish ship had been severely damaged, and two were completely engulfed in flames. Many of their guns were now out of operation, and she could see those gunners, who were unable to continue firing, now standing at the railing watching the battle.

The American gun crews, meanwhile, had no respite. They continued loading and firing, heaving 200-pound shells into the massive guns, even as the midday sun melted the pitch on the decks beneath their feet.

An hour and a half after the battle had started, three Spanish ships were out of action, and the remaining vessels, heavily damaged, broke off the engagement and began limping away from the fight.

"Shall we pursue, Admiral?" Captain Bradley asked.

Sampson stroked his chin, watching the battered enemy ships pull back. Then he shook his head.

"No," he said. "We've dealt them a terrible blow. Chasing them down would take it beyond war and into savagery. Set course for Tampa Bay, we're heading back tonight."

"Aye, aye, sir."

The *Oregon* signaled the fleet to withdraw, turning away on a course back to port.

"Secure from quarters," Admiral Sampson ordered. Moments later, a cheer went up from the deck. Battle gratings were lifted, and men, covered in grime, rushed topside, eager to breathe fresh air and to cheer their comrades aboard the other ships.

Marty watched them closely. These were the men who had fought the worst battle of all—the ones trapped below deck, working in conditions that would break most people. Down in the heat and the smoke, without even the satisfaction of seeing the enemy, they had endured. If a Spanish shell had hit the boilers, it would've been instant death for dozens of them—scalded alive. They hadn't seen the Spanish ships' shells fall wide, or their own shots land true. But in Marty's eyes, there was no doubt: they were the real heroes of this battle.

"Well, Miss McGuire, did you gather enough for a story?" Admiral Sampson asked, stepping up beside her.

"More than enough, Admiral," she replied.

"What angle will you take? The gunners' accuracy? The thrill of combat?"

"No, sir," Marty said, stepping over to the windows again. She looked down at the men who had just come up from the engine room. They were lined up at the rail, letting the spray from the sea wash over them, grateful for the cool breeze.

"I'm going to write about them," she said.

"The black gang?" Sampson asked with a slight smile.

"The black gang?"

The admiral chuckled. "It's what the crew calls the men in the engine room. It's not meant as an insult, believe me. In fact, they wear it like a badge of honor —because of all the soot and smoke that clings to them down there."

"I can't imagine what they went through," Marty said, shaking her head.

"I can," Sampson replied easily. "I started as an engineering officer myself." He looked at her with a knowing smile. "I knew I was right to bring you along. I doubt there's another reporter out here who'd recognize that those men are the real heroes today. You write about them, Miss McGuire, and you'll have a friend in the navy as long as I'm around."

"Thank you, Admiral," Marty said. "And thank you for letting me come on this mission."

ADMIRAL SAMPSON SENT a fast destroyer ahead to carry the news of their victory, so by the time the fleet entered Tampa Bay, the harbor was buzzing with celebration. Whistles blared from the ships already at anchor, and sailors crowded the rails, hanging from the lines and shrouds to cheer. Soldiers rushed to the shore, waving their hats and shouting as the gig carrying Marty and the officers made its way to the dock. They were treated like returning heroes.

The great rejoicing wasn't just because of the victory at sea. With the Spanish fleet either destroyed or crippled, the way was clear for the invasion of

Cuba. Generals Miles, Shafter, and Wood had all insisted that no troopships would sail until the Spanish navy was no longer a threat. The risk of losing thousands of men to enemy fire at sea would have been too great a blow, perhaps even forcing the US to withdraw from the war. Now, the soldiers who had been sweltering in the heat, tormented by mosquitoes, and growing bored with inactivity could at last rejoice, for the word had come down. As soon as they could get loaded, they would proceed to Cuba.

Marty wasted no time hurrying to the telegraph office to file her story, written during the return voyage.

"Are you Miss McGuire?" the telegraph operator asked as she stepped in.

"Yes, I am."

"I've got a message for you." He reached into a cubbyhole and handed her an envelope. Her eyes fell on Nelson's name scrawled across the front.

She opened the letter:

Dear Marty,

Are you surprised to hear from me like this? When I learned where you had gone, I figured the fastest way to reach you was to leave a message at the telegraph office. You're a woman with a sense of mission, and that means this will be the first place you go.

I've secured a room at the Tampa Bay Hotel—a feat in itself, trust me. Like you, I'm a man with a mission, and right now, my mission is to have a quiet dinner with you. Meet me in

Room 604 at seven tonight. You can tell me all about the naval battle then.

Sincerely,

Nelson.

Marty smiled. Though she hadn't admitted it, even to herself, she had been concerned about Nelson's reaction to her going with Admiral Sampson. Only now did she realize how relieved she felt knowing he wasn't upset.

"Everything all right, miss?" the telegrapher asked.

"Yes," Marty replied. "Everything's just fine."

Ten

The western sky bled red and orange as the sun sank into the Gulf, leaving the water streaked with shadows. The air was calm, the bay quieter than the open sea, with only the soft hiss of waves rolling in and pulling back. Nelson leaned on the balcony railing outside his suite, watching the horizon darken. He had been waiting for this moment for over a week, and the thought of seeing Marty again brought a smile to his face. It was strange how much he'd missed her. He'd resisted her involvement in the beginning—now, all that seemed foolish.

A knock at the door pulled him from his thoughts. "The table is ready, Colonel," a voice called from inside.

Nelson stepped back into the room, dismissing the hotel staff with a nod. The penthouse suite was everything he'd paid for: elegant, polished, and quiet. He glanced at the table—china, silver, crystal, all laid out as if it were for royalty. The champagne, still chilling, was a luxury, but one he didn't mind splurging on. This wasn't just any reunion.

Checking his reflection in the mirror, Nelson adjusted his white mess uniform. Around his neck, on a blue ribbon, hung the Medal of Honor. It was the first time he'd worn it since the president had put it on him, and the irony of it wasn't lost on him. He'd been decorated by the Commander-in-Chief, but in his mind, Marty McGuire held a higher rank. He walked over to the champagne bottle and, grabbing the neck between his palms, gave it a twirl.

IN ANOTHER ROOM in the same hotel, Marty was getting ready for her reunion with Nelson. She, too, was giving some thought to what she should wear. Most of Marty's clothes were of the type she could wear while being active. She had a half-dozen dresses that *Harper's Bazaar* identified as *Ladies' Sportswear*, such as the kind women wore while hiking or playing golf. She also had a few ladies' hunting dresses, which were much simpler and easier to handle than all the flounces on the more stylish gowns. She even had two outfits that were called *faire le bicyclette*, or bicycle trousers. *Harper's* had declared that they were quite proper for women, even though they were trousers, because, in the words of the magazine, the Turkish trousers were "long and ample, and made of such fullness that when standing upright, the division is obliterated, thus preserving m'lady's dignity."

Marty had packed one gown and she pulled it out —sky blue silk, Parisian in design, with fine detailing in dark blue braid. It wasn't flashy, but it had an understated elegance. As she dressed, she thought of Nelson. They hadn't seen each other in days, and though she never admitted it aloud, she was looking forward to this moment.

On her way to the elevator, she passed a few fellow reporters. They tipped their hats but didn't linger. If they noticed her dress, they didn't say anything, and that suited her just fine.

When the elevator doors opened, Nelson stood waiting at the suite's entrance, his mess uniform crisp, the Medal of Honor gleaming around his neck. "I see we both dressed for the occasion," he said, a grin tugging at the corner of his mouth.

Marty smiled. "It's been a while. I thought I'd make an effort."

Nelson stepped aside, letting her in. "I wanted to make tonight special. It's been nine days."

Marty took in the room, her eyes lingering on the elegant table setting. "This place…it's incredible. It must've cost a fortune."

"It did," Nelson admitted. "But it's worth it. This might be our last quiet evening together for a while." He stepped closer, placing his hands on her shoulders. "Tomorrow's going to be hectic. Roosevelt and his Rough Riders are pushing to get transport, and I've got to be ready."

"The Rough Riders?" Marty asked. "So it's true. Roosevelt's leading them personally?"

Nelson nodded. "Yeah, he's been wrangling to get his men on ships bound for Cuba. Word is, he's determined to be in the thick of it, not just sitting behind a desk. He's got his hands full. Roosevelt's a force of nature—he's made it clear he wants his Rough Riders to be at the front when we go ashore.

I'm just hoping he doesn't decide to commandeer the *Conqueror*."

"He wouldn't try that, would he?" Marty asked.

Nelson chuckled. "You don't know Theodore Roosevelt. The man's relentless. He's already got half the army in awe of him, and if he sets his sights on something, he'll do whatever it takes to get it. But we've got orders—our Lightning Cavalry is supposed to be on the *Conqueror*. Still, I wouldn't put it past him to try and take it over."

"He sounds like trouble," Marty said.

"He's the kind of trouble you want on your side in a fight," Nelson replied. "I respect him. He's tough, and he'll lead from the front. The Rough Riders are lucky to have him."

Their conversation shifted to other topics as they sat down for dinner, sharing stories from the past week. Marty spoke of the battle, the intensity of the fight, and Nelson updated her on the Lightning Cavalry's training. The meal was simple but good—broiled red snapper and cold shrimp, paired with white wine. By the time the champagne was brought out, they were both relaxed.

When the table was cleared, Nelson moved to the sofa, pulling Marty gently beside him. He kissed her, a brief but firm connection. When they pulled apart, Marty smiled.

"I've missed you, Colonel."

"And I've missed you." Nelson kissed her one more time and then stood up. "Let's get you back to your room before I get too comfortable. Tomorrow's going to be a long day, and Roosevelt won't wait for anyone."

Marty got to her feet. "Think you can keep him from hijacking your ship?"

Nelson smirked. "We'll see. But it's Roosevelt—he'll try, and I'll be ready."

As they walked to the door, Nelson gave her a reassuring look. "We'll get through tomorrow. Whatever happens, we'll handle it."

Marty nodded. "I know we will. And, Nelson, thank you for this evening."

MARTY WOKE up early the next morning. She dressed quickly in one of her more practical outfits—bicycle trousers—ready for the day. Afterward, she rested on the bed until the sound of voices in the hallway stirred her. It was about five-thirty. She swung her legs off the bed, opened the door, and spotted a group of five reporters already getting ready to head out.

"Morning, Marty," Richard Davis greeted her with a nod, the other reporters echoing the sentiment.

"Should've joined us last night," one of the reporters said with a grin. "We had a hell of a time, and it's a good thing, too. Last night here—the invasion force heads out today."

"She couldn't come. She's a woman," one of the others quipped.

"No, she's a reporter," Davis shot back, cutting off the exchange.

Marty felt a small satisfaction at that. Not long ago, they'd have written her off without a second thought. Now, they were seeing her for what she was—one of them.

"I had a fine enough evening," Marty replied, keeping her tone light.

"How? I saw you head to your room last night, but I didn't see you come back downstairs."

Marty smiled.

"It doesn't matter," Davis interjected. "Whatever she did, it's her business. Now, what do you say we grab breakfast while we can? Something tells me we won't be eating this well for a long time."

"Good idea," one of the others said. "Come on, Marty. You can fill me in on what it's like to be under fire. Never had a shell come my way, and I don't know if I'll run for it when it happens. Got to give you credit for staying cool."

"Where was I supposed to run? I was on a ship," Marty replied dryly. The group laughed, the sound bouncing down the hall loud enough that a hotel guest —dressed in pajamas and a nightcap—opened his door to glare at them.

The group made their way downstairs, taking over the dining room like they owned the place. It was already busy, but Davis, taking charge, sent one of the guys ahead to snag a large round table before someone else could grab it.

As they settled in, one of the reporters, the one working for Hearst, leaned back in his chair, flashing a grin. "Well, fellas, I don't need to remind you who I work for. Mr. William Randolph Hearst, richest man in the newspaper business. I figure it's only right that he buys us breakfast today."

The group roared in agreement. "Hearst should cover the whole damn day," one of them joked.

When the waiter came over, the Hearst man didn't miss a beat. "We're reporters," he said, not waiting for the rest of them to chime in. "We're about to head off to a war zone, so bring us ham, eggs, and plenty of coffee. And don't stop until we tell you to."

The waiter turned to Marty. "And for the lady?"

The Hearst reporter grinned, but without missing a beat, he added, "We're all reporters here. Just bring her the same."

BY THE TIME breakfast was over, the hotel lobby was jammed with men and luggage. Marty learned that nearly a hundred reporters were certified to cover the invasion, and most of them were crammed into the lobby, jostling for transport assignments. Marty had already drawn a spot on the *Conqueror*, so she didn't need to be a part of the shoving and pushing, but she stood on the sidelines, watching the others.

The scene was something to behold—reporters dressed in all sorts of gear. Some wore hunting jackets, others in white ducks, and a few even sported military uniforms, minus the insignias. A few, Marty noticed, were as immaculately dressed as if they were going to a party.

The variety of equipment made Marty laugh quietly to herself—canteens, binoculars, cameras, notepads, and belts of ammunition hanging off them like decorations. Some even carried machetes and pistols, as if they were headed into battle themselves.

Richard Davis spotted Marty standing just outside the crowd, watching the others as they shouted and shoved for a ship assignment.

"Are you going to wait for whatever is left?" he asked.

"I have my assignment. The *Conqueror*," Marty replied.

"Well then, I'd suggest you get down to the docks sooner rather than later," Davis said with a knowing grin. "Some of these boys are gonna figure out that possession beats any official assignment. Once they realize it, they'll be rushing the ships, assignment or not."

Marty nodded. "Thanks. I'll just do that." She remembered then that Nelson had warned her about this kind of thing with the troops as well. No sense in waiting around.

She grabbed her bag and slipped outside. Several hacks were drawn up, waiting for the onslaught they knew was about to start. She got in the first one and directed that she be taken to the docks.

When they arrived, Marty stood up in the hack to get a good view of the scene. The docks were packed—dozens of regiments preparing to board the ships, supply trains lined up on the roads, and the entire quay swarming with at least ten thousand men. It was a far cry from the orderly embarkation she had witnessed back in New York. There, soldiers had marched to the sound of military bands, a steady rhythm carrying them forward. Here, it was chaos, pure and simple. No music, no fanfare—just the grim determination of officers and quartermasters trying to get their men and supplies on board.

The driver turned to her. "Here you are, miss."

"Thanks," Marty replied, paying her fare before climbing down.

She moved through the crowd, taking in the scale of it all—tents, crates, and equipment piled high, exhausted soldiers in line, trying to haul their gear aboard. The sun was already punishing, and sweat dripped from every face she passed.

Then she spotted him—Colonel Theodore Roosevelt, locked in a heated exchange with another officer. The colonel was doing what Roosevelt did best—seizing the moment.

"The *Yucatan* has been assigned to the Seventy-first," the other colonel said, clearly frustrated. "That's our ship."

Roosevelt smiled, though there was no mistaking the steel behind it. "Well, it seems we've got it now."

"But the assignment—" the officer began again.

"I had verbal authorization to board," Roosevelt interrupted. "I suggest you make other arrangements for your men."

Marty couldn't help but smile. At least Roosevelt hadn't taken the *Conqueror*.

Shaking her head, she moved on, eventually locating the quartermaster general. A few choice words about the herculean task he was facing got him talking, and he proudly rattled off the logistics of the operation.

"It's the largest military expedition ever to leave the United States," he said, clearly pleased with himself. "We've got 819 officers, 15,058 enlisted men, 30 civilian clerks, 272 teamsters and packers, 107 stevedores—along with 2,295 horses and mules, 114 six-mule army wagons, 81 escort wagons, 16 light guns, four 7-inch howitzers, four 5-inch siege guns, one Hotchkiss revolving cannon, eight 3.6 mortars, and four Gatling machine guns."

Marty grinned to herself. And one female reporter, too.

Eleven

The *Conqueror* was packed tighter than expected, with two regiments now crammed aboard. It wasn't as long a trip as the one from New York, but the crowded conditions turned what might have been bearable into a constant burden for the men. Elbow room was a luxury, and every space felt like it was being squeezed tighter by the minute.

Colonel Nelson Pickett was in his element, though. The added people on the ship meant added responsibilities, and he was occupied in sorting out space and order when Marty came aboard. Their only acknowledgment was a smile and a nod of the head. Both knew there was no time for more. Marty found herself a corner, keeping well out of the way and observing as the chaos unfolded.

Once the flotilla set off, forming up just outside Tampa Bay, it became clear this was no ordinary operation. Thirty-two transports, one towing a barge, another towing a schooner filled with fresh water, slowly edged forward. The naval vessels encircling the convoy were the real muscle, guarding against any Spanish threat that might appear on the horizon. But as the hours wore on, it became clear there wouldn't be any fight. The Gulf was as quiet as a graveyard.

On board the *Oregon*, Marty recalled her previous voyage to Cuba—quick and efficient, taking less than twenty-four hours...this was nothing like that. The convoy crawled along at speeds that were laughable. Sometimes they moved at a rate of seven miles an hour, sometimes four miles an hour, and sometimes they didn't move at all. The line of ships stretched nearly thirty miles long, often sitting dead in the water for hours. There was no danger in sitting still, though, because there wasn't a Spanish ship in sight. The flotilla had the ocean all to themselves.

Marty had only been on a few sea trips before, mainly one-day trips from Key West to Cuba to visit her mother's family, but this one was something else entirely. The other transports couldn't seem to hold a line to save their lives, losing formation and forcing the navy's smaller gunboats and torpedo boats to chase them down and herd them back into place. Officers barked sharp commands through megaphones, and for a while, things would get straightened out. But soon enough, another vessel would drift, and the process would repeat. It reminded Marty of sheepdogs chasing after wayward lambs.

At one point, the *Oregon* made a slow, deliberate pass along the line of transports. Marty couldn't help but feel a sense of pride seeing it glide by, knowing she'd been aboard during its first action. The sailors, who were wearing white uniforms, were met with cheers from the soldiers, who waved enthusiastically from the transports as the battleship sailed past.

The days dragged on, and while Marty caught glimpses of Nelson here and there, he was always surrounded by his men, very much engaged in his duties. Even though she was only a few yards from him at times, it might as well have been miles. They exchanged greetings, but that was it—no time for any conversation. And Marty accepted that.

On the fifth day, the convoy approached the northern coast of Cuba, moving slow enough to be a tempting target for the Spanish, though none appeared. At one point, they passed a Spanish barracks, and a few soldiers on the ships waved. Strangely, the Spanish soldiers waved back, as if the war hadn't reached this part of the world yet.

Marty had seen blackout conditions enforced on the *Conqueror* during their trip from New York, but here, many transports didn't bother. Signal lights flashed through the night, some ships were lit up like cities, and from General Shafter's vessel, the sounds of a ragtime band drifted across the water, which, in Marty's opinion, seemed completely out of place in the tension of the moment.

When Marty sat down to write about the conditions, she wanted to capture the reality of what the soldiers were enduring: the crowded decks, the restless waiting, the surreal calm before the storm that everyone knew was coming.

THE HOLDS below deck are more crowded than when we first departed from New York, with two regiments now packed together. Fortunately, the sea is calm, and with the portholes open, a fair breeze flows through, giving the men some relief and allowing them to rest with a measure of comfort.

Many have taken to sleeping on the deck under the stars. The sentries make their rounds, stepping over or sometimes on the men sprawled out on every available inch of space, but there is little grumbling. The soldiers are weary but accustomed to the rough conditions.

The daily rations consist mostly of coffee, hardtack, canned beef, and tinned tomatoes and beans. Some of the more resourceful fellows manage to create a kind of stew from these meager provisions, making the most of what's at hand.

This morning, as we near Cuba, the rugged peaks of the Sierra Maestra come into view, their slopes draped in a haze of blue mist. It is a striking scene, and the men gather at the railings to take in the sight. They are not only admiring the beauty but also anticipating the moment when their boots will finally touch Cuban soil. The excitement, tempered by the unknown challenges ahead, is palpable among the ranks.

MARTY SAT on a stanchion at the stern of the *Conqueror*, finishing her article. The sun was setting, casting a deep orange hue over the water, and the ship's constant hum was the only sound, aside from the occasional shuffle of boots on deck. She had just put away her pencil when a lieutenant approached, his face set in that no-nonsense military expression she'd come to expect.

"Miss McGuire?" he asked, tipping his field cap.

"Yes?" Marty answered, slipping her papers into her bag.

"The colonel sends his compliments, ma'am, and requests your presence in the wardroom with General Shafter and Admiral Sampson."

"Yes, of course," Marty said.

She followed the lieutenant through the ship,

passing familiar decks and passageways. The air below was stuffy, the kind of heat that clung to your skin, but it barely registered as her curiosity about the meeting grew.

When she entered the wardroom, Admiral Sampson and General Shafter stood up, greeting her with a nod. Nelson was already standing, arms folded, his eyes catching hers for just a moment before turning to the officers.

"Admiral, I believe you've met Miss McGuire before," Nelson said.

"Indeed I have," Sampson said, a grin tugging at the corners of his mouth. "She was with us on the *Oregon,* stood right on the bridge when we engaged the Spanish. Held herself together better than some of my men."

General Shafter gave her a once-over, a mixture of respect and curiosity. "Then you think she would be of service for this mission?"

"No question," Sampson said. "Sharp as they come."

Marty blinked, taken off guard by the exchange. "Mission?"

Nelson stepped forward. "Marty, we're going ashore tonight to meet with the Cuban patriot general, General Calixto Garcia. His cooperation is vital to what we're doing here, and we need someone who can speak Spanish fluently. That's where you come in."

General Shafter added, "We'll need you to help smooth over any misunderstandings. But that's not all."

Nelson's tone shifted, his eyes locking on hers. "There's more to it than just that. We want you to keep one ear open for any conversations that might take place around us, even if it is not directed at us. You may hear something that would be of great importance to us. Will you do it?"

Marty straightened. This was no small request. It was dangerous, no doubt, but it was exactly the kind of challenge she thrived on. "I would be glad to," she said.

Admiral Sampson nodded approvingly. "Good. We'll bring the dinghy alongside and head ashore after dark."

As the admiral and general prepared to leave, Shafter paused at the door, glancing back with a grin. "Coming, Nelson?"

"In a moment, sir. I need to go over a few things with Miss McGuire first."

Shafter chuckled. "It was Marty a minute ago, I believe."

Nelson flushed slightly but recovered quickly. "Yes, sir. I guess it was."

The two officers left, and the door swung shut. The room was suddenly still, just the two of them now. Nelson's gaze lingered on Marty for a beat longer than usual. Then, without warning, he pulled her close and kissed her, the intensity of it surprising her. When he finally pulled back, Marty caught her breath, her heart still racing.

"I didn't expect that," she said, half-amused, half-shocked.

Nelson shrugged, a half-smile creeping onto his face. "I've been waiting for that since we left Tampa."

Marty raised an eyebrow. "And here I thought you were all about discipline."

"About tonight," Nelson said, turning back to the mission. "Are you sure you want to come ashore? It won't be easy. I won't say there will be no danger involved."

She gave him a steady look. "This whole operation has some element of danger, doesn't it? I willingly assumed that risk when I came down here, and yes, I would love to go ashore. I'm honored to be asked."

Nelson nodded, respect clear in his eyes. "That's what I thought you would say."

Just then, the door opened, and two stewards entered, one carrying a bucket of coal, the other with a coffee pot.

"Excuse me, sir. We didn't know anyone was in here," one of them said, looking slightly embarrassed.

Nelson stepped back, his grin returning. "Go on, get your work done. We're finished here anyway."

AFTER SUNSET, Marty McGuire climbed down the small access ladder to the dinghy waiting alongside the *Conqueror*. The boat rocked gently in the dark water, and one of the sailors reached up to steady her as she stepped in. From this vantage point, the ship loomed above her like a steel cliff, its white sides rising out of the water and curving inward at the waterline before bowing outward toward the portholes, where heads poked out, watching with curiosity. The men aboard knew something was happening, and their eyes followed the movement of the small boat below.

Behind them, about forty feet away, a bilge pump gurgled as it discharged water into the sea, the rhythmic sound breaking the stillness of the night.

Nelson Pickett was the last to come down the ladder, his boots hitting the bottom of the dinghy with a solid thump. Once everyone was aboard, the sailor in charge gave the order, and the small craft pulled away from the *Conqueror*, heading toward the beach. The palms ahead swayed slightly in the breeze, their dark silhouettes standing against the faint outline of the Cuban coast.

"There's the signal, Admiral," a sailor called out as a light flashed three times from the shore.

"Steer for the light," Admiral Sampson commanded from his seat.

The dinghy cut swiftly through the waves, rising and falling with the surf. Marty's face was splashed with salt spray, but she ignored it. Her mind focused on what was in front of them. She recognized that this was more than just a meeting—this was history in the making, and by a quirk of fate, she was right in the thick of it.

As they neared the shore, a group of Cuban men, stripped to the waist, rushed out to meet them. They pulled the dinghy onto the beach and then hauled it far enough back so that everyone could step out dry-footed. Marty, along with the others, climbed out, her boots sinking slightly into the soft sand.

A double line of Cuban officers formed a guard of honor, their uniforms worn but their faces proud. Marty caught the surprised looks of some of the men when they saw her, but those expressions quickly turned to respectful smiles.

At the end of the line stood Colonel Juan Alvarez, tall and imposing, his eyes sharp as he offered a crisp salute. "Welcome to Cuba, friends and liberators. I am Colonel Juan Alvarez, Chief of Staff to General Calixto Garcia. I will take you to him."

The Americans introduced themselves, and when it

was Marty's turn, Alvarez's gaze lingered, his expression shifting from curiosity to admiration. "And you, señorita?"

"I am Marty McGuire, a correspondent for the *New York Banner*," she said in English before switching to fluent Spanish. "I recently met your sister, Francesca. She is well and sends her regards."

Alvarez's face lit up with a broad smile. "What a wonderful surprise," he said. "You not only speak our language, but you speak it like a Cuban. How is that?"

"My mother is Cuban," Marty explained before turning to the Americans to translate the exchange for them.

Alvarez nodded and gestured inland. "Señorita, gentlemen, the general is waiting. Please, follow me."

They moved inland, following a narrow path that wound through the thick palmettos and brush. The night air was still, filled with the scent of the tropics, and the distant sound of the sea gradually faded as they trekked further from the shore. After about fifteen minutes, they arrived at a small palm-frond hut, where General Calixto Garcia stood waiting. He was a small man with a white mustache and a deep scar across his forehead, a reminder of the failed suicide attempt that had almost claimed his life during his time as a Spanish prisoner.

"The people of Cuba welcome you," Garcia said in a gravelly voice. "I have maps laid out inside. Let us discuss the liberation of my country."

They gathered around a rough-hewn table inside the hut, where a hand-drawn map of the island was spread out. Marty, Nelson, and Alvarez stood back, observing and listening. The discussions were serious, focused, as Admiral Sampson and General Shafter debated the best course of action.

Sampson's plan was bold: land troops on both sides of Santiago's harbor entrance and assault Morro Castle. Afterward, the navy would engage the Spanish fleet and clear the harbor of mines. But Shafter, ever the cautious commander, balked at the idea. The high cliffs of Santiago were formidable, and he had no desire to repeat the British disaster from decades earlier.

The back-and-forth continued until Shafter finally turned to Nelson. "Colonel Pickett, would you explain the plan we've worked out?"

Nelson stepped forward, pointing to the map. "The idea is to land here, at Daiquiri, about fifteen miles east of Santiago, and at Siboney. These locations are less fortified, and we can establish a foothold before pressing inland."

Sampson looked skeptical. "There's a heavy swell against the beaches there. It won't be easy to land."

Before Nelson could respond, Colonel Alvarez interjected. "Pardon, Admiral. But the plan, how do you say it, *merecedor*?"

Marty translated. "Deserving."

"*Sí*, deserving. Colonel Pickett's plan is sound. There are only about three hundred Spanish troops at Daiquiri. We can drive them off and stage diversions elsewhere to keep the Spanish occupied."

Sampson considered this for a long moment, his fingers drumming on the edge of the table. "Can you clear the beaches before Wednesday?"

Alvarez nodded. "*Sí.*"

"General Shafter, will your men be ready to land by then?"

Shafter gave a curt nod. "They're ready anytime."

Sampson glanced at Nelson, then at the others. "June 22nd, then," he said. "That will be our landing date. Gentlemen, let's return to the ship. Perhaps June 22nd will join the ranks of our country's most celebrated days."

Twelve

As the sun rose the next morning, Nelson, Dan, the commanding officer of the other regiment, his executive officer, and General Shafter stood on the bridge of the *Conqueror*, looking out toward the distant shoreline. The American ships lay anchored as close to the shore as they dared, but several hundred yards of heavy waves stood between them and the beach. Beyond the beach, a limestone bluff stretched for miles, towering 250 feet high, with blockhouses built along the ridge, giving the Spanish a commanding view of the landing site.

Shafter lowered his field glasses, a deep frown etched across his face. "If Linares can hold off Alvarez's attack, he'll have more than enough men here to shove us right back into the sea."

Nelson glanced at Dan, who was stone-faced, his own binoculars scanning the coastline.

"Who's Linares?" asked the executive officer of the other regiment, who stood nearby.

Dan answered without lowering his binoculars. "The Spanish commander."

Shafter grunted. "Alvarez swears there are only two hundred Spaniards up there, but if Linares managed to sneak his full army back into position, it'll make Custer's little fiasco up in Montana look like a Sunday-school picnic."

All eyes were trained on the shoreline. Suddenly, Dan pointed. "Smoke, General—there. And more over there…and there."

Shafter's eyes followed Dan's direction. "Hell, it looks like Linares did sneak back in. They're burning the place to the ground."

Nelson remained calm, his brow furrowed in thought. "Why would they show us?" he muttered.

Shafter turned toward him. "What did you say?"

Nelson crossed his arms, staring hard at the fires. "If Linares had ten or twelve thousand men dug in, waiting for us, would he really be lighting fires and letting us see them?"

Shafter tilted his head, his frown deepening. "What are you getting at, Nelson?"

Nelson unfolded his arms and gestured toward the bluffs. "Even if Linares has his whole army up there, we still outnumber him. His two biggest assets would be his defensive position, which is the bluffs, and the element of surprise. Now he certainly wouldn't have any reason to come down off the bluffs to meet us at the surf, would he?"

A slow smile spread across Shafter's face as he stroked his chin. "You're right. If he were up there in force, he'd be hiding, waiting for us to land before launching his attack."

The other executive officer still looked skeptical.

"But what about all that smoke? What if they're so sure of their position they don't care if we know they're there?"

Shafter shook his head. "No, they're bluffing. They're lighting every fire they can to make us think the place is crawling with troops. Nelson's right."

The officer pursed his lips but didn't argue further. Shafter turned back toward the shore. "We're going in. Nelson, signal the fleet. Prepare for landing."

Nelson nodded. "Yes, sir."

Within moments, signal flags were raised to the topmast of the *Conqueror*. The orders rippled down the line, and soon, the distant thundering of naval guns filled the air as the bombardment began.

The *Conqueror* had no artillery, so her men were already climbing down the nets, rifles slung over their backs, loading into the small boats bobbing in the waves below. The naval barrage lit up the shoreline, shells smashing into the bluffs. Rapid-fire cannons and machine guns sounded along the cliffs like long drumrolls while the five, seven- and eight-inch guns boomed and thumped like great bass drums. The shells ripped through the trees, smashed the cliffs, uprooted great palms, and tore out great chunks of earth.

Marty appeared on the bridge as the last echoes of the bombardment began to fade away. Dressed in her bicycle trousers, she carried a small leather case that contained her writing materials and a change of clothes. When Nelson spotted her, he was pleased with how sensibly she had dressed and with the efficiency of her luggage. Despite the chaos around them, he allowed himself a brief smile.

"Good morning," he said.

"Morning," she replied, her eyes scanning the shore. "Are we about ready to land?"

"Almost," Nelson said. "How about you? Ready?"

Marty raised an eyebrow. "I'm surprised you're not trying to stop me."

Nelson shrugged. "It wouldn't matter if I tried. You'd find a way ashore either way. But you'll be going in Dan's boat."

"Dan's boat?" she asked, her voice sharp.

Nelson raised a hand to cut her off. "I'm in charge of this landing, and I assign the boats. I expect things to go smoothly, but if I'm wrong and there's trouble waiting for us, you'll be safer in Dan's boat, which will be the last to go. Or you can stay aboard the *Conqueror* for three days."

Marty sighed, her lips pressed into a thin line. "Fine. I'll be in Dan's boat."

Nelson nodded. "Good. Dan, take charge of her."

Dan grinned, clearly enjoying his assignment. "Yes, sir."

Marty glanced back at the scene unfolding on the beach. "Do you mind if I watch the operation from the deck until it's time?"

Dan waved a hand. "Go ahead. I'll come get you when it's time for us to head in."

Marty hurried down to the deck, stepping aside as she watched the men and horses being loaded into the boats. The thick smoke from the bombardment drifted inland, obscuring the beach ahead and offering some cover for the landing party. A dozen steam launches were ferrying the boats toward shore, each pulling a smaller craft filled with soldiers. As they neared the breakers, the men cut loose, paddling hard through the crashing surf toward the sandy beach. The launches would return for more men, bringing wave after wave ashore—each one adding a thousand more to the ranks.

She watched tensely, her eyes tracking Nelson's boat as it rode the rough surf. The thick clouds of smoke gradually parted, revealing glimpses of the shoreline—a mix of soft, pale sand and dense tropical foliage. Towering palm trees with broad fronds swayed in the breeze, their roots tangled with low-growing mangroves that clung to the shore like twisted claws. Beyond the tree line, dense patches of jungle rose, filled with thick-trunked mahogany and silk cotton trees, their canopies casting shadows on the ground below. Long vines hung from the branches, swaying with the breeze, while the occasional burst of color from tropical flowers stood out in the greenery. The air was heavy with the scent of salt and damp earth.

The surf crashed relentlessly against the beach, making every landing difficult. The Spanish army might be hidden in the tangled mass of trees, waiting to strike. Marty held her breath, half expecting to see a volley of rifle fire erupt from the jungle. But when Nelson's boat hit the shore and the men rushed across the sand into the cover of the trees, nothing happened. A soldier emerged from the jungle a moment later, waving his hat toward the ships, signaling all clear. Cheers erupted from the men still aboard.

It took three more landing waves before Dan appeared beside Marty and nodded. "Your turn."

Without hesitation, she scrambled down the netting and into the boat. The surf slapped hard against the hull as the small boat rocked and dipped, fighting the waves. The closer they got to shore, the more treacherous it became. Boats that weren't being opposed by Spanish troops found their enemy in the pounding waves. Marty saw boats heading for a nearby pier, only to be smashed against the pilings by the furious sea. Two soldiers from the Tenth Cavalry were thrown into the churning water and crushed between a boat and the pier. Several other boats and one of the steam launches were capsized by the heavy seas, but the two Tenth Cavalry troopers were the only men killed in the entire landing operation.

When Marty finally set foot on the shore, the oppressive heat of the Cuban sun hit her like a wall. Nelson was already on the beach, establishing a temporary headquarters. His men worked to secure the horses, struggling against both the animals' fear and exhaustion. The beach itself was strewn with palm fronds and driftwood, while the tropical jungle loomed just beyond, thick with underbrush and the constant drone of insects.

The horses proved to be more difficult than the men. The horses had been loaded onto large lighters, then pulled close to the shore by the steam launches. As the boats reached the shallows, the animals were pushed into the water, where they were caught by men in small boats, led to the breakers by their halter shanks, then turned loose to be washed ashore. Some managed to reach land, but others floundered, disoriented by the waves. The men on shore tied them to picket lines, where they stood quietly, dripping wet and exhausted, a picture of dejection and weariness.

"Colonel, look!" one of the men shouted, pointing toward a group of horses that had broken away.

Marty followed his gaze and saw a dozen horses swimming in the wrong direction, heading out to sea, their panic driving them farther from shore. She gasped, horrified by the sight of the struggling animals.

"Oh, Nelson, can't you do something?" she cried.

Nelson didn't hesitate. "Bugler! Sound *To The Post*!" he ordered.

The bugler sprinted to the water's edge, raising his instrument to his lips. The call echoed across the beach, a familiar sound to cavalry horses. The animals in the water heard the bugle and, as if by instinct, turned in unison and began swimming back toward shore. Marty clapped her hands in relief as the men cheered, watching the horses make their way back.

By the end of the day, six thousand American soldiers were ashore without a single Spanish shot fired. Nelson's Lightning Cavalry was now on land, but they wouldn't be riding anytime soon. As Marty moved through the camp, she noticed the condition of the beach and jungle surrounding them. The men set up temporary bivouacs in the sand, their tents pitched beneath the swaying palms, while the jungle loomed menacingly just beyond. Thick ferns and creeping vines covered the ground, making every step a battle against the natural world. The sounds of monkeys echoed from deeper in the trees, along with the occasional screech of tropical birds that darted between the canopy.

Nelson called her over to a small wooden shack near the beach. "Marty, take a look at this," he said, handing her a piece of paper he'd found inside.

She glanced at the letter. "It's from Colonel Diaz to General Linares," she said as she translated. "He's pleading to stay and defend this position with three thousand men."

Nelson shook his head. "Linares was a fool to pull him out. Now we've got a foothold."

Just then, a soldier stuck his head into the shack. "Colonel, the American flag's been raised on the blockhouse. Colonel Roosevelt and the Rough Riders did it."

Nelson smiled slightly. "Roosevelt trying to steal some glory, huh?"

Dan approached. "What's next, sir?"

Nelson nodded toward the jungle. "We move on Santiago. But first, we march to Siboney. The horses are spent, they'll need to be led. So, for now, we're foot soldiers."

THE MARCH INLAND was hot and grueling. Marty kept pace easily with the soldiers, her eyes taking in the strange and wild beauty of the Cuban landscape. Every now and then, gunfire would echo through the trees, sending the soldiers diving into the ditches along the road. But each time, it turned out to be a false alarm. By nightfall, they reached Siboney, where they bivouacked, awaiting orders to advance.

Marty knew that the majority of newspaper writers who were part of the morning's operation would be writing stories about the landing, so for her first dispatch, she chose to write about Siboney.

From the Shores of Siboney

By Marty McGuire, Special Correspondent

Siboney, once a quiet and unremarkable hamlet of no more than a thousand souls, has, overnight, been transformed into a bustling center of military activity.

General Shafter has chosen this site to transfer the unloading of men and supplies, establishing his headquarters for the ordnance, quartermaster, commissary, and medical corps. What was once a small village is now the focal point of America's march into Cuba.

By our standards, Siboney is scarcely a town at all. A few humble, weather-beaten houses dot the shoreline, and the most imposing structure in the vicinity is a sawmill, now taken over by our engineers. A storehouse nearby serves the commissary. To the west, a sluggish creek snakes its way into a stagnant pond ringed by swamps. These marshes, dark and brooding, are breeding grounds for the dreaded vapors that seem to call forth the scourges of malaria and yellow fever.

Last night, our first ashore was one we will not soon forget. Sleep was a luxury no one enjoyed as our troops continued to be unloaded from the ships into the surf until well past two o'clock this morning. But darkness was no hindrance, for two mighty warships anchored nearby illuminated the shore with their brilliant searchlights. The beach glowed under the fierce beams, as bright as the grand ballroom of the Fifth Avenue Hotel, where, not long ago, the Lightning Cavalry enjoyed their farewell dinner. How distant that memory seems now.

Behind the warships, the ocean shimmered under the light of the full moon, its surface a silvery expanse stretching toward the horizon. On land, hundreds of campfires flickered, casting their warm glow on weary soldiers who gathered around, drying their uniforms and hoping the smoke might drive away the swarms of mosquitoes that plagued them. Alas, the smoke did little to deter the relentless insects.

In the surf, men stood shoulder to shoulder, helping their comrades ashore. Without the threat of Spanish resistance, the landing took on the air of a game—pontoons and boats charging through the waves, only to be swept ashore by the breakers, like children's sleds hurtling down the water chutes at Coney Island. Yet, despite the almost festive atmosphere, there was no mistaking the gravity of the situation. To witness an army of this size land on hostile shores in the dead of night is a sight seldom seen in the annals of war. The fact that this enormous task was completed in less than twenty-four hours, from the thunderous barrage of our naval guns to the final wave of troops landing to the sound of laughter and cheers, makes it all the more remarkable.

This morning, the scent of coffee, bacon, and beans fills the air as the men prepare their first meal in over a day. Many went without food yesterday, either too caught up in the day's excitement or unable to spare a moment for rest. Now, the beach buzzes with the activity of men recharging their bodies for what lies ahead.

Yet, there is an unease among us. We know the Spanish army is here. We see their blockhouses and rifle pits stretching along the bluffs, but why have they chosen not to resist us? This is a question that lingers on every soldier's lips. General Shafter and Colonel Pickett have spoken of our good fortune in landing unopposed, but there is a growing sense that this quiet is deceptive. General Linares, it seems, is biding his time. Every man on this beach knows the Spaniards have something planned for us—we just don't know when or where they'll strike.

COLONEL CARLOS DIAZ crouched in the shade of the thick trees just behind the outskirts of Siboney, and he looked down on the mass of American soldiers swarming the beach. For two days, the Yankees had unloaded men and equipment ashore, doing it as easily as if they were arriving routinely at a train station. Not a shot had been fired to stop them.

He spat in frustration. If General Linares hadn't been such an old woman, they wouldn't have given up the coastline so easily. Diaz could have done more with half the men. He knew every ridge, every low spot along the shore, and he'd already pictured where to place the artillery. A few well-placed cannon and riflemen would have broken this landing. But now the Americans were on Cuban soil and in numbers far greater than Linares had predicted.

Grumbling under his breath, Diaz stood and made his way down toward the invaders. His unshaven face and ragged peasant clothes made him blend easily into the surroundings. Cuban refugees were everywhere, their dirty clothes and gaunt faces common sights. Diaz moved easily through the streets of the town, stepping over puddles as he edged closer to the American lines.

He passed through the chaos of the encampment—soldiers bustling around campfires, unloading gear, and laughing as they cooked their breakfast. His heart raced when a shout came from behind.

"Hey, you!" a soldier shouted.

Diaz froze, muscles tensing. Had they recognized him? If so, he could be shot on sight, out of uniform and clearly spying.

"You, Pancho!"

Diaz exhaled quietly, his fingers unclenching at his

sides. The soldiers had no idea who he was. How could they? Just a couple of American soldiers with no clue about the local terrain, let alone the commander of Spanish troops in this sector.

"How do you know his name's Pancho?" another soldier chimed in.

"Because they're all named Pancho, that's why!" The first one chuckled. "Or maybe it's just the Mexicans."

Diaz forced a smile. "Yes?" he asked in a thickened accent.

"You speak English, Pancho?"

"Yes, a leetle," Diaz said, dragging out the words.

"You seen any Spaniards around here? We came to fight, not sit around on the beach all day."

"No Spanish troops, *señor*. I think they go."

"Figures. Cowards probably high-tailed it the moment they seen us." The soldier puffed out his chest. "We're the fightin' lightnin'. That's the Lightning Cavalry, and we're here to whup the Spanish back to Spain where they belong."

"Yeah, we're here to free your people," another added. "That's what you want, right? Freedom?"

Diaz nodded. "Sí, *señor*."

The first soldier cocked his head. "You hungry, Pancho? How about some bacon and beans?"

"No, *señor*," Diaz said. He saw the coffee. "I drink coffee."

"Coffee? Hell, why not. Here." The soldier handed him a tin cup and poured it full. Diaz accepted it gratefully, his eyes darting up and down the beach as he sipped. He noted the absence of Hotchkiss guns—a small mercy, as those rapid-fire weapons could devastate his troops. The Americans might be overconfident, but their sheer numbers couldn't be ignored. They outnumbered his men three to one, a ratio that would be insurmountable now that they were entrenched on Cuban soil.

Diaz handed back the cup, muttering a quick thanks before continuing his slow stroll along the shoreline, his mind calculating, analyzing. He had much to prepare for. Lost in thought, he didn't notice Eddie Stone, a young soldier, sitting nearby with a notebook in hand, busily sketching the man who had just shared their coffee.

MARTY WALKED DOWN onto the beach to talk to the soldiers and get their impressions of the landing. She needed to keep her connections with these men strong, as their firsthand accounts would be critical to her reporting as the war progressed.

"Hey! Miss McGuire!" A voice called out from the nearest group of soldiers. "You want to join us for breakfast?"

She recognized the young artist Eddie Stone among them. Marty made her way over, offering a polite smile. "I wouldn't want to take anyone's meal."

"Heck, we've got plenty to go around," one of the soldiers said, patting a log next to him. "Have a seat."

Before long, they handed her a pan filled with bacon and beans, along with a spoon.

"You want some pepper? Helps the beans go down easier," a soldier offered.

"No, thank you. This will do just fine," she said, thinking how ironic it was. She had just written an article about this being the first decent meal many of the men had in two days, and now she realized she was in the same boat—having not eaten since the day before.

As they ate, the soldiers shared stories about the landing. One recounted how his boat capsized, and he thought he'd drown. Another sheepishly admitted to losing his rifle, fearing his sergeant's wrath. Mosquitoes, they all agreed, were everywhere.

Marty's gaze fell on Eddie's sketch pad. "Have you been drawing much, Eddie?" she asked.

"Not really," Eddie said, looking down, his shyness showing. "This is the first one."

He handed the pad to her. Marty examined the sketch—a Cuban peasant. But there was something about this man, something that stood out. The defiance in his posture, the hard set of his jaw, the pride in his eyes. This wasn't just any refugee.

"May I use this for my article?" she asked. "I'll make sure your name will be on it and the paper will pay you."

Eddie's face lit up with pride. "Sure, Miss McGuire, but you don't need to pay me."

"Nonsense. You've got a talent here, Eddie. You should think about doing this for a career after the war."

The other soldiers chimed in. "Yeah, Eddie, better than driving an omnibus for the rest of your life."

Eddie nodded, his grin widening. "All right, Miss McGuire."

After breakfast, Marty wandered the beach, taking in the sights for future stories. She exchanged a few words with a group of Cuban children, who quickly giggled and ran off when she spoke Spanish with them.

Finally, she returned to where Nelson had set up his temporary headquarters. Colonel Juan Alvarez was there, greeting her with his usual charm.

"Ah, the lady with the golden tongue," Juan said in Spanish. "Why do the Americans let someone as lovely as you come to war? Don't they know it's dangerous for beautiful women?"

"Isn't it dangerous for everyone, Colonel?" Marty asked

Juan laughed, glancing at Nelson, who was approaching.

"What are you talking about?" Nelson asked.

"Just a little flattery," Juan said, flashing a smile. Switching to Spanish, he asked, "Does he have a reason to be jealous, Miss McGuire?"

"He does," she replied, switching back to English. "And he also has a right to ask that we speak in English."

Juan shrugged, grinning at Nelson. "My congratulations, Colonel. You seem to have the advantage over me with this young woman. But I'm used to fighting against great odds. After all, I've been fighting the Spanish for many years now."

"Then let's get to the point," Nelson said, unimpressed. "The Spaniards are still here."

As Nelson and Juan began discussing the next move toward Santiago, Marty placed Eddie's sketch on the table. She stepped over to the edge of the tent and looked back toward the beach, where the soldiers continued their preparations. Behind her, the conversation between the two men continued, though Juan's sudden exclamation made her turn around.

"Where did you get this?" Juan asked, holding up Eddie's drawing.

"What's wrong?" Marty asked.

"This is Colonel Diaz," Juan said, his voice growing serious. "The commander of the Spanish forces in this area. Where did you get it?"

Nelson leaned in, his brow furrowing. "That's Diaz?"

"*Sí*," Juan confirmed. "He's the commander of all Spanish troops in this area, who are under General Linares,"

"Where did you find this, Marty?" Nelson asked.

"One of the soldiers, Eddie Stone, drew it. They said a refugee came down to the beach, had coffee with them."

Juan shook his head. "He's not just any refugee. He's here to spy. He's seen everything we have."

Nelson called out to his second-in-command. "Dan! Get ten men, have them study this drawing, and comb the beach for this man. If you find him, bring him in."

Dan nodded and left immediately, but Juan looked skeptical. "You won't catch him. Diaz is too clever. If he's been here, he's already seen what he needs to see."

"How clever can he be?" Nelson muttered. "He let someone draw him."

Juan smiled grimly. "You'll find out how clever, Colonel. When you march on Santiago, Diaz will be waiting."

Thirteen

Nelson scanned the Cuban refugees one last time, but Colonel Diaz was nowhere to be found. Either the colonel had finished his leisurely inspection of the American troops and their equipment, or he realized someone was searching for him and slipped away unnoticed. Regardless, the scouting party returned empty-handed.

"Colonel, if you'd like, I'll take two of your men and locate where Colonel Diaz has positioned his troops," Juan offered, adjusting the brim of his hat as the tropical sun beat down from a clear sky.

Nelson nodded. "Do it."

Dan stepped closer, lowering his voice. "What's the plan if we find them?"

"We're going to attack," Nelson said flatly, glancing toward the coastline where waves gently lapped the shore, the deep blue of the sea contrasting with the bright sand. Palm trees swayed, their fronds rustling in the light breeze, a stark contrast to the tension simmering in the camp.

Dan's brow furrowed. "You know General Shafter isn't going to like this. He ordered no engagements without his direct orders."

"He also said we could fight if we were attacked," Nelson replied.

Dan smirked. "Always good at finding the gray area, aren't you?"

Nelson's expression remained hard. "We find Diaz's troops and take the ground they're on. If he doesn't fight, fine. If he does…" He let the words trail off.

Dan laughed. "Always a way to push the limits, Nelson."

"Go pick two men to go with Colonel Alvarez and prepare the troops. We move soon."

"Right."

Marty had been watching the exchange in silence. The thought of the Lightning Cavalry going into action excited her, as she was sure it would excite the men. But it frightened her, too. She had been with them since New York, witnessing their drills and exercises, watching the camaraderie form. Now, the Lightning Cavalry, New York's own, *her* regiment, was about to go into battle. This wasn't just a story—this was war, and the thought of them spilling blood on foreign soil made her stomach tighten.

She wandered outside the headquarters, looking toward the jungle that bordered the beach. Dense foliage pressed in from the tree line, the vibrant greens of the palms and ferns blending into a tangled mass of vines. Somewhere out there, Diaz and his men waited, hidden in the undergrowth.

Near the horses, Colonel Alvarez tightened the cinch on his saddle. When he caught sight of her, he flashed a confident smile, one that carried a hint of arrogance. Marty returned a tight nod, uninterested in whatever he might have been implying.

"Would you care to come with us, Señorita?" Juan called, switching to English.

Before she could respond, Nelson cut in. "She'll remain here."

Juan raised an eyebrow. "She is a reporter, is she not? She will be exposed to many dangers before this is over, Colonel Pickett. You can't shield her from everything. You may as well let her get used to it now."

"She'll be exposed soon enough," Nelson said, his jaw tightening.

Marty took a breath. "Nelson, you do intend to let me come along on the attack, don't you?"

Nelson looked at her with a pained expression on his face. The dilemma was clear. He couldn't leave her behind without risking her safety. The beach was crawling with Cuban refugees—some loyal to Diaz and others simply caught in the crossfire. Any of them could signal Diaz if they learned of the impending attack.

"Yes," he said finally. "I'll let you come along with the main body on the attack. But I'll not send you on a scouting mission with Colonel Alvarez."

Juan chuckled from his saddle. "Colonel Pickett, which are you the most frightened of, me or the Spanish?"

"Neither," Nelson said, his tone even.

Juan smiled at Marty. "I'm sorry, I would have let you come along, *Señorita*."

"That's all right," she replied coolly. "I'll wait."

At that moment, Dan returned with two sergeants—both seasoned men. One had fought in the Civil

War, and the other was a veteran of the Indian campaigns, a survivor of the Battle of Little Big Horn.

"Did Major Calhoun brief you two?" Nelson asked.

The Civil War veteran scratched his chin. "Not exactly, sir. He said you needed a bit of scouting done."

"Correct. Colonel Diaz and his troops are very close by. We don't know exactly where they are, but we do know they are near because Diaz was seen this morning, walking up and down the beach."

The younger sergeant scowled. "What? You mean here? He was in plain sight?"

"Exactly. He was disguised as a Cuban peasant."

"Well, there are damn sure enough of them around, sir. They're all over the place."

"Nelson, what if some of them are Diaz's men?" Dan asked. "If they are, and if they get word that we are planning an attack, they'll get back to Diaz."

Nelson's eyes swept the beach, where clusters of Cubans wandered, some lounging in the shade of palms, others tending to fires. "You have a point. All right, have a platoon round up all the Cuban peasants who are wandering around the beach, and hold them back until after the attack is launched. Don't let any of them leave until it's too late."

Dan nodded. "I'm on it."

Nelson turned back to the sergeants. "Go with Colonel Alvarez. Find out where the Spanish are, their numbers, and if they have artillery or Gatling guns. I need an estimate."

"Understood, sir," the older sergeant said, and both men swung into their saddles, ready to ride.

Juan listened to the orders with mild amusement.

He had been fighting for years in these jungles, and the Americans were only now stepping into the fire. "Gentlemen, are we ready?"

The two sergeants spurred their horses forward, following Alvarez into the thick trees. Marty watched them until they disappeared into the tangled green. Just before Juan vanished from view, he glanced back at her. She quickly looked away, unwilling to give him the satisfaction of thinking she cared.

Marty returned to the beach, watching as the men were told they'd soon be heading into battle. She studied their reactions, curious about how they would respond. Almost to a man, they were charged with excitement, eager to release the pent-up energy that had built during their long journey—first from New York, then across the waters from Tampa. Now, with the promise of action, they were ready to blow off steam in the most dangerous way possible.

She walked along the stretch of sand, where soldiers prepped for the fight ahead. Rifles were cleaned, ammunition checked, canteens filled. Occasionally, one of the men would approach her, holding out a packet of letters, a photo, or some small keepsake.

"Miss McGuire, could you hold on to this for me? In case…well, just in case."

Marty gave each of them the same reply. "I'll be right there with you, so I'm sure you'll come through just fine. Besides, wouldn't it comfort you having this with you during the battle?"

The men would nod, sometimes embarrassed, as if realizing they had revealed too much of their own fear. "Yeah, maybe you're right," they'd mumble. Then, more boldly, "It'll take more than a few Spaniards to bring me down."

She was nearing the end of her stroll when Dan called out to her.

"Marty? Do you have a minute?"

She turned and walked over to where he stood. "Sure, Dan, what do you need?"

"We've got a group of Cuban peasants gathered over here, near the old lumber shed. They're confused and angry—and scared. Do you think you could explain to them what's going on?"

"You want me to tell them about the attack?"

"Go ahead. If there's a spy among them, they already know by now. It might help calm the others."

Marty nodded. "All right."

She followed Dan to the makeshift holding area, where nearly a hundred refugees were gathered. Angry questions were being thrown at the guards, none of whom spoke Spanish. The lack of answers only made the situation worse.

"They're scared," Marty said quietly as she approached.

Raising her hands, she called out in their language, "Please, don't be frightened! You are in no danger."

One voice shouted from the crowd, "A beautiful woman is with the soldiers, Mamma Mia."

"Please," Marty called again. "I will try to answer your questions if you quiet down."

Immediately, the voices dropped. Someone called out, "Why are we here?"

"You've been brought here for your own protection," she explained. "Our commander expects a battle soon, and he wants to keep you safe."

"Since when do soldiers care about the peasants?" another voice demanded.

"These aren't Spanish soldiers," Marty replied firmly. "They are American soldiers, and they're here to help you drive out the Spanish. When this war is over, Cuba will be free."

"Maybe we won't worry about the Spanish, but now we have to worry about the Americans!" came another shout. "It's American guns pointed at us, American soldiers holding us here!"

"I told you, they are only keeping you from harm," Marty said.

The same voice replied, "Or from joining the Spanish."

Marty paused, then spoke the truth. "That, too. We know there may be Spanish spies among you. If there are, we can't risk letting them warn the Spanish about our plans."

The man considered this before nodding. "All right, we'll stay until the battle is over. But after that, we wish to be free."

Marty turned to Dan. "They've agreed to stay until after the battle. Can I tell them they'll be freed then?"

Dan nodded. "Yes, you can."

Marty relayed the message, and a cheer erupted. "Viva Cuba Libre! Viva los Americanos!" The crowd's mood shifted as they applauded. Even the guards, caught off guard by the sudden goodwill, smiled.

"Thanks," Dan said as they walked away. "You kept things from getting messy."

"I'm glad I could help," she replied.

Dan grinned and then chuckled to himself.

"What is it?" Marty asked, noticing his amused expression.

"Just thinking about Nelson," Dan said, still grinning. "Ever since we arrived, everyone's noticed he's been different."

Marty raised an eyebrow. "Different?"

"He's a happy man, Marty. Happier than I've seen him in a long time, and I think we both know why."

Marty smirked. "Just doing my part for the cause."

Before Dan could respond, they noticed the two sergeants who had gone scouting with Juan returning, riding quickly toward headquarters.

"The scouting party's back," Dan said. "Let's see what they found."

NELSON WAS ALREADY on his way back to the building when they arrived. They all entered the headquarters together, where the two men stood waiting for their briefing.

"What did you find out?" Nelson asked.

The senior sergeant cleared his throat. "You're right, Colonel. We ought to attack. The Spanish are positioned where they could bottle us up on this beach if they wanted to."

"How many men?"

"That's the strange part, sir," the other sergeant said. "They've only got about five hundred men. With fifteen hundred, they could hold us off all day."

"They're well fortified?" Nelson asked.

"Yes, sir," the senior man replied. "They've got trenches dug on a 250-foot ridge, thick brush covering the approaches. No way around them. If they had enough troops, we'd be stuck here until the fever took us."

Nelson frowned, rubbing the scar on his face. "It doesn't make sense."

"What doesn't?" Marty asked.

"The Spanish have the numbers and the fortifications. They could've denied us this beach, but they didn't. They could've reinforced the ridge, but they haven't. Why?"

"Colonel Alvarez said they plan to make their big stand at Santiago," the sergeant said.

Nelson nodded but still looked troubled. "It seems like a mistake to me."

A knock at the door interrupted them, and Nelson turned. Standing in the doorway, smiling broadly, was a general in uniform.

"Uncle Joe!" Nelson exclaimed, striding over to shake his hand. Dan and the sergeants snapped to attention while Marty looked on curiously.

"Nelson, you're looking good," the general said. "Better than I ever did at your age. Must be from your Uncle George's side of the family."

Nelson grinned. "Marty, men, I'd like to introduce my mother's brother, General Joe Wheeler."

Dan smirked as he added, "I think I know General Wheeler well enough, Nelson. We are all part of the same family, even though it was Molly who inherited the fighting blood from her uncles."

The sergeant perked up. "Fightin' Joe Wheeler? Late of the Confederate forces?"

"I'm afraid so, Sergeant," Wheeler replied with a chuckle. "But that was a long time ago."

The sergeant nodded. "Fought against you back then, General. Good to be on the same side this time."

"How does it feel to be back in the blue, sir?" the sergeant asked.

Wheeler laughed. "Like I've been on furlough and just now returned to my own colors."

"What brings you here, General?" Dan asked.

Wheeler pointed toward the back. "There's a Spanish force on that ridge, and I'm afraid if Linares thinks it over, he'll move another thousand men and trap us here. Nelson, you need to attack right away."

Dan and the sergeants exchanged amused glances.

"What's funny?" Wheeler asked.

Nelson smiled. "We just came to the same conclusion, Uncle Joe. We're preparing for an attack now."

Wheeler laughed heartily. "With my blood for military genius and General Pickett's for looks—though I'm not sure what good that'll do—you'll go far, boy. When do we attack?"

"We, General?" Nelson asked with a raised brow.

"Don't worry, don't worry," Wheeler said, waving off any concerns. "I'm just here to observe. You're still in command."

Nelson checked his watch. "Dan, spread the word. We begin the advance at noon."

AT NOON, the Lightning Cavalry started out, their march cutting through a dense, suffocating forest. Thick vines hung down all around them, and the air was heavy with humidity. The oppressive heat was squeezing every ounce of moisture from their bodies, and soon, they were drenched in sweat. Gnats and biting flies swarmed relentlessly, adding another layer of misery to their long march. The canopy overhead was so thick that the sunlight barely broke through, casting the trail in a perpetual, muggy gloom. The men swatted at the insects with halfhearted slaps, too weary to do more than endure.

When they finally got through the trees, a high ridge—jagged and unforgiving—was in front of them. It was not just steep, it was also treacherous, with loose rocks and crumbling soil that threatened to give way with every step. The troops paused for a moment at the base, staring up at the climb that was ahead of them. Marty could see the change in their expressions. Gone was the bravado that had carried them through their earlier march. Now, a collective sense of unease settled over the men. It wasn't quite fear, not yet, but it was close.

A corporal rode back to find Marty. His face was flushed, and sweat dripped down his temples as his horse snorted and shifted uneasily.

"Miss McGuire, the colonel sends his regards, ma'am, and informs you that you are to stay here with Captain Baker and the reserve company."

Marty eyed the steep incline, its jagged rocks interspersed with patches of thorny underbrush. She knew that soon the men would dismount, leaving their horses behind as they began the climb. The ridge offered no cover, and the Spanish would be waiting at the top, hidden behind stones and natural barriers, rifles aimed downward. It would be a massacre if they weren't careful. She shuddered at the thought of becoming one of the targets. Staying with the reserves seemed a very wise decision.

"Very well, Corporal," she replied, her voice steady despite the tension within her.

The corporal, clearly relieved, allowed a grin to cross his face. "Thank you, ma'am. The colonel told me to keep you back even if I had to hold you down myself. Glad you ain't gonna make me do that."

As the horse-holders gathered, each managing four nervous mounts, the Lightning Cavalry was suddenly reduced by one-fourth of its strength. Marty watched as the horses were led into the shelter of the trees, their snorts fading into the distance. Meanwhile, Captain Baker's voice rang out with authority.

"Mount-holders to the rear! Reserves on line, ready to advance!"

Though the reserves wouldn't be engaged unless absolutely necessary, their presence was a reminder that battles were often decided by the final push, and sometimes, just sometimes, a well-timed reserve could turn the tide. But Marty knew that for many of the men heading up the ridge, there would be no need for reserves—they would never make it back.

She found a large rock offering some cover as she watched the men begin their slow, torturous climb. Nelson was among them, bending at the waist, moving carefully, one foot in front of the other. The color-bearer beside him clutched the American flag, which fluttered faintly in the slight breeze. Marty's heart tightened as she whispered a prayer.

"Please, God, protect him," she said softly. Then, feeling a pang of guilt, she quickly added, "Please protect all of them."

The climb was brutal, and even from her position, Marty could see the strain on the soldiers' faces. The rocky slope was loose and treacherous, and every misstep could send a man tumbling back down. Still, the men pressed forward, moving in slow, deliberate strides. So far, not one shot had been fired from the enemy above.

Suddenly, a bugle call pierced the air. Marty turned toward Captain Baker, her eyes wide.

"What's that?" she asked. "Is he signaling a charge?"

"No," Captain Baker said. He smiled at her. "As steep as that hill is, I reckon they're chargin' just about as fast as they can now. That bugle call is to bring the machine guns to the front."

Marty's attention shifted back to the machine gun crews, who were now pushing their way through the men. They were easy to pick out, because they had pack mules carrying the barrels of the guns.

When the weapons got to the front, the advancing army stopped and spread out along the hillside. A moment later, Marty heard the rapid, staccato tapping of the machine guns echoing off the ridge.

Marty spotted little puffs of smoke rising from behind a makeshift wall of stones at the crest of the hill. The sounds of the firing drifted down to them now, growing more intense with each passing second. Marty thought of corn popping in a pan, how it starts slow and builds to a crescendo, with so many of the kernels popping at once that the individual pops can't be discerned. The battle was like that.

Before long, the first of the wounded appeared. Two men were carrying a stretcher, and Marty felt a cold wave of dread wash over her. The soldier's leg was soaked in blood, and though she fought to remain composed, the sight made her stomach churn.

"Medics, prepare for the wounded!" Captain Baker called, and Marty saw two men open a box filled with medical equipment.

"Hit in the thigh," someone said, though his information wasn't needed. Everyone who saw the wounded soldier knew where he had been hit, and because he was the first casualty, there wasn't a man who didn't come over to see him.

Soon, the wounded came in a steady stream—some on stretchers, others limping or being helped down. The line of casualties grew longer with each passing moment, and the air became thick with the sounds of men groaning in pain, the frantic shouts of medics, and the relentless crack of gunfire.

"Soldier?' Captain Baker yelled at one of the wounded who was able to walk. "How goes the fightin'?"

"Bad," the soldier replied. "They're dyin' up there…dyin' all around me." Then he added, his voice shaking, "They ain't bringing the dead back down. There ain't enough medics to do it. They can only mess with the wounded. The dead…they're just layin' up there."

It was enough to rattle anyone, and it didn't take long for the talk to spread like wildfire. All around her, Marty heard men grumbling and speculating, many convinced they were on the losing side of this fight.

"Hold up! Hold on!" A grizzled sergeant bellowed over the rising panic, his voice cutting through the chatter. "He's just been shot, and he's hurtin' real bad. Don't blame him for panickin'. But look up there! Does it look to you like we're gettin' beat? We're still moving up the hill, ain't we?"

Marty followed the sergeant's pointing hand, and sure enough, the Lightning Cavalry was still advancing in surges, small groups of ten and twenty men at a time pushing upward through the hail of Spanish fire.

"The sergeant's right!" another voice rang out. "We're still in it! Go get 'em, boys!"

"Go get 'em!" another soldier shouted, his voice full of renewed hope. "Save some for us!"

The air seemed to shift, and Marty felt it—the raw determination that replaced the fear. The men were rallying, their voices rising over the chaos of gunfire.

"Thanks, Sergeant," Captain Baker said gratefully. "I thought I was about to lose 'em there for a moment."

"I've seen it before, Cap'n," the sergeant replied. "Back in the War between the States. A man gets hit, and he don't know nothin' but the pain. He panics, and it spreads like a disease. These boys ain't been in battle before. They don't know how to deal with it yet. You just gotta settle 'em down."

Marty glanced up at the ridge again, her heart in her throat. The American line was still moving, though the pace had slowed to a crawl. Her breath caught in her chest as she watched Nelson, bent low, leading his men forward. He was so close to the top. So close.

Suddenly, a soldier came stumbling down the hillside, heading straight for Captain Baker.

"Cap'n, Colonel Pickett says to bring your men up now," he panted, his face slick with sweat. He turned to Marty, his expression softening for a moment. "Ma'am, the colonel says you're to stay put till he sends for you."

"Very well," Marty agreed, her stomach tightening.

"Keep your head down, Miss McGuire," Captain Baker said with a reassuring smile.

"You do the same, Captain," Marty replied, her voice wavering slightly despite her attempt to stay calm.

Baker's men let out a cheer as he stood up and motioned for them to advance. They surged forward with renewed energy, but as they pushed up the hill, the shouts of enthusiasm soon turned to grunts.

Behind her, Marty heard the wounded soldiers laughing softly, their voices thick with pain but tinged with dark humor.

"What's funny?" Marty asked, turning to one of the men.

"General Wheeler," one of the soldiers wheezed. "Just before I got hit, he was wavin' his sword around, shoutin', 'We've got the Yankees on the run!' He still thinks we're fightin' the Civil War."

Another soldier chimed in, his face pale but his lips curled into a grin. "Look at Cap'n Baker and his fool company, tryin' to run up that hill like it's a parade ground. They'll learn soon enough you can't run up it without gettin' plumb tuckered out."

Sure enough, within minutes, Baker and his men were forced to slow, their once-quick strides turning into a slow, steady climb. But they kept moving, inching their way toward the top.

The added firepower from Baker's reserves made all the difference. The American line began to surge forward again, groups of ten, then twenty, then whole companies pushing toward the crest of the hill. Marty caught her breath as she watched the flag bearer raise the Stars and Stripes high above the ridge.

"She's ours, men! She's ours!" one of the wounded soldiers shouted, his voice raw with emotion.

The cry was echoed by a loud hurrah from the soldiers below, their cheers ringing out across the battlefield as the American flag fluttered proudly at the top of the ridge. Marty's chest tightened with a mix of relief and grief—relief that the battle was over, grief for the men who wouldn't return from that ridge.

An hour later, Marty stood at the crest of the hill, her chest heaving from the exertion of the climb. Even after the battle had been won, the ascent was punishing. She glanced down the slope and thought of the men who had advanced under fire. A lump formed in her throat as she realized how lucky she had been to stay back, shielded from the hell those men had faced.

She climbed to the very top, then looked back down toward the beach and the little village deep in the shadow of the hills. From this vantage point, she could see the blackened ruins. Smoke still curled from the wreckage, caught in the light breeze that swept across the hilltop.

"Hello, Marty," a familiar voice said.

She turned quickly, her heart skipping a beat. Nelson stood there, a shadow of the man she'd seen earlier that morning. His face was smeared with sweat and the gritty residue of gunpowder, and his eyes had a hollow gaze that saw far beyond the present, into places no one should ever have to visit.

"Nelson!" she cried, rushing toward him. Without thinking, she threw her arms around him, clinging to him as if she could hold him back from that faraway place his mind had wandered to. He wrapped his arms around her in return, his grip steady despite the weight of what had just happened. For a moment, they stood there, two souls pulled together by the gravity of survival.

"Thank God you made it through," she whispered, her voice cracking with emotion.

"I did," he said quietly. "But not all of my men were as lucky."

Marty pulled back slightly, her relief overshadowed by the grim reality of his words. His tone was flat, worn down by the loss. "How many?"

"Forty-two wounded," he said. "Eight killed."

Her heart sank. The number felt like a punch to the gut. She hadn't known all the men, but after days of following them, reporting on their every move, she felt a connection to them. And now, knowing that some would never return home, a sense of guilt twisted inside her. She was relieved that Nelson was alive, but that relief felt hollow, almost selfish, in the face of so much death.

"Seven enlisted men…and one officer," Nelson continued.

Marty swallowed hard. "Who…who was the officer?"

She knew all the officers, had shared meals with them, listened to their stories. The men were too numerous to know individually, but the officers had faces, names, personalities.

"Captain Baker."

Marty gasped, her hand instinctively flying to her mouth. "Captain Baker? But…he was with the reserves."

Nelson's face tightened. "I know. He was one of the last casualties we took."

For a moment, Marty couldn't speak. Captain Baker had been the one to watch over her, to offer reassurances during the heat of battle. Now, he lay among the dead. She followed Nelson's gaze and saw the bodies, eight of them, laid out beneath makeshift pieces of canvas. The men who had fallen on the ridge had yet to be brought down. She had heard the reports, but seeing them there, motionless, erased any distance between her and the brutal truth.

Nelson's voice broke the silence, low and heavy. "Now you understand why I told you once—there's no glory in battle."

Marty didn't respond right away, couldn't. Her eyes were drawn to the canvas-covered bodies again, and for the first time, she truly felt the weight of those words. War wasn't about flags waving on hilltops or grand victories in the field. It was about this—sweat, blood, death. She looked at Nelson, standing there with the grime of battle still clinging to him, and realized that for men like him, this wasn't victory. It was survival, nothing more.

FOURTEEN

THE LIGHTNING CAVALRY LEFT A SMALL SECURITY detail at the top of the ridge, ensuring the ground they had fought so hard to win remained in their hands. The rest of the regiment bivouacked at the foot of the hill, not far from where Marty had watched the battle unfold. Control of the ridge opened the path to Santiago, where rumors said General Linares's entire army was waiting, ready for the next fight with the Americans.

As Marty moved among the soldiers, she noticed the subtle shift in their mood. The night before, they had been bold and challenging, almost jovial at the thought of going to battle, but now the bravado was gone. Their morale was much better than she would have thought. The men had been tested, and they came through the test. But now they knew what it was like to be terribly frightened and to see their friends killed and wounded. Nearly everyone there had a story to tell of a very close brush with death, and the experience had sobered them.

Marty made her way to the makeshift field hospital, where the wounded were resting as comfortably as possible. As early as possible the next morning, many of them would be evacuated back to one of the ships that had been designated as a hospital ship. But for this one last night, they were still with their comrades.

One soldier called Marty over. "Miss McGuire, could you write a letter to my folks for me? I'd do it myself, but…" he lifted his arm, the bandage covering his shoulder already seeping with blood. "It's just easier this way."

Marty nodded and found a place to sit, the last gleam of twilight casting long shadows over the camp. She took out her notepad, pencil poised as the soldier began to speak, his voice calm, almost reflective.

Dear Ma and Pa,

There's something purely awesome about a soldier dying on the battlefield. One second, the fella next to you is alive—just as alive as you are. He's strong, maybe scared, or mad, or dead-set on making it up that hill. And then, in the next breath, there's a sound—like a dull thump—and he's gone. That's how quick it happens. One moment, you're two men in a fight, and the next, you're just one.

It's funny, though. I heard every bullet that hit the men around me. I could hear the impact—sharp and quick, like a snap. But I didn't hear the one that hit me. It didn't come from the front, it came from somewhere off to the left. I was trying to be the hero, rushing up the hill, when the bullet found me. I didn't yell, didn't wave my arms like you might imagine. I just dropped, like a piece of hay cut down by a scythe. I lay there in the brush, and for a while, I watched the other men keep going past me. Funny thing was, I wasn't hurting, and I wasn't scared. Lying there felt like the natural thing to do.

Some soldiers found me after a bit and carried me back to the aid station. When I got there, one of the surgeons took one look and told me to make peace with God. He said I wasn't going to make it. But even then, I wasn't afraid. I wasn't even all that interested, if I'm honest. It just didn't seem like a big deal anymore.

Later on, another doctor came by, said I might just pull through. And now here I am, writing this letter. By tomorrow, I'll be headed to a ship, and who knows after that. I figure my soldiering days are over. I won't be charging up any more hills. But at least I got my licks in while I could.

Your loving son,
Billy

Marty finished writing, her fingers trembling slightly as she set the pencil down. She looked at Billy, lying there with a calmness she could hardly understand. The letter was simple, straightforward, but it held so much in those few lines. It spoke of the randomness of life-and-death on the battlefield, the quiet resignation of a man who had faced death and found it strangely unremarkable.

"Do you want me to add anything else?" Marty asked, her voice soft.

Billy shook his head. "No, ma'am. That'll do just fine."

Marty added a short postscript at the bottom of Billy's letter, explaining to his parents that his writing arm was bandaged and that was why she had written the letter for him. She mentioned how the bullet that struck Billy had not only torn through his arm but also grazed his side, puncturing the chest wall. But she'd spoken to the doctor, and he was optimistic. Billy, it seemed, would make it. She hoped those words would bring some comfort.

After folding the letter carefully, she sealed it in an envelope and handed it to the regimental mail clerk, who was collecting letters with a somber expression. Marty watched as the clerk tucked it away. It would be days, maybe weeks before Billy's parents received it, but the letter would be on its way home, just as Billy would be—eventually.

She turned and began wandering back through the bivouac area to her own tent. The mood among the men was markedly different from the night before. There were no crackling fires lighting up the camp, no songs or laughter echoing through the trees. Men sat quietly, staring into the darkness, the weight of the day's battle pressing down on them. They had seen enough for one day.

Nelson wasn't with the men. He had ridden back to Siboney to confer with General Shafter, and Dan had told her he wouldn't be back until the early hours of the morning. Marty wished he was here, not only because she wanted to see him, to feel the comfort of his presence, but because she knew how exhausted he must be. He hadn't slept much in days, yet while the others were collapsing from sheer fatigue after the battle, Nelson had ridden off again.

She reached her tent and lay down, the images from the day swirling in her mind—the gunfire, the fallen men, Billy's words echoing softly in her ears. And yet, despite it all, she fell asleep almost instantly. Her body, like the men's, had reached its limit.

"YOU HAD no right to bring on this battle!" General Shafter's voice was sharp, cutting through the tent like a knife. His face was flushed, his frustration barely concealed as he stood with his hands on the map table, glaring at Nelson.

Nelson stood his ground, his expression calm despite the rebuke. He had expected this, knew it was coming, but still, the force of Shafter's anger stung more than he had anticipated.

"General, I beg to differ with you," General Wheeler interjected, stepping forward before Nelson could respond. Wheeler had come with Nelson to brief Shafter on the outcome of the battle, and he wasn't about to let the victory be turned into a reprimand. "If Colonel Pickett had not acted quickly and decisively, General Linares could have reinforced that ridge. With command of the high ground and a well-dug-in position, they could have held us off indefinitely."

Shafter's lips tightened, but he didn't interrupt. Wheeler continued. "We would have had no choice but to put back to sea and try to land someplace else, and even that's assuming Congress would let us try again. It was a risk, sir, but it paid off. It was a great victory. You shouldn't be angry with Colonel Pickett. You should be congratulating him."

Shafter's face hardened, and he leaned back, crossing his arms. "Victory or not, Wheeler, this army does not succeed by ignoring orders. It's about discipline, structure, and coordination. If every officer acted independently, we'd be in chaos." He turned his sharp gaze on Nelson. "Do you have any idea the risks involved? You could have compromised this entire campaign."

Nelson met his eyes without flinching. "With

respect, General, I knew the risks, and I acted on the information we had in the moment. Waiting for further orders could have meant losing the ridge entirely. I couldn't afford to wait."

Shafter studied him. He didn't speak for a long moment, clearly weighing the situation. "I don't like it," he finally muttered. "You went against protocol, undermined the chain of command."

Wheeler opened his mouth to speak again, but Nelson raised a hand, stopping him. "General, I understand your concern. But the situation demanded action. We had to move quickly, and now, because of that, we control the ridge. General Linares has lost his advantage."

For a moment, it seemed as if Shafter was about to fire back again, his frustration mounting. But then he sighed, his shoulders slumping slightly. His hand rubbed through his hair as he looked away, a small smile beginning to form. "Maybe you're right, Colonel," he said. "Maybe I'm just too damn tired to see it clearly right now. But I'll admit…the ridge is ours. And for that, you deserve credit."

He extended his hand, his smile now more genuine. "So I should be congratulating you. A job well done, Colonel—despite my orders."

Nelson hesitated for only a second before taking the offered hand, relief washing over him. "Thank you, General. I'm glad we could secure the ridge."

Shafter nodded, his expression serious again. "Perhaps next time we can work together more closely, rather than having to sort things out afterward."

"Of course, sir," Nelson replied, his voice steady. He knew how close the reprimand had been but was grateful the situation had been defused.

Shafter straightened and unfolded the map on the table before him. "Now, we must focus on Santiago," he said, motioning for Colonel Humphrey to join them.

Humphrey, the quartermaster general, stepped forward, pointing to the ridge Nelson's forces had captured earlier in the day. "We've received reports from the Cubans about the road between Siboney and Santiago," he began. "This ridge, as you can see, controlled the road, just as you observed, Colonel Pickett. If the Spanish had still held it, we'd be in serious trouble. Even now, the road ahead will be difficult. It crosses over high ground, through ravines, and rivers with no bridges. Our supply wagons will barely fit through some of the narrower passages. The Spanish could easily set up an ambush at any point."

Shafter nodded grimly. "That's where your cavalry comes in, Colonel Pickett."

Nelson leaned in, studying the map closely.

"I want your men to move ahead," Shafter continued. "You'll clear the road, secure it, and hold it while we bring the rest of the army and our supplies through."

"Understood, sir," Nelson replied as he calculated the challenges ahead. "When do you want us in position?"

"With first light," Shafter said, glancing at his watch. "That's just over two-and-a-half hours from now."

Nelson nodded, feeling the exhaustion sink in. It had been days since he'd slept more than a few hours at a time, but he would follow orders. "I'll return to the bivouac and prepare the men. Will you see to it that my wounded are evacuated?"

Shafter gave a nod. "Yes, of course. They'll be taken care of."

With a sharp salute, Nelson turned and left the tent, his thoughts already on what was ahead of him. But first, the long ride back to camp, then the march to Santiago.

IT SEEMED to Marty that she had barely closed her eyes when she heard the unmistakable sounds of the bivouac being broken. She poked her head through the front of her tent and saw the soldiers moving about in the dim, pre-dawn light. They were rolling up their bedrolls, saddling their horses, and filling their canteens. Nearby, Dan stood adjusting his saddle.

"Dan, what is it?" Marty asked, her voice still groggy. "What's going on?"

"General Shafter's orders," Dan said, his tone grim but accepting. "We're to secure the road so the army can move the supplies through."

Marty frowned. "Now? He wants you to do it now?"

Dan offered her a tired smile. "Afraid so."

"These men are exhausted," Marty said, her frustration rising. "They fought a hard battle yesterday."

"At least they got a couple of hours of sleep," Dan replied with a shrug. "Nelson didn't even get that."

"Nelson hasn't slept at all?"

"Nope." Dan's voice was calm, but there was a hardness in his expression. He was used to the grind of soldiering, but Marty could see it was wearing on him, too.

"Well, I'm going to see him. I'll make him—"

Dan reached out, his hand on her arm, and his grip was firm. "No," he said sharply, his voice more commanding than she had ever heard before.

Marty blinked in surprise, staring at him. It wasn't like Dan to speak to her this way.

He took a deep breath and softened his tone. "Marty, listen. If you go to him now, with everything else he's got on his mind, you'll just be reinforcing what he's already trying to fight. He's got the weight of the entire regiment on his back. Don't add to it. Be his support, not another burden."

She sighed. "You're right," she admitted, her voice low. "It just seems so unfair to expect him, and the rest of you, to just go and go and go with no rest."

"We'll rest when the road's secured," Dan said. "It'll all be fine. Nelson's used to this. It's what being a soldier is all about."

Marty held her tongue, though the words were on the tip of it: *I hope Nelson will tire of this soon and leave the army*. But she knew what the army meant to Nelson, and she knew that the quickest way to end their friendship would be to suggest he find some other profession.

HALF AN HOUR LATER, with the first gray light of dawn creeping over the hills, the Lightning Cavalry moved out. Marty rode with them, learning—just as the men had—to rest in the saddle, her body swaying with the movement of the horse as exhaustion settled deep in her bones.

By nine o'clock that morning, the road was secured without resistance. Nelson posted guards along the route, ensuring it was safe for the supply wagons and the rest of the army. When the task was complete, the column halted at the far end of the road, waiting for the first of the army to come through.

Marty found a spot under a large palm tree, grateful for the shade. She leaned back against the trunk, watching the weary soldiers gather in small groups, slumped against their packs. Moments later, Nelson appeared, moving toward her with the slow, deliberate steps of a man who had pushed himself beyond his limits. He sat down beside her with a heavy sigh, his face drawn with exhaustion.

"I guess I owe you an apology," Nelson said, his voice gravelly.

Marty glanced at him, surprised. "Why?"

"I was pretty sure, by now, you'd be ready to go back to the beach," he said, a faint smile tugging at his lips.

She laughed softly. "Don't think I haven't thought about it," she admitted.

Nelson chuckled, the sound rough in his throat. "I admire your honesty."

He reached up and brushed his fingers gently across her cheek, and Marty looked into his eyes. She had never seen anyone look so utterly worn out. His face, streaked with dirt and sweat, told the story of everything he had endured—leading his men into battle, securing the ridge, and now this. All without a moment's rest.

"The practical side of me says I wish you would go back to the beach," Nelson said quietly. "But…there's a part of me that's glad you're here."

Marty reached for his hand, lifting it to her lips, and kissed his fingers gently. "I love you, Nelson Pickett," she whispered.

He smiled, a tired but genuine smile, and nodded. "I love you, too," he said. "Though I have to admit, sometimes I feel like a bit of a scoundrel."

"Why?" she asked, her brow furrowing.

"Because," Nelson said, "I'm surrounded by men who have loved ones waiting for them back home. But I have the unfair advantage of having you here with me."

Marty's heart tightened at his words, but she spoke gently. "I'm not here for your privilege, Nelson. I'm here because this is where I need to be."

He sighed, his head leaning back against the tree trunk. "I know," he said softly. "But I still can't shake the feeling."

Marty glanced at him, seeing the way his eyelids drooped, the exhaustion pulling him under. "Nelson, how long has it been since you slept?" she asked.

"I got an hour or so on the beach last night," he mumbled, eyes half-closed.

"That was two nights ago," Marty corrected.

"Yeah… I guess it was," he murmured, his voice trailing off.

"Why don't you lie down here? Just for a little while. I'll keep watch."

Nelson surprised her by nodding. "Maybe I will," he said, his voice barely above a whisper. He stretched out on the ground, folding his arms behind his head, but Marty gently moved him so his head rested in her lap.

"Don't worry about me," she said softly. "Just rest."

But he didn't hear her. Nelson was already asleep, his deep, steady breathing filling the quiet around them. Marty smiled faintly and brushed his hair back from his forehead, feeling the weight of his exhaustion settle over them both. She sat there, still and quiet, as the rest of the army slowly moved through the road his men had secured.

By noon, half the army had passed through, fanning out across the flatlands toward Santiago. Marty scribbled notes for her article, glancing down occasionally at Nelson's sleeping form, grateful that—at least for now—he had found a moment of peace.

Dispatch from the Field: The Lightning Cavalry After the Battle

By Marty McGuire, Special Correspondent

Yesterday, the men of the Lightning Cavalry became the first American soldiers to engage Spanish troops in battle. By now, most of you reading this will already know the outcome—victory was ours, though not without a heavy price. We lost eight brave souls, men who fought with courage and determination. The full details of the engagement have been filed in a previous dispatch, but this one is for the families of those soldiers. I hope to offer a glimpse of how your sons, husbands, and sweethearts are faring today, in the calm that follows the storm of battle.

Let me begin by saying this: the men are doing well, considering the circumstances. Exhaustion weighs heavily on them, as it does on us all, but their spirits remain strong. Even as I write this beneath the welcome shade of a palm tree, I can see dozens of them catching what sleep they can while their comrades keep watch. There's a quiet stillness here now—the quiet that comes after the chaos of battle.

The engagement is now being referred to as the Battle of Las Guardia, named after the ridge the Lightning Cavalry stormed and secured from the Spanish.

The ridge's name, fittingly enough, means The Guardian, *for it sits like a sentinel over the vital road between Siboney and Santiago de Cuba. Had the Spanish reinforced the ridge, it would have blocked our entire advance. But with the enemy driven off, the road is now clear, and the American Expeditionary Force is making its way forward.*

After the battle, the Lightning Cavalry was tasked with securing the road—ensuring no hidden ambushes lay in wait along the narrow, deeply cut paths and ravines. The men, weary though they were, took to the task without hesitation. The road was found to be clear, and now, as I write, the rest of the army is pouring through, a sight both magnificent and sobering.

From this vantage point, I can see the long columns of soldiers, their rifles gleaming in the sunlight as they march toward Santiago. Behind them, pack mules trudge along, burdened with supplies: ammunition, medical stores, and everything else needed to wage war. Farther back still, the wagons roll—laden not with weapons but with the salt pork, beans, coffee, and sugar that keep these men going. This is the lifeblood of the army, just as important as the weapons they carry.

We can see the outskirts of Santiago clearly now, some seven or eight miles distant. The land between here and the city appears mostly level for the first few miles, before rising into low hills just outside of Santiago. Those hills, as of this morning, appear deserted, but I've heard officers discussing plans to move artillery onto the heights. From there, it's expected that General Shafter will begin shelling the city.

For those back home, the thought of shelling a city may sound grim. But we must remember: Santiago is the key. It's where General Linares and his army are likely to make their stand. Though we haven't yet faced the bulk of the Spanish forces, there is no doubt in anyone's mind that Santiago will be the decisive battleground in this campaign.

Until then, we wait. The men are tired but resolute. They know the fight is far from over, and they will meet it head-on when the time comes.

For now, I send this dispatch with the hope that it brings some small comfort to those back home, knowing that your soldiers are here, carrying on in the face of exhaustion and danger, with their eyes set firmly on victory.

Nelson opened his eyes to find Marty finishing up her notes. He glanced at the sun hanging overhead, then at her, a grin tugging at his mouth.

"Morning," he said, stretching. "Or is it afternoon by now?"

"Just after noon," Marty replied, not looking up from her scribbling.

Nelson pushed himself to his feet, scanning the road below. The wagons were rolling through the draw, undisturbed.

"Looks like we're getting through the draw all right," he said.

"It seems that way," Marty said.

Nelson rubbed his neck, then shifted his gaze back to her. "Are you hungry?"

"A little," she admitted.

He smirked. "How about some pork and beans? I could whip up a batch."

Marty chuckled, her eyes still focused on her work. "Sounds about like the last meal I had."

"What was it?"

"Pork and beans."

Nelson laughed softly. "Well, you haven't really had it until you've tasted mine."

"Oh?" she said, finally looking up from her work. "You've got some secret recipe the others don't know about?"

"Been fine-tuning it for years," Nelson said, already heading to his horse to grab his gear.

In no time, he had a small fire going, the bacon sizzling in the pan. He tossed in pepper and a few pinches of something from a cloth bag and then opened a can of tinned beans to add to the mixture.

Marty sniffed the air. "I have to admit, it smells better than the usual stuff."

"Told you," Nelson replied with a grin, poking at the fire. "Best you'll get out here."

Just as Marty was about to respond, a voice cut through the moment. "Colonel Pickett."

Nelson didn't turn, but kept stirring the pot. "General Shafter," he said, his voice calm. "What can I do for you?"

Shafter's tone was tight, all business. "I want to ensure there's no repeat of yesterday's...premature action."

Nelson's jaw tightened slightly, but he stayed casual. "General, if we hadn't taken that ridge, your wagons wouldn't be moving through the draw right now."

"We would've taken it," Shafter shot back, stepping closer. "But on my command and with a coordinated plan. What would you have done if the Spaniards had reinforced their position? You had no reserves. If you'd waited for my orders, you would've had an entire regiment at your back."

Nelson's gaze didn't waver. "Sir, we didn't need them."

"A lucky break, Colonel," Shafter snapped. "But that's not strategy. Now I'm concerned about Santiago. I don't want you charging ahead with your cavalry again."

Nelson rose to his feet, meeting the general's stare. "Sir, we're the cavalry. Your eyes and ears. You're telling me you don't want us to scout the heights around Santiago before you move in?"

"That's exactly what I'm saying."

Nelson's eyes narrowed. "You want to move your artillery into position without clearing the heights first?"

Shafter's face flushed. "Colonel, see to your regiment. Leave the strategy to me." His gaze shifted, settling on Marty with clear disapproval. She met his eyes, unflinching, the weight of Nelson's confidence grounding her.

Shafter gave a sharp nod, as if dismissing them both, before turning on his heel and marching off.

Marty let out a breath. "I've gotten you in trouble, haven't I?"

Nelson chuckled, his laughter quiet but rich with humor. "You? Trouble? I doubt it." He scooped the beans into her tin plate, handing it to her. "But you'll have to enjoy this on your own. Duty calls."

He grabbed a bite for himself, then strode to his horse. Swinging into the saddle, he gave her a quick salute. "Thanks for the pillow," he said, grinning. Without another word, he turned the horse and galloped off, disappearing into the dust and heat.

Marty watched him go, then spent the rest of the afternoon mingling with the men. Eddie Stone came up to her with a sketch of Las Guardia Hill, the drawing depicting the tension and energy of the battle. Marty took it from him.

"This is fantastic," she said. "I'll send it back to New York—your drawings add so much to my articles."

Eddie beamed as she tucked the sketch into her satchel, already thinking of the half-million papers that would soon carry the story of what had unfolded on that ridge.

THE AMERICANS MADE no effort whatever to observe blackout discipline that night. Below the ridge, the flatlands were dotted with a hundred campfires, flickering like stars scattered across the earth. No one cared if the Spanish knew their position—the Americans were confident, and there was no need for caution tonight.

Marty stood on the small rise where Nelson had rested earlier, gazing down at the campfires. She was listening to the soft whisper of sound that reached her ear. There was laughter in bursts, clashing songs, and the low buzz of conversations that blended together. It was the sound of an army at rest, and she wasn't quite ready to give it up for sleep.

From behind, she heard the familiar crunch of boots climbing the hill. She didn't have to turn to know it was Nelson. The steady rhythm of his stride was unmistakable, and soon enough, he was beside her, silent for a moment as he took in the same view.

"I thought you'd be asleep by now," he said quietly.

Marty shook her head. "No, not yet. There's something about all this..." She gestured to the camp below.

"It's strange. I know it's war. I know it's awful, but..." She struggled for the right words. "It's...magnificent in a way. Like watching something bigger than yourself unfold."

Nelson chuckled, a deep, warm sound. "Careful who you share that with. That's a secret men have kept for centuries."

Marty smiled, glancing at him.

They stood in silence for a moment, both absorbing the scene below. There was a comfort in standing side by side, a shared understanding of the chaos and calm that came with war. Nelson shifted slightly, his voice taking on a quieter tone.

"It's not about the thrill of it. It's knowing you're part of something, that what you do out here means something," he said, his eyes scanning the horizon. "That's what keeps us going."

Marty nodded, her gaze still on the flickering fires below. "I think I understand that."

"I'm glad you're beginning to understand the way of a soldier's life."

"I'm doing my best," Marty said.

Nelson took her hand in his and they stood looking over the scene below them, but neither of them spoke.

Finally, Nelson dropped her hand as he straightened. "You should get some rest. Tomorrow's going to come fast."

Marty nodded, her voice quiet. "You too, Nelson."

He gave her a small, lingering smile before turning and walking back down the hill, disappearing into the shadows. Marty stayed where she was, watching the fires below burn steadily into the night.

FIFTEEN

AS NIGHT SLOWLY GAVE WAY, THE FIRST LIGHT OF DAWN was casting a pale glow over the army encamped in the flatlands below the ridge. The hundred campfires that had burned so brightly the night before had dwindled to a few smoldering embers. Now, in the early morning stillness, thousands of soldiers sitting or lying about were just beginning to wake up to the new day. A thin, diaphanous haze of smoke hung over the campground, and there drifted on the morning air the smell of bacon and coffee from those industrious soldiers who had risen before dawn.

Marty stirred in her small tent, still wrapped in the warmth of sleep. Crawling out into the cool morning air, she reached for the wash pan near her gear, filling it with water from her canteen. The cold splash of water on her face shocked her fully awake, and as she scrubbed her skin, the events of the past two days ran through her mind. The battle for the ridge had been intense, the energy of the camp almost tangible afterward, but last night had been different.

She paused, staring into the basin. The moment with Nelson still lingered, though it wasn't something she could name outright. Standing on that rise with him, watching the fires flicker below, something had passed between them. She wasn't sure what it was, but she knew it was important.

Drying her face, Marty glanced around, wondering where Nelson was. She wondered if he was already on the move, making preparations for the day's march. The army would go to Santiago today—everyone knew it. The real fight was coming, and this morning felt like the calm before a storm.

Standing up, she stretched the stiffness from her body and looked over the camp. Men were milling about, some gathering in small groups to eat, others still trying to wake up. The mood was quiet, almost somber. Even though there was the usual banter and the occasional burst of laughter, there was an edge to it all. The battle for Santiago was in front of them, and everyone could feel it.

Shaking her head, she forced herself to focus. There was work to be done. She had an article to write, and her readers back in New York were waiting for every detail. War wasn't just about battles, after all—it was about the men, the movements, the moments in between. It was her job to capture it all, to bring it to life for people who had never seen the horrors of war up-close. She couldn't afford to let her thoughts stray, not now.

Pulling her notebook from her bag, Marty began jotting down observations: the haze of smoke still lingering in the air, the soldiers' tired but determined faces, the sound of distant gunfire that echoed from the hills like a reminder of what was coming. She could already feel the tension mounting, the way the men were steeling themselves for whatever awaited them in Santiago.

Her pencil hovered over the page for a moment as she considered the day ahead. There was no telling how things would unfold once the army moved. Everyone knew the Spanish were waiting for them, and Santiago was their stronghold. It would not be an easy fight. But something inside Marty had changed over these last few days. She was no longer just an observer of this war—she was part of this, whether she wanted to be or not. The men, the battles, the emotions—all of it had seeped into her in ways she hadn't expected. And maybe, just maybe, so had Nelson Pickett.

For now, though, she pushed those thoughts aside. She had an article to write, and Santiago wouldn't wait for her to sort through her feelings.

The New York Banner

Dispatch from Cuba—July 1898

By Miss Marty McGuire, Special Correspondent

The Calm Before the Storm

At dawn today, the great American army that now occupies the flatlands below the ridgeline of Las Guardia stirred from its slumber. Yesterday, this very ridge saw the bloody conflict that secured our foothold on this island. But as the morning light bathed the land, there was a strange serenity in the air, as if nature itself had forgotten the violent clash that had so recently echoed over these fields.

The camp, which the night before had been alive with the flicker of countless fires, now smoldered in the thin morning haze. A few remaining embers dotted the landscape, but the men were awake, rising from the earth like weary giants, shaking the dust from their shoulders as they prepared for the march to Santiago. The air here is thick with anticipation, a feeling both heavy and electric, as the men steel themselves for the task ahead. The city of Santiago, still held by Spanish forces, looms in their minds. Today will likely see our boys advance once more—this time toward the heart of Spanish power on the island.

It is a curious thing, to stand amid an army on the cusp of battle. One might expect the mood to be somber, but instead, there is an odd peace here—a quiet determination that seems to settle over the men like the soft dew that lingers on their uniforms. There is laughter still, though it is quiet, subdued. The usual banter that fills camp life has been tempered by what we all know is to come.

This morning, the smell of bacon and coffee drifts through the air, a welcome comfort in these strange times. Soldiers who rose before dawn stoke the last of the fires, their tin cups clanking as they share what will likely be their final hot meal for some time. They sit together, speaking in low tones, their faces drawn but resolute. These men, young and old, are well aware of the price that war demands, but they do not shrink from it. Instead, they rise to meet it, with the quiet bravery that has come to define them.

As I walk among the rows of tents, I see the faces of those who have become more than just soldiers to me. In these past weeks, I have learned their names, their stories—who they are beyond the uniform. They are fathers, brothers, sons. Some have seen battle before, while others are tasting it for the first time in this war.

But despite their differences, there is a shared sense of purpose here, a unity that transcends their individual fears. It is the knowledge that they are part of something larger than themselves—a fight not just for territory, but for the very ideals upon which our nation stands.

The air is heavy with humidity, and even in the early hours of the day, one can feel the oppressive heat that will soon press down upon us. Yet, the men do not complain. Their eyes are fixed on the horizon, where Santiago waits. There is no turning back now. Victory feels close enough to touch, and yet it is far enough away that every man here knows the cost will be dear.

As I stand here, looking out over the vast encampment, I cannot help but be struck by the weight of history that we are living through. This is not merely a battle for Cuba—it is a battle for the future, for the very soul of our own nation. The men here fight not just for glory, but for a world in which liberty, justice, and peace might take root.

And as the sun begins to rise over this camp, casting its golden light on the faces of those who will march into the fray today, I am reminded that these soldiers are more than just figures in a grand campaign. They are the heart of America—strong, steadfast, and unyielding in their pursuit of victory.

What the day will bring, none can say for certain. But this much I know: as long as there are men like these standing firm in the face of adversity, the future is bright, and the banner of freedom will continue to fly high.

Marty read over her work, making small adjustments where needed. Her thoughts drifted to the people back home, the readers who would see this article in the paper. She hoped her words had captured the sense of awe and deep respect she felt for these men—men who, with such quiet courage, were ready to follow the orders of their commanders, no matter what awaited them on the battlefield.

NELSON WAS six miles away from the encampment. He had been forbidden by General Shafter to conduct a reconnaissance in force, but the general had not said anything that would prevent him from conducting a small scouting expedition to see what lay ahead. He and Dan had ridden out before dawn, and now they were approaching the hills where General Shafter intended to put his artillery to shell the city of Santiago.

Nelson had just passed on a remark about something funny Marty had said the day before, and Dan laughed.

"Now, tell me truthfully, Nelson," Dan said. "Aren't you ready to admit how foolish you were to try and deny yourself the love of a good woman?"

"No," Nelson said. "I was right all the time."

"You were right?" Dan exclaimed in a disbelieving voice. "Now that you've met Marty, you have seen how rare the love of a good woman is, and yet you still insist that your attitude toward women has been right all along?"

"Yes," Nelson said. He smiled broadly. "Don't you see? If I had allowed some woman to work her charms on me earlier, I would be married now. Suppose I was married, and I met Marty? Then where would I be?"

Dan laughed again. "Oh, so now you are willing to

take credit for an intelligence you don't have, are you? Are you trying to say that, all along, you knew Marty would come along, and you were just waiting for her?"

"Sure. You didn't really believe all that stuff I was saying about never wanting to get married, did you?"

"Are you and Marty going to marry?"

"Well, I haven't asked her, but if she'll say yes, then the answer is yes," Nelson said. "Do you approve?"

"Approve? I think it's wonderful!" Dan enthused. "I hope you know that I intend to be your best ma... *uhng*!"

An instant later, Dan let out a strange grunting sound, and Nelson heard the sound of a rifle shot. He looked in the direction of the sound and saw a puff of smoke rising from behind a boulder a hundred yards away. Almost immediately, a half-dozen Spanish soldiers began running toward him. None of them were mounted, but all were armed, and several were shooting at him. They didn't stop to take aim, and their shots went wild.

"Dan!" Nelson shouted.

Dan held his hand to his chest and looked down, almost in surprise, as he watched the bright, red blood spill through his fingers.

"I've been shot, Nelson," Dan said as if he couldn't believe it. He started weaving, then fell off his horse. He lay flat on his back, staring up at the sky, as if still unable to believe that this had happened to him. The six Spanish soldiers were still rushing headlong toward them, screaming threats and challenges.

Nelson drew his carbine from his saddle scabbard and raised one leg up and across his saddle. He leaned forward and put his elbow on his knee, then using that as support, he took a very careful, deliberate aim at the

Spanish soldiers. He picked the one who was ready to fire next. Nelson squeezed his trigger. The Spaniard went down. Nelson levered another round into the chamber of his carbine, then aimed at the next Spaniard. One more trigger squeeze, one more Spanish soldier down. Calmly and deliberately, he operated the cocking lever a third time and dropped one more of his attackers. With three shots in a space of less than five seconds, he had cut by half the size of the attacking force.

The three remaining soldiers looked around and saw the grim efficiency with which the American was decimating their ranks. They stopped their charge, then turned and ran back to the safety of the hills. Nelson could have dropped all three of them quite easily, but he didn't. Instead, he sheathed his rifle and jumped down to see to Dan.

"Dan! How bad is it?"

Dan had been trying to stop the flow of blood from his chest, but the entire front of his blouse was now red and sticky. Dan's face was pale, and his eyelids were fluttering.

"I've got to stop the bleeding," Nelson said. He crushed his campaign hat, then slid it under Dan's shirt, up against the wound. Next, he stripped out of his own shirt and wrapped it around Dan's chest, then he tied it tightly over the top of his hat.

Dan tried to chuckle, and when he did, flecks of blood came out of his mouth. Nelson knew that his lungs must be filling with blood, and he knew that was bad. Dan was drowning in his own blood.

"You know what they say," Dan said. "A sucking chest wound is God's way of telling you to slow down."

"I've got to get you back to a doctor," Nelson said. "I've got to get you up on your horse."

Nelson let go of the reins of his horse so he could work with Dan. He tried to lift him, but Dan cried out in pain.

"Wait, Nelson, wait!" Dan said. He lay there and gasped for a moment.

"I've got to get you back," Nelson said. "If I don't, the Spanish will come again."

As if to underscore his statement, the Spanish soldiers fired another volley from the protection of a distant group of rocks. One of the bullets slammed into the saddle of Nelson's mount, and the horse bolted and ran. Nelson whistled for it, but the horse kept going. Dan's horse would have run as well if Nelson hadn't been holding onto the animal's reins.

"Did one of the horses bolt?" Dan asked.

"It's all right. We'll double up."

"No," Dan said. "Go on, Nelson. Leave me here."

"I'm not leaving you."

"I won't make it."

"Yes, you will."

"Molly," Dan gasped.

"What?"

"Molly," Dan gasped again. "What's she going to do without me?"

"She's not going to have to do without you, Dan. I told you, I'm getting you back."

Dan smiled weakly. "Who are you kidding, Nelson? I've been in as many battles as you. I know what this wound means. I want you to tell Molly that my last thoughts were of her. Tell her…" Dan stopped. His breathing became more labored.

"Dan? Dan?" Nelson called.

Suddenly, an easy, peaceful smile spread across Dan's face.

"It's really true, Nelson," he said in a voice that was strangely unmarred by pain. "There really is a Fiddler's Green. I'll wait for you there."

Dan's facial muscles relaxed and his breathing stopped.

"Dan? Dan?"

There was no answer. Nelson looked at his friend in disbelief. Just a moment ago, they had been laughing and talking together, and now Dan was dead.

"Save me a place, Dan," Nelson said quietly.

Suddenly, there was a sound like an angry wasp, then a puff of dust, and the retreating whine of a spent bullet as one of the Spanish soldiers shot at him again. Nelson looked around and saw that the Spanish were running toward him again. This time, there were ten soldiers.

Nelson reached down, picked Dan up, and threw him belly down across the front of his saddle. He climbed on behind Dan's body, then slapped his legs against the horse's flanks. The animal responded immediately, and Nelson galloped away from the Spanish, whose shots were now so wild that he couldn't even hear the whine of their bullets.

NELSON's riderless horse had galloped into a camp a few moments earlier, and now a dozen or more people were gathered at the edge of camp, looking toward the distant hills. One of the people was Marty.

"It could mean anything, Miss McGuire," one old sergeant said. "Colonel Pickett might have gotten off to check somethin', the horse spooked, then run off. I've seen that happen lots of times."

"Sarge!" one of the men called. "This here horse warn't just spooked. Lookie here, they's a bullet lodged in his saddle. He's been shot at."

"Oh!" Marty gasped.

"That still don't prove nothin'," the sergeant said with an angry glance toward the soldier for upsetting Miss McGuire.

A couple of the men had field glasses, and one of them spotted a rider coming in their direction from a couple of miles away.

"Here comes a rider, but there's only one."

"Who is it?"

"I can't tell," the man said. He paused for a moment, then added. "No, they's two people on that horse. One of 'em ridin' 'n the other belly down across the saddle."

"Dead?" another asked.

"It sure looks like it."

"Who is it, man? Who's ridin' 'n who's belly down?"

"Ain't no question to that, is there, Sarge? You seen whose horse come back, didn't you?"

The sergeant looked toward Marty, who bit her lower lip and fought hard to keep from crying out. She clenched her fists so tightly that the fingernails dug into her palms.

Please, dear God, she prayed silently. *Please let it not be Nelson*. Even as she prayed, she knew that if the man draped across the saddle wasn't Nelson, it would have to be Dan. She didn't want it to be Dan either, but pray God for forgiveness, if it had to be one of them, she would rather it be Dan than Nelson.

"The colonel's been killed," one of the soldiers said.

Marty felt her knees grow weak, then her head began to spin. Suddenly everything went black.

"ARE YOU ALL RIGHT?" he asked quietly, his voice softer than usual.

Marty's eyes fluttered open, and the sight of him brought immediate relief. "Nelson? You're alive! You're all right!" She tried to sit up, but the world spun around her, and she had to lie back down, her heart still racing.

"Take it easy," Nelson said, his hand steady on her shoulder. "You fainted."

Marty nodded, letting out a shaky breath. "I thought…I thought you were…what happened? Your horse came back without you, and then we saw…" She stopped, her hand flying to her mouth. The truth hit her like a stone. "Oh, Nelson, it's Dan, isn't it? Dan's been killed?"

Nelson's expression darkened. He gave a slow, somber nod. "Yes."

Marty blinked hard, but she couldn't stop the tears from sliding down her cheeks. "What happened?" she asked in a small, broken voice.

"We were ambushed by the Spanish," Nelson said, his voice tight, as though each word took effort. "We didn't see them coming."

Marty's eyes welled up even more. "Oh, poor Molly," she whispered, her voice trembling.

Nelson's gaze shifted, and a pained look crossed his face. "Yes," he said quietly. "Poor Molly."

Marty sat up again, this time more steadily. "Where is he?" she asked softly. "Where's Dan?"

"He's back there," Nelson said, his voice distant, his eyes staring into the horizon. "They're…they're putting him in a canvas sack. We'll bury him in a few minutes."

"So…so soon?" Marty gasped, the speed of it all taking her by surprise.

Nelson's face hardened. "It's better this way. It's not good for morale to leave the dead lying around for long."

"But…can't you send him back to New York? To Molly? She deserves to bury her husband," Marty pleaded, her voice breaking.

Nelson's expression grew even more closed off. His voice, when it came, was rough, colder than she'd ever heard it. "This is war, Marty. You evacuate your wounded and you bury your dead. That's how it's done. Molly knew that when she married him. She knew he might end up dead and buried on some distant battlefield. Anyone foolish enough to marry a soldier knows that risk."

He turned and walked away before Marty could respond, his words left hanging in the air. His tone frightened her, and the way he had said *anyone foolish enough to marry a soldier* made her heart tighten. Did that mean her? Marty caught her breath, a lump forming in her throat. She wanted to run after him, to demand an answer to the questions swirling in her mind, but she stopped herself. Now wasn't the time. Nelson had just lost his best friend. He was hurting, and this was a pain she couldn't soothe, no matter how much she wanted to.

IT WAS LESS than an hour later when word passed through the camp that Major Daniel J. Calhoun of the Lightning Cavalry was about to be buried. Slowly, soldiers drifted toward the makeshift grave, a hole dug hastily in the dry earth. The body, wrapped in a canvas sack, lay on the ground, nothing more than a lump of fabric and blood-soaked dirt. It looked so small, so utterly lifeless, that it was hard to believe this was Dan—a man so full of life, now reduced to an inert figure sewn into rough canvas.

General Wheeler stepped forward, standing beside the grave with a grim but steady expression. His voice broke through the thick silence.

"I knew Major Calhoun—he was married to my niece," Wheeler said, his voice roughened by years of battle but clear. "He was a brave soldier, a loyal officer, and a good man. Some of you here may not know about Fiddler's Green, but let me tell you, it's where Dan is right now. It's a cool spot, under the shade of trees, near a stream where the air is always clean and crisp. That's where every soldier who's ever heard *Boots 'n Saddles* blown from a bugle goes when they pass on."

He paused, looking at the men gathered around. "Dan's there now, likely having a drink with the men who went before him. I expect Captain Baker's there too, and the soldiers who fell on Las Guardia Hill. And who's to say General Custer isn't there, with his men from the Little Big Horn?" His voice softened. "I've got good friends of my own there, waitin' for me—men who wore both blue and gray, and they'll be ready when my time comes."

Wheeler's gaze grew distant, as though he could

see the fabled place himself. "Now, I know some of you may be thinkin' this doesn't quite square with what you learned about heaven. But if you stop and think for a moment, it's not all that different. Heaven is where we all want to go, isn't it? And Fiddler's Green...well, that's a place where soldiers go to meet their old friends again, to rest and wait for us to join them."

The men stood in silent reverence as four soldiers lowered Dan's body into the ground. The canvas sack, so impersonal, disappeared into the earth, taking with it the man they had all known.

The bugler stepped forward, raising the instrument to his lips. The sound of *Taps* cut through the still air, the mournful notes drifting out over the camp, echoing against the distant bluffs. Each soldier stood frozen, listening to the somber melody, the final farewell to a fallen comrade.

"Day is done,
Gone the sun,
From the lake,
From the hill,
From the sky.
Rest in peace,
Soldier brave,
God is nigh."

As the last note faded, mingling with the echo that seemed to hang in the air, the soldiers who had come to the impromptu funeral began to turn away, their faces solemn, their hearts heavy. Those who had known Dan fought against the tightness in their throats, their eyes stinging with unshed tears. Even those who had only come out of respect or curiosity felt the weight of what they had witnessed.

Each man there knew it could easily have been them lying in that canvas bag. And each one, though they didn't say it aloud, wondered if General Wheeler was right. Was there really a Fiddler's Green? Was there really a place where they could be reunited with their comrades when their time came?

As the crowd dispersed, Marty stood rooted to the spot, her chest tight, the air around her suddenly too thin. She felt the weight of Dan's death pressing on her, but also the sting of Nelson's earlier words, still fresh in her mind. She glanced toward him, standing apart from the others, his face a mask of control. He hadn't cried, hadn't let himself show the emotion she knew was inside him.

But she could feel it. She could see it in the way his shoulders sagged ever so slightly, in the way his hands clenched into fists at his sides. Nelson was hurting, and despite everything, Marty longed to reach out to him.

But she didn't. She had nothing to say.

Later that day, as the sun began to set and the campfires were rekindled, Marty tried to find Nelson. She wanted to comfort him over the loss of his friend, and, in truth, she wanted his comfort as well, because Dan was also her friend. She remembered that Dan had been her ally in the early days of her campaign to get Nelson to accept her. Now, that smiling, friendly ally was gone, and she was going to miss him terribly.

When she saw the sergeant major, she asked, her

voice almost hesitant, "Sergeant Major, have you seen Nel—Colonel Pickett?"

The sergeant major, his expression unreadable in the fading light, nodded. "I believe he had some business back in Siboney, ma'am. Won't be back till tomorrow."

"Siboney?" Marty repeated, surprised. "He went all the way back to Siboney?"

"Yes, ma'am," he confirmed.

"Thank you," she murmured, though the words felt hollow.

Marty returned to her tent and sank down in front of it, her eyes watching the sun disappear in the western sky. She stayed there, motionless, as dusk fell on the distant hills, then crept toward the trees until, finally, the whole valley was swallowed in darkness, except for the scattered campfires flickering in the night. The warmth of their glow did nothing to touch the cold ache that had settled in her chest.

As the soldiers' songs drifted through the camp once again, they sounded different to Marty tonight. The melodies, which so often had been lively and filled with camaraderie, now felt laden with sorrow. It was as if the camp itself mourned Dan. Of course, that wasn't true. There were thousands of men out there, and only a handful even knew his name. It was her grief, her loss, that cast a pall over the melancholy music.

Marty watched as the stars popped out, one by one. She looked up at them and saw that they were no different tonight than they were the night before. And yet, last night, Dan had been on earth to enjoy them. Tonight, he was gone, and the stars felt colder, more distant.

Her thoughts drifted to Molly, so far away in New York. As far as Molly knew, Dan was still alive. She was probably going to bed this very night, whispering a prayer for his safety, for God to keep her husband from harm's way. Marty's throat tightened at the thought. How cruel was fate, to let Molly pray with hope in her heart when, in truth, Dan was already gone—buried beneath foreign soil in a canvas sack.

Marty imagined the long days ahead, the two weeks or more it would take for the news to reach Molly. For those days, Molly would carry on, believing Dan was alive, thinking of him with love, and waiting for him to come home. But Dan would never come home. He was gone, and the weight of that knowledge pressed down on Marty, making the air feel thick, as though she could hardly breathe.

She stayed there sitting in the dark, watching the stars multiply. The world kept spinning, the war kept raging, and the stars kept shining—but for Marty, everything had changed. The loss of Dan was a wound that would take a long time to heal, and as she sat alone in the quiet of the camp, she wondered if it ever truly would.

Nelson stood on the beach at Siboney, staring out over the moonlit water. The fleet's ships were anchored offshore, their silhouettes dark against the sea. The quiet lapping of the waves contrasted sharply with the turmoil in his mind. He had come to Siboney to request General Shafter's permission for a reconnaissance. If there were that many Spanish so far from Santiago, Nelson was convinced there had to be more hidden in those hills. Shafter's artillery would be slaughtered if they didn't clear the heights first.

He could have waited, could have made the request when the general returned to camp the next day. But he couldn't face Marty tonight. Not now. He knew she would want to talk, would ask him about Dan, would need answers. And he didn't want to give them. He didn't want to tell her that Dan had been killed because they were laughing, joking, talking about her, about life, about love. How could he tell her that Dan was dead because he, Nelson, had let down his guard?

Nelson clenched his fists, the cool night air doing nothing to ease the guilt that gnawed at him. He should have been alert. He should have seen the ambush. If he had been doing his job as a commander —no, as a soldier—Dan would still be alive. Dan, his best friend and his sister's husband, was gone because he had failed him.

And it wasn't just the failure in that moment—it was everything. Dan had been thinking about Molly as he lay dying, his final words full of regret for leaving her behind. But Nelson knew the truth—Dan shouldn't have been thinking about Molly at all. He shouldn't have been married. A soldier has no right to be distracted by love, by the pull of family, by the fragile hope of a life beyond the battlefield. And yet, Dan had given in to that hope. He had married Molly, and now she was a widow, left alone, because Dan had made the mistake of believing he could have both—a wife and a soldier's life.

Nelson's jaw clenched tighter, the muscles in his face twitching as the wind whipped against his skin. He couldn't allow himself to make the same mistake. He wouldn't. Tomorrow, when he returned to camp, he would tell Marty what he should have told her long ago: there was no place for her in his life, not while the war raged, not while he was still a soldier. He had to let her go before it was too late, before he hurt her the way Dan had hurt Molly.

He rubbed the scar on his cheek, a habit when his thoughts turned dark. She wouldn't understand. She would cry, and it would tear him apart to see it. But it had to be done. He wouldn't let her suffer like Molly—left with nothing but memories and grief. Marty deserved more than what he could give, and he would have to find the strength to push her away, even though that was the last thing he wanted to do.

Nelson turned and began walking down the beach, the line between the wet and dry sand shifting beneath his boots. The wet sand shimmered like silver in the moonlight, an eerie, haunting beauty that somehow reminded him of Marty.

"No," he muttered, trying to shove the thought of her from his mind.

"Sir, did you say something?" a nearby soldier called to him, his voice breaking the stillness of the night.

Nelson didn't turn, barely aware of the man's presence. "Just clearing my throat," he said.

He picked up his pace, pushing further down the beach, away from the sounds of the camp. He hadn't realized he had spoken out loud, but it didn't matter. He had to put a stop to this.

———

AFTER FINISHING HER MORNING ROUTINE, Marty spotted Nelson riding back into camp. She smiled, waving at him, but he didn't acknowledge her. He didn't stop by her tent, didn't even come to see her once he'd handled the military business.

By noon, Marty couldn't take it anymore. She'd been watching Nelson's tent all morning, seeing officers come and go, but Nelson stayed out of sight. Her patience finally gave way. Taking a deep breath, she stood up, squared her shoulders, and marched toward his tent.

The guards stiffened as she passed, but she ignored them, stepping through the tent flap into the dim, shaded space. Nelson was seated behind a makeshift desk, shuffling through papers. He looked up, his expression unreadable.

"Yes, Miss McGuire? What can I do for you?" His voice was cold, distant. The sudden chill in his tone made her stomach knot.

"Nelson, I need to talk to you," she said, her voice quieter than she intended.

"I'm sorry, but if you're looking for something for the press, I've got nothing new to share."

Marty blinked, confusion creeping in. "What?" she asked, her voice tight. This wasn't the conversation she expected.

Nelson's eyes met hers, but they held none of their usual warmth. "You want a story, don't you? About the Lightning Cavalry?"

"What's going on?" she whispered, glancing at the sergeant major standing nearby.

The sergeant major, sensing the tension, cleared his throat. "Colonel, I've got a meeting with the first sergeants. I should see to it."

Nelson glanced at him, then back at Marty. "That meeting isn't until two."

"Yes, sir. Just want to make sure everyone's on time," the sergeant major said, tipping his hat to Marty before slipping out.

The moment he left, Marty stepped closer to Nelson. "What's this all about?" she asked, trying to hold steady, though her voice wavered. "You didn't say anything when you left last night. You didn't come to see me this morning. I don't understand."

Nelson leaned back, his jaw clenched. "I didn't realize I had to report my every move."

The coldness in his voice hit her like a slap. Marty's throat tightened. "Nelson, what's wrong? What did I do?"

Nelson's hand went to the scar on his cheek, rubbing it absently. He sighed, the hard edge in his demeanor softening but not disappearing. "You didn't do anything," he said, though the words offered no comfort.

"Then what is it?" Marty asked.

Nelson's eyes darkened, and suddenly, he slammed his fist on the table, his voice rising. "I got Dan killed!"

Marty flinched, shocked by the outburst. "What? Nelson, you were scouting. The sergeant major explained. Things happen on scout missions, you know that."

"Do they?" Nelson said bitterly. "Did the sergeant major tell you how two seasoned officers could be riding on a scout with as much vigilance about them as if they were riding through Central Park? No, he didn't. We were talking about you, Marty. I let my guard down. I let *you* into my head, and because of that, I wasn't paying attention. I got Dan killed because I was thinking about you instead of the mission."

Marty felt her heart sink. "Nelson, I'm so sorry," she whispered, the weight of his words pressing down on her.

Nelson rubbed a hand through his hair, his anger fading into something more resigned. "It proves what I've always known," he muttered. "A career officer has no business being in a serious relationship. Especially not in war."

Marty bit her lip, struggling to hold back tears, but they came anyway, silently slipping down her cheeks. "I see," she managed, her voice steady despite how she felt. "I think I'll speak with General Shafter about reassignment."

Nelson nodded, his face hard. "That's probably for the best. I'll have the sergeant major arrange for someone to help with your things."

"That won't be necessary," Marty said, her voice cool. "I can take care of myself." She turned and strode out of the tent without a second glance, her head held high though her heart felt heavy.

She didn't see the tears in Nelson's eyes as he watched her go.

Sixteen

General Shafter had granted Marty the same freedom he'd given all reporters—to move through the American Expeditionary Force as they wished, covering whatever part of the war caught their attention. It wasn't a special favor for her, and most of the other correspondents had taken full advantage, drifting between units. But Marty had stayed with the Lightning Cavalry, even when the others roamed. She owed those men something, after all. They'd trusted her, shared their stories, and let her be their voice to the loved ones back home. The letters they sent her made that clear enough—wives, sweethearts, and mothers wrote back, thanking her for her articles.

But Nelson had changed everything. Whatever was left of their relationship made staying with the Lightning Cavalry unbearable. Seeing him every day, knowing things were strained—that wasn't an option. The only way forward was to detach herself from the unit and join the pool of other reporters, covering the war wherever it led.

The hills surrounding Santiago were no longer quiet. Dan's death on a scouting mission proved as much. And yet, despite this obvious evidence, General Shafter still seemed ready to ignore it, and he kept his army in position totally inactive, for several days.

Richard Harding Davis, the most experienced of the correspondents, made no secret of his feelings about the general's strategy. He expressed his feelings one night around a campfire shared by all the reporters in the field.

"This is criminal," Davis said, his voice hard. "I've been forward enough to see the Spanish in the hills. They're just strolling leisurely around through their rifle pits like they're on a damn picnic, as if they had all the time in the world. And why shouldn't they think that? We are certainly giving them time enough to prepare for us. Every day we sit here, they dig in deeper, the network of pits grows longer and more complex. Soon, they'll have the positions so well fortified that we won't be able to drive them out of there with ten times the artillery we have now."

A few of the other reporters murmured in agreement, though not as openly. One of them finally spoke up, "Surely, Richard, General Shafter knows what he's doing."

Davis snorted. "Does he? They're parading through El Caney every day, waving their flags like they've already won. Hell, I'm starting to think they've made Shafter an honorary general."

The others laughed, though it was the kind of nervous laugh that came when no one wanted to be the first to agree. Davis had earned his immunity—he wasn't worried about upsetting the wrong people. His reputation was too strong. If Shafter tried to send him away, Davis had enough clout to get back in with a phone call to Washington. The rest of them weren't so lucky. A wrong word could mean getting sent home on the next ship.

Marty kept her thoughts to herself. Criticizing Shafter felt wrong, not because of loyalty to the general, but because it felt like a betrayal of the army Nelson served. She should have been bitter. The army had, in a way, become the *other woman* in Nelson's life. But her feelings didn't work that way. Even now, she couldn't bring herself to be anything less than protective of the men out there, fighting for what they believed in.

Davis wasn't done. "You know who's actually doing something? Colonel Juan Alvarez. If I spoke Spanish, I'd be with him right now. That's where the real news is."

The conversation drifted after that, but Marty's mind stayed on Davis's last words. She *could* speak Spanish. And if Nelson had shut her out, there was no reason to hold back in her work. She was here as a journalist, and she wasn't about to waste time wallowing in personal problems.

BY THE END of the night, Marty had casually gathered the information she needed—where Colonel Alvarez's headquarters were located. Tomorrow, she'd be there, following the story, doing her job.

At dawn, Marty set out for Colonel Alvarez's headquarters, five miles away. The route wasn't dangerous, as it didn't lead toward the Spanish-occupied hills. She felt confident traveling alone, knowing she could pass as a Cuban woman if necessary.

Marty's previous meeting with Alvarez had been brief, but it left an impression. Alvarez was a man who spoke with the authority of years spent in battle, someone who didn't shy away from speaking his mind. Marty admired his passion, even if his views on the Americans had struck her as a little blunt. This morning, as she approached his camp, she anticipated a deeper conversation—one that might offer her more insight into both the man and the conflict.

As she neared the camp, she saw Alvarez waiting, leaning casually against a post, watching her approach. His eyes, dark and piercing, held the same intensity as before.

"*Señorita* McGuire," he greeted her with a slight nod

"Good morning, Colonel," Marty replied, adjusting the strap of her bag on her shoulder. "I came for the story you promised."

Alvarez straightened, pushing off the post with an easy grace. "Ah, the story. Yes. Come, walk with me."

They walked together toward the camp, his horse trailing lazily behind them. The Cuban camp came into view, and Marty noted the stark contrast to the American camp. Tents were scattered randomly, guitars and drums filled the air with lively music, and women danced around fires while children played in the dirt. It was far from the orderly, regimented atmosphere of the American forces.

Marty couldn't hold back her curiosity. "Is this really a war camp, Colonel?" she asked, her tone betraying a mix of confusion and disbelief.

Alvarez chuckled, glancing sideways at her. "It's

exactly what it looks like, *señorita*. A camp of soldiers, their families, and life in between battles."

"But it's nothing like the American camps. There's no order here, no drills," Marty said. "It almost feels like…a celebration."

Alvarez's expression hardened slightly. "Ah, but that is the difference, isn't it? The Americans come here to wage their war, to fight the Spanish and return to their homes. For them, this is but a campaign—something to win and be done with. But for us, this war is not new. It is not a campaign. It is life."

He paused, his voice sharpening. "I've fought the Spanish since I was a boy. At fifteen, I was already on the battlefield. Now, I am thirty, and still, I fight. For us, the war does not end. So yes, we sing, we dance, we laugh, because that is how we survive."

Marty listened quietly, absorbing his words, but when he continued, his tone became pointed. "Look closely, *señorita*. The Spanish will fall, but if your Americans linger too long, we will fight them as well."

Marty stopped in her tracks, turning to face him. "How can you say that? The Americans have come to help you—people are dying to end this fight."

Alvarez met her gaze without flinching. "Yes, they are dying. But that is what they signed up for, is it not? They came to play the role of savior, to write their stories of valor and sacrifice. But this is not their land. This is Cuba."

The tension hung between them for a moment. "Tell me, why are you really here, Marty?"

She hesitated, taken aback by the shift in his tone. "I came for a story. The truth."

"And what do you see here?" he asked, gesturing to

the camp. "A party? A gathering of people with no care in the world?"

Marty frowned, looking around at the women, the children, the music. "Honestly…yes. That's exactly what it looks like."

Alvarez smiled grimly. "Then you are not seeing clearly yet. But you will." He paused, watching her carefully. "You can ride, can you not?"

Marty blinked, caught off guard by the question. "Of course."

"Good," he said, his voice dropping slightly. "You wanted a story, and tonight, you will have one. We are going on a raid."

"A raid?" Marty's pulse quickened. "You're willing to let me come with you?"

Alvarez gave a small nod. "You came here for the truth. The truth is not found in the safety of camps or in idle conversation. Tonight, you will see what we do in this war. But you will need to blend in."

Marty's heart pounded, a mixture of fear and excitement rising in her chest. "I can do that."

Alvarez looked her over, nodding in approval. "Go to my tent. I will have someone bring you clothes—pants and a shirt. You'll stand out less in those."

"Are you sure?" she asked, her voice steadying as she fought back her nerves.

Alvarez smiled faintly. "If you wish to live longer in this war, you do not want to stand out. Trust me."

Marty took a deep breath, nodded, and headed toward his tent. Whatever happened next, she knew this story would be unlike anything she had ever written.

HALF AN HOUR LATER, Marty had removed her *faire le bicyclette* and replaced it with a man's trousers and a shirt. Her hair, now bundled under a wide-brimmed hat, gave her the look of a young boy from a distance.

Juan introduced her to a young Cuban woman named Carlotta Fernandez, her sharp features softened by the flickering campfire. "This is Marty," Juan said in Spanish, "an American reporter."

The woman raised an eyebrow, her English strained but clear. "Women work on newspapers in America?"

"Not many, I'm afraid," Marty replied, her Spanish smooth and flawless. The woman's eyes lit up at hearing her own language spoken so well.

"You speak like one of us," the woman said, smiling.

"My mother taught me," Marty explained. Her Spanish roots, a legacy from her mother, seemed to break any barrier, and soon, the woman, Carlotta, invited her to share a meal that night.

Over the firelight, the two women sat, exchanging stories. "Are you Colonel Alvarez's wife?" Marty asked.

Carlotta laughed, a short burst of genuine amusement. "No. Colonel Alvarez has no wife, though he could have any woman he wanted. I am with Lieutenant Carillo. One day, when this war is over, we will find a priest, and then I will be his wife."

Marty paused, choosing her next words carefully. "Does it bother you, living like this?"

Carlotta's expression hardened. "Living like what?"

"Here, in the field, alongside the soldiers. I meant no offense, just that it must be difficult."

Carlotta's gaze softened, and she shrugged. "Difficult? Maybe for someone who doesn't know war. But I am with my man, and that is enough."

Marty let the simplicity of Carlotta's words sink in. There was no room for sentiment here, no room for questioning the realities of life. The Cubans had learned to live with war. It was their way now, just as it was for the men who fought. There was no separation of roles, no questioning of why a woman like Carlotta would be here. War was everything. Marty wondered if she could have done the same for Nelson, if only he had let her.

As the night went on, Carlotta shared stories that would never grace the pages of Marty's newspaper. Stories of blood, sacrifice, and survival. It was a glimpse into a world that the outside world would never understand. Marty noticed how, even in this conversation, there was a tension underlining every word that Carlotta openly shared.

The music, the laughter, the clatter of plates—everything seemed normal, but there was something just below the surface. Marty knew the raid against the Spanish was coming. Her heart was pounding, but the camp showed no such anxiety.

It wasn't until well after it got dark, when the camp's activity had died down, that Juan reappeared from the shadows. The firelight reflected his eyes to be a mixture of excitement and calm.

"Are you ready?" he asked.

"For the raid?" Marty was still uncertain, expecting more warning or preparation. "You're still going through with it?"

Juan's grin was faint, almost patronizing. "Why wouldn't we? The night is still young."

"I thought it was too late," Marty said.

Juan chuckled, a low, dangerous sound. "Raids are best when the enemy is asleep in their beds. Come."

Marty followed him into an area illuminated by small, low-burning fires. A group of men was gathered there, tending to their horses in silence. These were the same men who had been singing and playing guitars earlier, the same ones who had joked with the children and flirted with the women. Now, their expressions were stoic.

"Here," one of the men said, offering Marty half a coconut shell filled with powdered charcoal. "Use this."

"What for?" she asked.

"To darken your face," Juan explained. "The moon's out. You don't want to give yourself away." He smeared some of the charcoal across her face before she could protest, his movements quick and practiced. Marty winced but said nothing, realizing how necessary this small detail was. Around her, the other men were already rubbing the charcoal on their faces.

Every move the men made was for a specific purpose. Their loose clothing was tied down, while their boots were wrapped in strips of cloth to silence any sound. They emptied their pockets, tied straps on their saddles, and prepared for the raid with a cold professionalism.

"These are guerrillas now," Juan said quietly, almost proudly. "The Spanish call us that—irregulars. We take pride in it."

Marty couldn't help but admire the transformation. These men had been farmers, craftsmen, and laborers once, but war had changed them. Now, they were soldiers of a different breed—silent, swift, and deadly.

She wiped more of the charcoal across her face, accepting the darkness.

The guerrilla fighters moved silently, disappearing into the thick shadows that clung to the terrain. Marty rode among them, her heart pounding in her chest. The fear was there, but she masked it with the excitement that she felt. She was here, in the middle of something no other reporter would dare—a guerrilla raid deep in the heart of enemy territory.

The group avoided the main roads, instead weaving through the treacherous Cuban landscape with a familiarity born from years of fighting in these hills. The terrain was made up of steep ridges, deep gullies, and rocky outcroppings that could break a horse's leg if one wasn't careful. But these men knew every inch of it. They used the dry riverbeds and hidden ravines like secret pathways, moving with the confidence of those who had made this war-torn wilderness their home.

After about an hour of steady riding, Juan raised his hand, signaling to stop. They had reached a small rise overlooking Santiago. Marty could make out the city below, though only barely—the buildings were ghostly shapes in the moonlight. It was well past midnight, and most of the city slept, unaware of what was about to hit them.

A dog barked somewhere in the distance, and the sound of distant laughter floated up on the warm night air. Marty caught a glimpse of a door slamming shut, a brief moment that seemed so normal.

"Cervera," Juan hissed, his voice barely a whisper. "Take three men. Create a diversion on the south side. Once they respond, we will strike from the north. No unnecessary deaths—remember, we fight to free our people, not to kill civilians."

Cervera nodded, selecting his men before they disappeared into the night, heading toward the southern edge of the city. Marty, Juan, and the others waited, their breaths shallow as they watched the dark shapes move below. One of the horses shifted uneasily, sensing the tension in the air.

"These raids may seem like mere nuisances," Juan murmured, "but they keep the Spanish on edge. When the Americans strike Santiago, the defenders will be sleep-deprived and jumpy. That's when we'll have the advantage."

Marty nodded, her mind racing with questions. "Are they worth the risk, though? So many lives at stake…"

Juan stared at her, his face serious. "In war, everything is a risk, *Senorita* McGuire. We do what we must."

Suddenly, gunfire erupted from the southern side of the city. The raiders had made their move. A hammer rang out, pounding against metal—a makeshift alarm. Dogs barked frantically as shouts of panic spread through the streets. Spanish soldiers were waking up, scrambling to respond. The gunfire intensified, flashing brightly in the night.

"They think the Americans have slipped around them!" Juan laughed softly. "Listen to them, running to defend the wrong side!"

Marty watched the muzzle flashes in the distance, marveling at how surreal it all looked, but each flash carried a potential death with it, and she could never quite forget that.

Juan stood in his stirrups, his men now in a tight formation. He glanced at Marty. "Are you ready?"

Marty swallowed her fear. "Yes," she said quietly, her voice steady despite how she felt.

"Stay close to me," Juan said. "If I fall, find someone else. Keep low on your horse. You'll be harder to hit."

Marty nodded, lowering herself as close to the horse's neck as she could, feeling the animal's muscles bunch beneath her. The horse was tense, ready to run. Juan's hand hovered in the air, then sliced down sharply.

The raiders charged.

They swept into Santiago hitting from the north as the Spanish defenders scrambled to cover the wrong side of the city. Marty's heart raced as she kept pace with Juan, their horses pounding down the narrow streets. The defenders, confused and disoriented, fired blindly. Juan and his men whooped and yelled, adding to the chaos as they rode straight into the heart of the city.

Juan aimed for a barricade manned by a few Spanish soldiers, their rifles clutched tightly in their hands. Marty realized too late what Juan intended to do—he was going to leap the barricade. Panic flared in her chest, but she urged her horse forward, preparing for the jump. She had done this before, back in New York, but that had been in daylight, and the stakes had been nothing like this.

Her horse gathered itself and sprang over the barricade with ease, and Marty felt a rush of exhilaration that cut through her fear. For a brief moment, she understood what drove these men to fight.

"This way!" Juan shouted, veering toward a trench line where Spanish forces had hastily dug in. Marty followed, the sound of explosions and gunfire roaring in her ears. The other raiders were throwing makeshift bombs into the trenches, the blasts tearing cannons from their mounts and scattering soldiers like ragdolls.

The acrid smell of gunpowder filled the air. Marty could hear the buzz of bullets zipping past her head, and instinctively, she crouched lower, pressing herself against the horse's neck. She felt the powerful muscles beneath her straining, the animal surging forward as they raced toward the edge of the city.

With a sudden turn, Juan led them out, away from the burning barricades and crumbling buildings. Marty glanced back, seeing the raiders moving swiftly behind them, their whoops and hollers echoing through the streets. They were making their escape, and it was only then that Marty realized what they had done—they had hit the Spanish hard and were now riding free.

As the last of the city's buildings faded behind them, one of the riders let out a piercing war cry. The others followed, their voices rising in a spontaneous shout. Marty found herself joining in, surprising even herself. She finally understood what drove these men to fight—not just survival or pride, but the sheer, unbridled joy of being alive after facing death.

The mountains stood in front of them, the rocky slopes offering shelter, and the thick vegetation of the Cuban jungle swallowed them once again. Behind them, Santiago was a city in chaos, but for now, the raiders were riding free.

SEVENTEEN

THE CAMP ERUPTED IN SHOUTS AND LAUGHTER AS THE raiders returned, greeted by those who had stayed behind. There was good-natured bantering, with Marty caught in the celebration of the raid's success. She had been unarmed, of course. She had gone along as an observer only, and yet she felt the same sense of excitement as the men. Never had she been more alive than at this moment! What a thrill it was to ride into the very teeth of the enemy, then ride out again. Her skin was flushed and tingling from her adventure.

"Double the guard!" Juan Alvarez called as they dismounted amid the congratulations. "The Spanish may return the favor soon."

"The Spanish are nothing but frightened old women!" someone joked, and the camp roared in agreement.

"Colonel Diaz is no frightened old woman," Juan warned, his tone darkening. "Be on your guard."

One of the men took Marty's horse as she headed

toward her tent, wiping sweat and dust from her face. A young woman approached with a basin of water.

"I thought you might want to wash before Colonel Alvarez visits," she said with a hesitant smile.

Marty frowned. "Visits?"

"Sí, *senorita*. After every raid, he honors a woman with his company." The girl seemed earnest, unaware of Marty's surprise.

Marty shook her head, taking the basin. "That won't be necessary. Thank you."

The girl looked perplexed. "But, *senorita*, no one refuses *El Commandante*."

"This is one person who can, and will," Marty said as she disappeared into her tent.

Inside, Marty lit a small candle and began washing away the dust and grime. She peeled off the shirt she had worn during the raid, grateful for the moment of peace. The cool water on her skin was a relief after the tension of the night.

Without warning, the tent flap moved. Marty spun around to see Juan Alvarez standing there, his dark eyes shining, a smile curling at the edges of his lips.

"What…?" she said, instinctively folding her arms across her chest. "What are you doing here?"

"The candle," he said, gesturing toward the faint light.

"The candle?"

"It casts a shadow of you on the walls," he explained, stepping closer. "I watched you."

Marty's heartbeat quickened, not from attraction, but from the realization of the power he held here. "I appreciate your concern for my safety, Colonel, but I assure you, I'm fine on my own."

Juan's smile faltered. "Do you not find excitement

in battle? I saw it in your eyes during the raid. You thrived on it."

"I came for the story," Marty replied, stepping back.

Juan's expression darkened. "A story? Is that what you tell yourself?"

His hand reached toward her, but she stopped him, her voice firm. "Colonel, I trusted you to keep me safe on the raid. Don't make me regret it."

For a moment, their eyes locked, tension crackling between them—not the tension of unspoken desire, but of a conflict of wills. Juan stepped back, his gaze hardening.

"Very well, if that is how you wish it. There are many women who would be glad for my company." He tossed the shirt aside, backing out of the tent. "But if you change your mind, I'll be waiting."

Marty's muscles relaxed only when he was gone, though the camp's noise made her jump. Gunfire erupted outside—sharp, angry bursts of sound.

"It's Diaz!" someone shouted.

The tent flap swung open again, and Juan stumbled inside, clutching his chest. His face was pale, his voice weak. "You should have let me stay," he said, his voice a ragged whisper. "Now…it's too late."

Marty rushed forward as Juan collapsed. Blood oozed through his fingers, staining his shirt. "Juan!"

But he was already gone.

Before she could fully process his death, the tent flap opened once more. She looked toward the entrance and saw the man whose picture Eddie had drawn.

"Colonel Diaz!" she said.

Diaz was puzzled by her recognition.

"Do I know you, senorita?" he asked.

"No, I just recognized you, that's all."

Diaz smiled.

"You are a very beautiful woman, senorita, and while I am flattered to be identified by someone of your beauty, I fear recognition by a prostitute is bad for my reputation."

"A prostitute?" Marty gasped.

Colonel Diaz laughed. "Surely you aren't going to tell me you were Colonel Alvarez's wife?"

"No, I…" Marty said. She stood up. Perhaps for the time being, it would be safer for her if Diaz thought she really was a prostitute. "I'm not his wife," she finally said.

"I didn't think so," Diaz said. "Cover yourself—you're coming with me."

"Coming with you? Why?"

"Either you come with me…or you stay here and be shot."

"Shot?"

"Yes, shot."

"I don't understand. Why should I be killed?"

"There was a raid against Santiago tonight," Diaz said. "Six of my men were killed. In order to stop this sort of thing, I am going to kill twelve rebels. Seven were already killed in battle. That leaves five more to be executed."

"But, surely you wouldn't shoot a woman?

"Why not?" Diaz replied. "Three of the seven who have already been killed are women."

Marty heard a shot fired, and she jumped. Diaz chuckled at her.

"Make up your mind, senorita."

"All right," Marty said. "I'll go with you."

Diaz watched her carefully, then stepped back outside, allowing her a moment of privacy. Marty's hands shook as she dressed. Since coming to Cuba, she had seen enough death to harden her resolve. Whether she survived the night depended not on Diaz's mercy, but on her own wits.

Marty knelt down beside Juan. She put her hand on his neck, but the pulse of life had stilled. He was dead. She felt a sadness for him, but there were no tears. She had been shocked when Captain Baker was killed, then shocked and saddened by the death of Dan Calhoun. Now there was Juan Alvarez, and there would be more. Perhaps her own death was imminent. If so, it didn't matter. It just didn't matter. For several hours now, her own destiny had been out of her hands.

When Marty stepped outside, the sight before her was staggering. Lifeless bodies lay strewn across the camp. Among them, she recognized the young woman who had brought her the water basin earlier, her life snuffed out in what seemed like the blink of an eye.

Half an hour? Could all of this have happened in just half an hour?

"Can you ride?" Diaz's voice snapped her back to the present.

Marty nodded, her voice steady despite the chaos. "Yes."

"Bring the girl a horse," Diaz ordered.

A soldier handed her the reins, and with what little strength she had left, Marty climbed into the saddle. Her body ached, exhaustion gnawing at her from all sides—both physical fatigue and the emotional weight of everything she'd witnessed. Her mind, however, focused on one thing: staying upright in the saddle.

BY THE TIME they reached Santiago, the eastern sky was laced with red. As they neared the city, Marty noticed soldiers in their bright blue-and-scarlet uniforms, preparing for reveille. Many of the towns-people were out as well, and several of them stared at her in curiosity and suspicion as she rode by.

Diaz didn't break the gallop until they were in the center of the town square. He halted the group in front of a large church. He returned the salute of an officer who greeted him, then dismounted.

"Who is the girl?" a sergeant asked, his voice low.

Diaz's face darkened. "That is none of your concern," he snapped.

The sergeant paled. "Yes, Colonel. Forgive me."

Marty heard the conversation going on, and she knew that, somehow, it involved her, but she was so exhausted that, for the moment at least, it meant nothing to her.

"You," he barked. "Come with me."

She slid from the saddle, legs shaky beneath her. Diaz led her across the square and into the church. Inside, it was a strange and disorienting sight—the pews had been removed, replaced with soldiers' sleeping rolls and tables. Dozens of men moved about, their uniforms contrasting sharply with the sacred space.

"The church is our headquarters," Diaz said. "A brilliant choice, don't you think? The bell tower offers the best vantage point in the city. And I hear that your North American soldiers don't like to shoot at churches."

"Don't you think it's blasphemy to use a church in such a way?" Marty asked.

Diaz chuckled. "You, a whore, speak to me about blasphemy?"

They walked up to the apse, and though the altar had been stripped bare, Marty genuflected.

"Ha!" Diaz said. "A whore who has religion."

"Our Lord welcomes all in His church," someone said, and Marty looked over to see a priest standing nearby.

"Father," Marty said as she looked around the church. "You let them do this to a house of the Lord?"

The priest sighed. "I tried to stop them, my child, but there are some things I cannot control."

The weight of the past hours came crashing down on her. Marty's knees buckled, and she reached out, grasping the railing for support. The priest hurried to her side.

"Are you all right?" he asked, concern lacing his voice.

"I'm just…tired," she admitted, her voice trembling with the effort to stay composed.

"Tired?" The priest looked at Diaz, his expression hardening. "This woman is exhausted. What have you done to her?"

Diaz shrugged, his tone dismissive. "She was with the rebels. If she is tired, it is because of what went on in that rebel camp. She was the commander's woman, after all."

"No!" Marty protested, though her voice was weak. "I wasn't."

"Then what were you doing there?" Diaz challenged, stepping closer. "What were you to him?"

Her vision blurred, and her head drooped. "Please," she murmured. "I'm so tired."

The priest looked back at Diaz, his expression pleading. "Colonel, let her rest. It is inhumane to treat her like this."

Diaz stared at Marty for a moment, his eyes cold, before finally waving his hand dismissively. "Take her. Let her rest. I can wait."

"This way, my child," the priest said gently, leading her out of the church and into a nearby building.

Inside, the cool air and quiet soothed her frayed nerves. An elderly nun, Sister Theresa, met them at the door.

"Has she been hurt?" Sister Theresa asked, her voice soft with concern.

"Her spirit is wounded," the priest replied. "See that she gets some rest."

The nun nodded and guided Marty into a small room. There, a simple bed awaited her—the first real bed she had seen since arriving in Cuba. Sister Theresa led her to it, her touch gentle.

Marty didn't have the strength to respond. She lay down, and before she could even think about the events of the night, she was asleep.

"WE'VE STRUNG the telegraph wire all the way from here to the beach, Colonel," the sergeant major reported. "We're in contact with every major unit in the expeditionary force."

"And?" Nelson asked, the tension in his voice unmistakable.

"And they ain't none of 'em seen hide nor hair of 'er, sir. She's just…disappeared."

"Nonsense," Nelson snapped, slamming his fist into his hand. "She's a full-grown woman. A full-grown woman doesn't just vanish. She's out there, and I want her found!"

"Yes, sir," the sergeant major said. "We'll keep lookin'."

"What about the fleet?" one of the staff officers suggested. "Could she have returned to one of the ships? She was aboard the *Oregon* during the attack on the Spanish fleet."

Nelson shook his head. "It's unlikely…but I won't rule anything out. I'll try anything at this point."

"Yes, sir. We'll keep up the search," the officer promised, exchanging uneasy glances with the others.

Nelson's entire staff had noticed the change in him since Marty's disappearance. Where once he had commanded with calm authority, now he barked orders with impatience and barely concealed frustration.

There was another reason why everyone wanted to find Marty. She had become the good luck charm of the Lightning Cavalry. No one wanted to lose her.

"I'm heading back to the beach," Nelson said abruptly, grabbing his hat.

"Understood, sir."

Nelson mounted his horse and rode through the encampment, past soldiers idling in the sun. As he looked around, frustration continued to build. Through his field glasses, he had watched the Spanish preparing for the upcoming battle. They were working to strengthen their fortifications, and they were moving into positions in the hills so they could command the open-country approach to Santiago. The Americans were not engaged in similar preparations. They were not reconnoitering, and they weren't cutting new trails through the jungle. They weren't interfering with the Spanish in any way. Instead, the Americans spent their time foraging about for local varieties of food to spice up their rations, and they waited eagerly each day for the pack trains that brought mail from home. Many of the soldiers were busy bartering with the locals for tobacco. No one seemed concerned about the battle that would soon take place. It felt like a waste of precious time.

He rode through the narrow pass and descended toward the beach, where General Shafter had set up headquarters in a large house. Dismounting, Nelson handed the reins to a private and returned the salutes of the guards before heading inside.

"Colonel Pickett," General Shafter greeted him with a warm smile. "How are things at the front?"

"There's no front, General," Nelson replied curtly. "There's no fighting."

Shafter's smile faded. "Maybe not yet, but you're still in front of the lines. Don't tell me you're here to argue for an attack—I've already heard from Roosevelt on that front."

"No, sir," Nelson said. "I'm here for another reason."

Shafter raised an eyebrow. "That's a surprise. I thought you would have come to press the issue."

Nelson exhaled, his frustration showing. "We should be running patrols, at least. The Spanish are preparing, and we ought to know what they're doing."

"Odd you mention that," Shafter said, stroking his chin. "We had reports of shots fired in Santiago last night. None of your commanders are admitting responsibility, though. Any idea what that might've been?"

"No, sir," Nelson replied, shaking his head. "We've had no contact since Major Calhoun's death."

Shafter's expression darkened. "That was a tragic loss. Calhoun was a good man." He paused. "Are you sure you didn't send anyone into Santiago last night?"

"No, sir."

"Damned odd," Shafter muttered. "Damned odd."

Nelson hesitated, then asked, "General, have you seen Miss McGuire in the last couple of days?"

"No," General Shafter said. "Damn it, man, don't tell me she is missing! She was assigned to your jurisdiction. I'm holding you responsible for her safety."

"Yes, sir, but I'm afraid she is missing, General."

"Where is she?"

"I don't know, sir."

Shafter's fist came down hard on the desk. "Well, damn it, Colonel, you find her."

"I understand, sir," Nelson said. "We're searching for her now, but I need your permission to visit the *Oregon*. She did a story from there, and there's a chance she might have returned to the ship."

Shafter narrowed his eyes. "And if she's not there?"

"Then I'll have Admiral Sampson query the entire fleet. If she's aboard any vessel, we'll find her."

Shafter rubbed his chin, clearly irritated. "Colonel, the last thing I need is a congressional inquiry over Miss McGuire's disappearance. Get out there, find her, and make sure we don't have a political mess on our hands."

"I'll do everything I can, sir," Nelson promised.

Shafter glared at him, the weight of his words

heavy. "How the hell did you let her slip away in the first place?"

Nelson's voice was laced with frustration. "That, General, is a testament to my incompetence and ignorance," he said bitterly.

MARTY WASN'T on board the *Oregon*. Nelson hadn't really expected her to be, but he couldn't afford to leave any stone unturned. Every lead had to be followed, no matter how slim the chance.

Admiral Sampson met him on deck, his expression mirroring the same irritation Nelson had seen in General Shafter. He braced for another uphill battle, expecting to have to persuade Sampson to assist in the search. But to his surprise, it was the admiral who proposed making the inquiry. With a swift command, Sampson signaled the fleet under his own code, giving the search an immediate sense of urgency.

From atop the mast, flags were raised, the message rippling out ship-to-ship along the fleet that stretched twenty-eight miles down the Cuban coast. Nelson watched as the colors fluttered against the bright sky, each relay carrying the same hope—hope that was quickly dashed when the final response came back: *"Miss McGuire is not aboard and has not been seen."*

Nelson's chest tightened as he was told the result of the messages. He clenched his fists, the frustration growing. *Where could she be?* he thought.

"Thank you for the effort," he said.

"I wish you luck in finding her," Admiral Sampson replied. Then, almost as if to lighten the mood, he added, "It's nearly lunchtime. Won't you join us? I believe we have some fresh melon today."

Nelson paused, thinking of the cold beans and salt pork his men were choking down in the field. The contrast made his stomach turn. How could he sit here in comfort, eating fresh fruit, while his men went day after day on the same miserable rations?

"No, thank you, sir," Nelson said, shaking his head. "I need to get back to shore. My men are waiting."

The admiral studied him for a moment, then nodded. "Thinking of your men, eh?"

"Yes, sir," Nelson replied, though he knew his thoughts were split between his soldiers and Marty.

"Good man," the admiral said. "Good man."

Nelson didn't mention it, but he was also thinking of Marty. Where was she now? Was she in danger? What did she have to eat? He didn't want to think it, but was she even alive?

Eighteen

"*Señorita*? *Señorita*, wake up." Marty heard the soft voice cutting through the haze of sleep, pulling her back to consciousness. When she opened her eyes, a woman in a nun's habit was standing beside her.

"Are you awake now?" the woman asked.

Marty blinked, disoriented. "Where am I?"

"I'm Sister Theresa. Don't you remember? Father Damien brought you to me after you were captured."

Marty remembered. She had been captured by Spanish troops and brought to Santiago. She was in a small building behind the church, probably a cloister.

"Yes," Marty murmured. "I remember now."

"You've been asleep for twenty-four hours," Sister Theresa said. "I'm sorry to wake you, but you must take some nourishment."

Marty sat up, rubbing her eyes. "Twenty-four hours?" she repeated. "I slept that long?"

"Sí, *señorita*. You needed it. I've brought some rice. It's not much, but the soldiers have taken most of the food, and we are on strict rations."

"Thank you," Marty said, accepting the bowl. As she ate, the plain rice tasted surprisingly good.

"I think the Americans will come soon," Sister Theresa said, her voice low.

Marty looked up sharply. "Why do you say that? Has there been fighting?"

"No, but rumors are spreading. Some say there are a million Americans camped outside the city, waiting to attack."

Marty couldn't help but smile slightly. "There aren't a million," she said carefully.

"How do you know?" Sister Theresa asked, curious.

"Because I'm..." Marty stopped. The woman was in a nun's habit, and she had treated Marty kindly, but it was best to trust no one. Marty had nearly told her that she was an American. "I'm just sure, that's all," she concluded.

Sister Theresa sighed. "It's a shame. I was hoping there would be enough Americans to drive the Spanish out. The soldiers have brought nothing but suffering to our people."

"You're not loyal to Spain?" Marty asked, surprised.

The nun shook her head. "I have no fear in saying this to you, *Señorita*, but no, I am not. Spain is Catholic, yes, but their soldiers have defiled the church and our people. It breaks my heart."

"Neither am I," Marty said.

"But you are the woman of Colonel Diaz," Sister Theresa said.

"Why do you say that?"

"He came many times yesterday and last night to check on you."

"I'm his prisoner," Marty said.

"His prisoner?"

"I was with Colonel Alvarez when he was killed. Colonel Diaz took me prisoner."

"Colonel Alvarez is dead?"

"Yes," Marty said.

Sister Theresa crossed herself. "It is a pity," she said quietly. "Colonel Alvarez was a true patriot."

"Colonel Alvarez was a rebel who was lucky to be killed in battle," a stern voice said. "I wish I had been able to capture him so I could execute him in front of the good citizens of Santiago. Good morning, Sister Theresa. How is our guest this morning?"

"Good morning, Colonel Diaz," Sister Theresa answered. She excused herself and left the room.

Diaz laughed. "I don't think that one quite trusts me," he said.

"Can you blame her? You've made a mockery of all she believes in," Marty said.

"Oh, you mean the church? That monument to mankind's confession of servitude to the powers of superstition and ignorance? Yes, we have made a mockery of it. But the funny part is, we have done it all under the authority of His Catholic Majesty, King Alfonso the Thirteenth." Diaz laughed. "Don't you think that's funny?"

"I think it's disgusting."

"Oh, yes, I forgot," Diaz said. "You are the whore with religion. How I would like to be with you, but alas, I've no time for such diversions now. I must inspect the final defensive positions. Tonight, my pretty one. I will make you forget all about your Colonel Alvarez. I will show you what it is like to make love to a man who has no fear of God."

Marty thought of what he had just said about inspecting the defensive positions, and it suddenly dawned on her that if she could escape, this would be good information to have.

"Colonel Diaz?" she called, trying to make her voice sound as if she was really interested in him. "May I go with you?"

Diaz looked at her with surprise. "You want to go with me to inspect the defenses? Why?"

Marty had to be careful with this. She smiled coyly at him.

"Oh, I don't care about your defenses," she said. "That's your problem, not mine. I just want to test you, that's all."

"Test me? Test me how?"

"When you captured me, I recognized you. You said you were concerned about your reputation if it were known that a prostitute knew your name. But just now, you told me you had no fear of God. Surely a man who has no fear of God has no fear for his reputation."

Diaz laughed out loud.

"So, you want all the men to see you with me, is that it?"

"Precisely. The payment I want from you is your public acknowledgment of me."

Diaz held his hand out toward her. "You are a sly one. Very well, come along with me."

Marty followed Diaz outside the cloister.

"Sergeant, get a horse for the *senorita*!" he said.

"Si, Colonel."

SHORTLY, Marty was astride a horse and following Diaz through the streets of the city. For the next two hours, Marty rode beside him as they inspected the Spanish defenses around Santiago. Her sharp eyes absorbed every detail—the layout of the trenches, the positions of the forts, and the movements of the soldiers. She noticed a sizable gap in the northeast corner of the city's defenses, which piqued her interest.

"Why is there so much space between the forts here?" she asked casually.

Diaz laughed, dismissing the question with a wave. "That gap is nothing to concern yourself with. As long as we control San Juan Hill, we control the approach to the city."

Marty's gaze followed his pointing hand to the hill in the distance, where soldiers were stationed. Her instincts told her that this was a critical position.

"What if the Americans capture San Juan Hill? Then they will hold the high ground, will they not?" she asked.

Diaz laughed. "Do not try and determine military strategy, my dear. You aren't prepared for it. We know that the Americans' primary objective is Santiago. They are bold, vain men. They will try to take the city head-on…and they will fail." Diaz took out his watch and looked at it. "It is time to get back to the city."

At that moment, they were on the outskirts of Santiago, just behind the network of trenches. As they started back into the city, the road passed beneath a low-hanging silk cotton tree. Marty grabbed a limb and pulled it with her as she rode. Diaz, who was behind her, was looking off to his right and didn't see her. When Marty pulled the limb as far as she could, she released it. It slapped into Diaz with the impact of a baseball bat, unceremoniously dumping him from his horse.

"What are you doing?" Diaz shouted in surprised anger.

Marty wheeled her horse around, then grabbed the reins of Diaz's horse. She raced straight for the trench.

"Stop her! Shop her!" Diaz shouted.

The soldiers in the trench were so startled, they had no time to react. By the time they turned around to see what Colonel Diaz was yelling about, Marty had already urged her horse into a graceful leap over the trench, still leading Diaz's horse by its reins. When she was on the other side of the trench, she dropped the reins of Diaz's horse and bent low over her own animal. She was on the road, and she was getting away. She was going to make it!

Suddenly, her horse let out a little neigh, and down it went. Marty was thrown over the horse's head and she hit the ground hard.

For an instant, she didn't know what had happened. She lay on the ground with all the breath knocked out of her, looking up at the sky, trying to figure out where she was and how she got there.

Gradually, the breath returned to her body, and with it came a sense of location and the desperation of her condition. She managed to pull herself into an upright position, then she looked over at the horse. It was then that she saw why the horse had gone down. He had been shot.

The horse lay very still, killed either by the bullet that struck him, or by a broken neck from the fall. Marty wished now that she hadn't released Diaz's horse.

Before she could react, Spanish soldiers surrounded her, their rifles raised.

"Stop, *Señorita*, or we will shoot you!" one of them barked.

Marty sighed, knowing her escape had failed. Slowly, she raised her hands and began walking back toward them, her mind already spinning with what would happen next.

The church, serving as the Spanish military headquarters, also served as a military courtroom. Less than an hour after her failed escape, Marty found herself facing a military tribunal. The proceedings were moving quickly—too quickly for comfort.

Three senior officers, dressed in full military regalia, sat behind a table, serving as both judge and jury. A hastily appointed officer stood as her defense counsel while another represented the prosecution. Colonel Diaz, the man responsible for her capture, observed the trial from a corner of the room, his expression unreadable.

The prosecutor stood, reading the charges in a cold, formal tone. "The defendant, Carlotta Fernandez, is charged with espionage. She did knowingly accompany Colonel Diaz to observe the defensive positions of our forces and subsequently attempted to escape in order to relay this information to the American army."

Marty's appointed defense attorney, who hadn't spoken to her in any meaningful way, finally raised an objection.

"Objection, *señor*," he said, his voice weary. "There

is no evidence that the defendant intended to communicate this information to the Americans. She merely attempted to escape. The intent to spy has not been proven."

One of the senior officers behind the table leaned forward, looking toward the prosecutor. "How do you respond to this, *Capitán*?"

The prosecutor, barely containing a smirk, continued smoothly. "The defendant is not Carlotta Fernandez as she claimed. Colonel Diaz was led to believe she was Cuban, but we now know she is not. This woman is Marty McGuire, an American journalist. One of our informants at Siboney witnessed Miss McGuire speaking publicly to Cuban insurgents."

Murmurs rippled through the assembled crowd as the revelation sunk in.

The defense attorney turned toward Marty, surprise flickering across his face. "Are you an American?"

"Yes," Marty replied, her voice steady despite the tight knot in her stomach.

"If it please the court..." Marty's attorney said, standing and bowing slightly toward the senior officer.

"Yes?" the officer responded.

"In light of this admission, it is impossible to dispute the charge of espionage. Therefore, I plead the defendant guilty as charged and request leniency in sentencing."

"Wait!" Marty protested, rising from her chair. "I never told you I wanted to plead guilty!"

Her lawyer didn't meet her gaze. "As your appointed counsel, it is my responsibility to handle your defense as I see fit. This is the best course."

Marty's mind reeled at the betrayal. "But don't you have to consider what I want you to do?"

"No, *señorita*," he said quietly, eyes forward. "This is the court's proceeding, not yours."

"Excellency," the prosecutor said. "As the defendant stands adjudged guilty by her own lawyer, the prosecution will present no further evidence in this case. We ask that you sentence the defendant to death by firing squad, but grant her the right to a final confession and absolution by a priest."

The three officers conferred in hushed tones for a moment before the senior officer stood, placing a handkerchief on his head.

"*Senorita* Marty McGuire, this tribunal finds you guilty of espionage. You are hereby sentenced to death by firing squad at dawn on Calavera Hill. Do you have any final words?"

Marty's throat tightened, but she forced herself to stand tall. "No," she said, her voice barely above a whisper. Despite the terror coursing through her, she was determined to face them with dignity.

"May God have mercy on your soul," the senior officer said solemnly.

Two soldiers stepped forward and took Marty by the arms, leading her away from the church. As they passed by Colonel Diaz, his eyes glinted with satisfaction.

"What a stupid woman you are," he sneered.

Marty met his gaze, refusing to flinch. "My only comfort, Colonel, is knowing I won't have to worry about you putting your hands on me."

Diaz's face darkened with anger. "Whore," he hissed, slapping her hard across the face.

"Colonel Diaz!" the senior officer behind the table shouted. "Remove yourself from this court at once!"

Diaz glared at Marty, his lips curling into a cruel smile. "I will be there tomorrow," he said softly. "I will personally give the orders to the firing squad."

"I'll be dead no matter who gives the orders," Marty replied, her voice firm. "Do you think your words mean anything to me now?"

Red-faced, Diaz turned on his heel and stormed out of the church without another word.

MARTY WAS RETURNED to the small room where she had slept before, though this time a guard was stationed at the door. Inside, Sister Theresa waited, her face pale with worry.

"Is it true?" the nun asked quietly. "You are American?"

"Yes," Marty admitted, sinking onto the bed.

"And a spy?"

Marty shook her head, a bitter laugh escaping her lips. "No. I didn't intend to be a spy. I'm a journalist. As I told you, I was captured by Colonel Diaz. But none of that matters now."

Sister Theresa's eyes filled with sorrow. "A journalist at war is as brave as a spy."

"Or just as foolish," Marty said, wiping away the tears that had begun to fall. "I should have stayed with Colonel Pickett."

"Colonel Pickett?" the nun asked.

"Nelson Pickett," Marty replied, her voice softening. "He's the commander of the Lightning Cavalry… and the man I love. Or loved." She paused, her voice hollow. "By this time tomorrow, my whole life will be past tense."

NELSON DUNKED his head into the wash basin, scrubbing the grime and sand from his scalp with soap. The cool water trickled down his face as he rinsed his hair, the last remnants of the battlefield's grit slipping away. He was drying off when he noticed one of his men approaching. Beside the soldier, a figure in black moved in the shadows. At first, Nelson couldn't make out who it was, but as they drew closer, the unmistakable shape of a nun's habit came into view.

"Colonel Pickett? We picked this here woman up out at the advance lookout post. She's been babblin' somethin' in Spanish, but the only thing I could understand was your name."

"My name?" Nelson looked sharply at the nun. "She was saying my name?"

"Yes, sir."

Nelson sighed. "All right, Hobbs, thank you. I'll handle it from here. And send Lopez over. He can help translate."

Hobbs saluted and jogged off as Nelson turned to the nun. Her face was partially obscured by her wimple, but her eyes locked onto his with a sense of urgency.

"Colonel Pickett?" Her voice was soft but strained, and though she spoke his name, her accent was thick, nearly indecipherable.

"Yes, I am Colonel Nelson Pickett," he replied, hoping the hint of Spanish would help bridge the gap. "*Si, yo soy* Nelson Pickett."

She nodded quickly and pointed to herself. "Theresa."

"Sister Theresa?" Nelson asked, trying to piece it together. "All right, Sister Theresa, what can I do for you?"

She looked at Nelson with an expression that told him she didn't understand a word he said.

"Colonel Pickett, you want me, sir?" A soldier came up to his side, breathless from running.

"Private Lopez, find out what this sister is trying to tell me."

Lopez spoke to her in quick, fluent Spanish. Relief washed over her face as she responded in a hurried stream of words, her hands moving as if to emphasize the urgency.

Lopez's face paled. "*Madre de Dios*...it's Miss McGuire, Colonel. The Spaniards—" He paused, his voice catching. "They're going to execute her. They say she's a spy."

Nelson froze. "What?" His voice turned sharp. "What the hell are you talking about?"

Lopez translated as Sister Theresa continued, her voice growing more intense as she described what had happened. Nelson clenched his fists, his mind racing.

"They caught her near Santiago," Lopez explained. "She tried to get away, but they caught her again. They held a trial—if you can call it that—and sentenced her to death by firing squad at dawn."

"Where is she?" Nelson asked in a tight voice.

Lopez quickly relayed the question and then turned back to Nelson. "They're taking her outside of Santiago to the place where they execute all their criminals. I guess they figure they can get there, do the job, and then get back before we find out what's going on.

But the sister sneaked out in the dead of night to warn us. She took a big risk coming here, Colonel."

Nelson's jaw tightened. "Tell her that the United States Army is thankf…no, no, to hell with that. Tell her that I, personally, am very thankful to her for coming to me with this information. And tell her we are going to rescue Miss McGuire. Tonight."

Lopez translated the message, then Sister Theresa smiled and replied to his remarks.

Lopez chuckled under his breath. "She says Miss McGuire is wise to love such a brave man as you, Colonel."

Nelson cleared his throat, shifting uncomfortably. "That's—uh—that's not necessary to share with everyone, Lopez."

Lopez grinned. "No worries, sir. The men already know how you feel."

Nelson shot him a look but couldn't help a wry smile. "Thanks, Lopez, that'll be all. Express my thanks to the sister and see if there is anything she needs, like food or water. I'm going to have the sergeant major call for volunteers to go on the rescue mission."

"Colonel, I'd like to be the first to volunteer, sir," Lopez said, his voice firm.

"You'll be second in line," Nelson said. "I'll be the first."

THE SKY in the east was a dull gray, the first whisper of dawn still far from breaking. Marty sat on a rough wooden box in the back of a creaking wagon pulled by mules, her wrists bound loosely in front of her. Father

Damien sat beside her, the rhythmic jingle of the soldiers' bridles providing a steady, ominous beat. Two mounted soldiers led the way, with four more trailing behind—their rifles resting casually. They were the firing squad. Colonel Diaz was also riding along with them, though he kept a haughty distance. Whether he was keeping his distance from the firing squad or from her, Marty didn't know.

"I don't know where Sister Theresa is this morning," Father Damien muttered, worry etched in his voice. "It's unlike her to disappear. She should have been here to offer you comfort."

"I'm sure it was uncomfortable for her, Father," Marty said, her voice steady despite the tightening knot in her stomach.

"How generous you are," Father Damien replied, casting her a sorrowful glance. "Even now, you forgive her absence, just as our Lord forgave His persecutors on the cross. Think of our Lord, my dear. Take solace in that, my child. He suffered and died, and yet returned with the promise of eternal life for all who believed."

"Yes, Father," Marty responded, though her mind was far from thoughts of salvation. She didn't know how to explain to Father Damien that, though she was Catholic, she didn't need to hold onto that thought to comfort her. She didn't need comforting because, in truth, she wasn't frightened. She didn't know why. She knew she was going to die shortly, that this sunrise would be the last she would ever see, and yet, amazingly, she had never felt more calm or composed in her entire life. It was as if all cares and worries had been reduced to one infinitesimal grain of sand. She had less than fifteen minutes to live. It was as if someone had just told her that she had fifteen minutes to catch a train. When faced with certain death, death lost its mystery and its sting. She thought of the line from Shakespeare: *Death, where is thy sting?* The line comforted her. She'd better not tell Father Damien that she was comforted by a line from Shakespeare. She chuckled.

"What is it, my dear? Why do you laugh?" he asked, his voice lined with concern.

"Nothing, Father," she said, shaking her head.

Father Damien mumbled a prayer under his breath, crossing himself. He was afraid she was about to go crazy. All the signs were there. She had been very quiet ever since they had left Santiago. And now she was laughing.

The wagon jolted to a stop, and Marty looked up. The driver turned around and offered her an apologetic look. "We're here, *señorita*. Please, get down."

Marty slid off the box and stood beside the wagon. Only then did she notice it—the box she'd been sitting on. Her coffin.

Colonel Diaz barked an order, his impatience breaking the morning stillness. "Let's get this done," he said, spurring his horse forward. "We need to finish before the sun is above the horizon. I don't like being out in the open."

Father Damien stepped between Diaz and Marty. "Colonel, she is entitled to a final confession and to be granted absolution. It was promised to her."

Diaz's eyes narrowed. "Fine. But make it quick, Father. I want her dead and buried before the sun is fully up."

Father Damien led Marty a few paces away to a post rising from the ground. It was splintered and worn, stained with the blood of the condemned. Her heart stuttered as she realized this was where she'd be tied and shot. The weight of the moment pressed in, but she forced herself to breathe evenly.

"Bless me, Father, for I have sinned," Marty began, kneeling beside the stake. She hadn't even finished the first sentence when a sudden burst of gunfire shattered the quiet.

Shots rang out from the trees, sharp and violent, followed by a wild battle cry.

"Eeeeeyowww! Lightning Cavalry!"

Marty's head snapped toward the noise just as a line of American cavalrymen burst from the treeline, weapons flashing in the dim light. Chaos erupted around her—soldiers shouting, horses rearing, and Father Damien stumbling back in shock.

"Marty!" Nelson's voice cut through the melee. He rode out of the woods like a thunderbolt, a riderless horse at his side, and his face filled with a mix of fury and determination.

"It's Nelson!" Marty gasped. The calm that had settled over her was replaced by a surge of hope. "Father Damien, I'm saved!"

The Spanish who weren't felled by the first volley turned their horses toward Santiago and started running. The Americans gave a halfhearted chase, but the real purpose of their mission, Marty's rescue, had been accomplished.

Nelson galloped straight for her, his eyes locked on hers. As he reached the stake, he swung off his horse, rushing to her side. His arms wrapped around her, pulling her close with such force that she nearly lost her breath.

They didn't speak—there was no need. Their lips

met in a kiss, and in that moment, the world fell away. The danger, the fear, the soldiers around them—it all vanished. It was just them.

When Nelson finally pulled back, he grinned, his voice thick with relief. "Where have you been, girl? How in God's name did you end up here?"

"That's a long story," Marty said breathlessly. "But how did you know I was here? How did you find me?"

"Sister Theresa," Nelson said, his grin widening. "She risked everything to get word to us."

Marty's eyes lit up. "So, that's where she went."

Nelson nodded, his smile infectious. "That's where she went."

Father Damien, still shaken, stumbled toward them. "What…what just happened?"

Marty smiled at the priest, explaining what Sister Theresa had done, and Father Damien's eyes glistened with pride.

"Sister Theresa has done a brave and wonderful thing," he whispered.

Nelson glanced around. "Father, do you want to come with us? Santiago won't be safe for much longer."

Marty nodded. "The Spaniards have taken over his church and turned it into their headquarters."

Nelson raised an eyebrow. "Have they now? That's good to know."

Marty flashed a sly smile. "I've got plenty more information that'll be useful to you."

Nelson chuckled. "I'm sure you do. You've always had a way of getting into places you shouldn't be." His expression turned serious. "But was it worth almost getting yourself killed?"

Her smile faded as she looked at him. "When you take San Juan Hill, you'll see it was worth it."

Nelson laughed, shaking his head. "We're not attacking San Juan Hill. The plan is to take Santiago."

Marty gave him a knowing look. "Trust me. Once you see the defenses, you'll realize San Juan Hill has to fall first."

Nelson groaned, a playful grin tugging at his lips. "All right, Joan of Arc, let's get you to safety first. We'll worry about the generals later."

Nineteen

It was three o'clock in the morning on July 1st. Colonel Nelson Pickett stood in General Shafter's command tent alongside Colonel Theodore Roosevelt and Colonel Leonard Wood. The dim light of lanterns cast long shadows on the canvas walls as General Shafter, bedridden due to illness, addressed them from his cot.

"Gentlemen," Shafter began, his voice strained, "I regret to inform you that I overexerted myself yesterday. As a result, I will not be able to participate as actively in today's operations as I would like. However, new intelligence has made it clear that we must prioritize the capture of San Juan Hill."

Colonel Roosevelt exchanged a glance with Wood before speaking. "General, if I may, I believe our initial plan was to bypass the hill and push directly for the city from the south."

General Shafter shook his head. "That is exactly what the Spanish anticipate, Colonel Roosevelt. They've fortified the southern approaches heavily. But my latest intelligence suggests that their defenses in the northwest are vulnerable—once we control San Juan Hill, we'll have a clear path."

Colonel Wood leaned forward. "How strong are their positions on the hill, sir?"

"Our reports indicate approximately twelve hundred soldiers, and they are thin on artillery," Shafter replied, his gaze steady. "If we move swiftly, we can take it before they reinforce."

Roosevelt nodded, though still cautious. "I trust your information is reliable, General?"

Shafter's lips curved into a faint smile. "I have absolute confidence in the source, Colonel. Wouldn't you agree, Colonel Pickett?"

Colonel Pickett, who had been silent, thought of Marty's insistence about San Juan Hill. He allowed himself a small, knowing smile before responding. "Yes, sir. I agree with you completely. Taking the hill is the right course of action."

Shafter gave a brief nod. "Very well, then. Gentlemen, I will establish battle headquarters at the El Pozo house. Each of you will assign couriers to report back to me throughout the day. I will issue further orders from there."

The three colonels straightened to attention. "Yes, sir," they replied in unison.

"Dismissed."

With that, they saluted General Shafter before stepping out into the pre-dawn darkness. By the time Nelson returned to his regiment, the men had already broken camp. His battalions were assembled and ready, awaiting further instructions for the coming battle.

MARTY HAD RISEN EARLY, eating alongside the men. She shared the same sense of excitement and apprehension as the men, because Nelson had agreed to allow her to accompany the regiment to the line of debarkation. There, she would stay back with the reserve troops—close enough to see the battle unfold but far enough to remain safe. She was, perhaps, more anxious than anyone else. That was because she felt General Shafter's decision to attack San Juan Hill hinged on her intelligence.

Eight thousand four hundred American troops would face twelve hundred Spaniards, entrenched and well-armed. Though the numbers favored the Americans, the enemy held the high ground. That advantage could make all the difference.

"Here comes the colonel," someone murmured. Officers rose to their feet as Nelson rode into the camp, his presence commanding the men's attention. Marty remained at the edge, watching him dismount, his face calm and resolute.

Nelson addressed his officers. "Gentlemen, this is it. We've been lying around here for days now, wondering when something was going to happen. We've been watching the Spaniards dig in deeper and deeper every day, and now the time has come for us to earn our pay. We're going to take San Juan Hill."

"What about Santiago?" one of the officers asked.

"Leave Santiago to the generals. Our job is San Juan Hill. Take that, and we control the entire battlefield." Nelson's tone was sharp, decisive. "Go back to your units. We'll be in position to move by sunrise."

The officers saluted and dispersed to relay the

orders. Marty watched them leave, her nerves still buzzing with anticipation. As Nelson approached, she made her way to the campfire, pouring a cup of coffee from the pot simmering on the grill.

She brought the cup to Nelson. "Coffee?"

"Thanks," he said, taking it from her. His eyes lingered on her for a moment longer than usual, his brow creased slightly, as though he had more to say than orders for battle.

"Coffee warm enough?" Marty asked, her voice steady.

"Perfect," Nelson replied. He glanced down at the cup and then back at her. "Marty… I was a fool," he said. "I want to apologize. I shouldn't have… I've been thinking… I owe you an apology. I—"

Marty stopped him, placing a hand gently on his arm. "We've been through too much to apologize for things that don't matter."

Nelson's gaze softened. "Do you understand what you mean to me?" he asked, his voice quieter now, intimate, as if the words weren't meant for anyone but her.

Marty didn't need grand declarations. She understood. They both did. "I do," she said simply. "And I feel the same."

He nodded, his lips tightening into a brief smile. "Marty, if something happens to me—"

"Stop," she cut him off, her voice firm. "Don't talk like that. You've got a battle to fight, and we've both seen enough to know that worrying about what might happen won't change a thing. We'll deal with what comes when it comes."

Nelson exhaled, setting the coffee cup down, and in a rare moment, he pulled her close, his arms around her with a quiet intensity. No words passed between them, but everything was understood in that embrace. It wasn't about love spoken—it was about survival, about knowing that whatever happened, they had something real.

"I won't be killed," Nelson said, releasing her but keeping his eyes locked on hers. "I promise you, I won't be killed."

Marty smiled, not out of certainty but because that's what you do when facing the unknown. "Then we'll both hold you to it."

A voice called from the distance, breaking the moment. "Colonel, the troops are ready to move up to the line."

Nelson turned, all command again. "All right," he called back. "I'll be right there."

"We'll be right there," Marty added, her voice teasing, but with an edge of seriousness. She wasn't leaving him now.

Nelson chuckled. "Right. We'll be right there."

Together, they walked down the slope toward the waiting regiment. As they mounted their horses, the first light of dawn barely touched the horizon, and they rode toward San Juan Hill.

AS THE SUN ROSE, Marty could see the long line of American troops. They were all cavalrymen, but they were dismounted. They would attack San Juan Hill on foot.

Behind her, a rumble filled the air. Marty turned to see a battery of field guns being hauled into position on a nearby hill. The horses strained at the harnesses, nostrils flaring, their muscles taut as the artillery was dragged into place. The gunners worked quickly, unhooking the horses, wheeling the cannons around to face San Juan Hill. Marty could hear the clang of metal and the shouts of officers as the gun crews prepared to fire.

The first cannon roared, the blast sending a shudder through the ground. A cloud of white smoke erupted from the muzzle, and the recoil sent the cannon's wheels spinning back. Marty followed the arc of the shell as it whistled through the air, her breath catching in her throat. Seconds later, a burst of flame and smoke bloomed at the crest of the hill where the Spanish were entrenched.

More guns fired in rapid succession, filling the sky with smoke and thunder. The ground beneath Marty's feet trembled with each explosion, and the ridge was soon obscured by thick, hanging clouds of smoke. The air smelled of gunpowder and earth.

"Isn't that magnificent?" she muttered, half to herself, unable to tear her eyes away.

The moment was shattered by a sharp, rushing noise overhead. Marty flinched, her gaze moving upward as a shell burst in the sky above, raining shrapnel down like deadly hail. The whine of metal slicing through the air was followed by the sickening thud of debris crashing into trees and the ground around them.

"Shrapnel!" someone shouted. "Get down!"

Marty ducked instinctively behind a pile of rocks as another explosion rocked the regiment, this time in the center of one of the other units. Men screamed, and through the smoke, Marty saw bodies fall—some motionless, others writhing in agony.

"They've been up there too long," an officer growled nearby. "They've got the range on everything. It's going to be a hell of a job getting them out."

Before anyone could respond, a cry went up. "Balloon! Look, we've got a balloon aloft!"

Marty turned and saw it—an observation balloon rising slowly into the sky, a thin lifeline connecting it to the ground.

"Now we'll see those Spaniards!" another soldier crowed.

But Nelson, seeing the balloon, frowned, his hand brushing the scar on his face. "That's a mistake," he muttered. "I told them we needed that balloon days ago. Now it's too close to the front. All it's going to do is draw fire."

As if on cue, a burst of shrapnel tore through the air. The balloon jerked violently, punctured, and began its slow, inevitable descent, spiraling down like a wounded bird. The cheers of the Spanish could be heard even from where Marty stood.

The destruction of the balloon seemed to fire the Spaniards into a greater zeal, and the bombardment from the top of the hill increased, raking the Americans with deadly, accurate fire. Men scrambled for cover as shells exploded around them, spraying dirt and debris into the air. Marty saw more wounded men stagger back to the aid station, blood soaking through their uniforms, some dragging themselves across the ground, others carried on stretchers.

"Colonel, we're taking heavy casualties!" the sergeant major barked, running up to Nelson. "When can we move?"

Nelson's jaw clenched as he surveyed the field, the sounds of dying men mixing with the distant roar of cannon fire. "We need a coordinated attack. If we go up alone, we'll be torn apart by friendly fire."

But Marty could see the frustration in his eyes. Men were dying, pinned down by the relentless bombardment, and they hadn't even begun the charge.

More wounded poured into the field hospital, men clutching at bullet wounds or dragging shattered limbs. Marty overheard one of the injured soldiers curse through gritted teeth. "It's bad enough facing 'em when you're shooting back. This waiting…it's worse."

Suddenly, a shout rang out. "Major O'Niell's down! He's been killed!"

Nelson's face hardened. Major O'Niell had replaced Dan Calhoun as the regimental executive officer. Enough was enough.

"Sergeant Major!" Nelson barked, his voice laced with fury.

"Yes, sir?" The sergeant major ran up, eyes wide.

"I've had enough. I'm not waiting any longer for orders while our men are chopped to pieces by Spanish fire. I don't care whether Shafter gives us the word or not, we're going up! Prepare the men!"

A grin spread across the sergeant major's face. "Yes, sir!" he bellowed, already moving to relay the orders.

Nelson ran to the front of his men, the regimental flag bearer close behind him. Marty, watching from her cover, felt a surge of pride—and fear. The moment had come.

Nelson raised his saber high, his voice booming over the noise of battle. "Let's go!"

All along the line, men leaped to their feet, shouting war cries as they surged forward. Marty's heart pounded as she watched them advance—Nelson at the front, leading the charge. It wasn't just the Lightning Cavalry. The Tenth Cavalry and the Rough Riders joined the assault, their cheers blending into one deafening roar.

They moved in bursts—sprinting up the hill, dropping to their knees to fire, then surging forward again. Spanish bullets rained down, cutting through the lines, but the Americans pressed on, undeterred.

Marty could hear the rattle of Gatling guns opening fire, their rapid bursts ripping through the enemy positions. One of the Spanish blockhouses was completely subdued by the rapid-firing guns, and in the trenches near the blockhouse, a dozen Spanish soldiers broke and ran. The battle was over for them.

Along the rest of the hill, though, the Spanish riflemen stuck bravely to their posts, and their fire doubled and trebled in fierceness. The crest of the hill crackled and burst in roars and rippled with waves of tiny flame. Despite the killing rain of shot, the Americans continued to climb the hill, creeping steadily up, nearer and nearer to the top.

Just before they reached the crest of the hill, the Spanish did a courageous but foolhardy thing. They rushed out of their trenches and fortifications to meet the Americans head-on. Had they stayed under cover, they might have been able to direct enough firepower to break the back of the American assault. But once they exposed themselves, they were put at an immediate disadvantage, because they were outnumbered by their attackers. Soon, they realized their mistake and, somehow, managed to break off the fight and run. When the Americans realized they had won the battle, they let out a mighty cheer, and though several of them fired at the retreating Spanish, they seemed content with the fact that San Juan Hill had been taken.

Marty watched as Nelson reached the crest, standing tall among his men, the flag waving proudly beside him. The battle was over—but the cost had been steep.

For a moment, all was still as the smoke drifted away from the battlefield, leaving behind only the echo of victory.

SOMETIME AFTER THE BATTLE, with San Juan Hill now firmly in American hands, Marty climbed to the crest of the hill. Nelson stood at the ridge, his silhouette framed against the view of Santiago below. The city lay vulnerable, the trenches and fortifications visible from their vantage point, the path to the city now clear.

Marty stepped up beside him, her eyes sweeping the battlefield below. Nelson turned toward her, his gaze heavy but filled with relief. They embraced in silence, both feeling the weight of survival. She whispered a prayer of thanks that he had made it through.

"You were right," Nelson said, his voice gruff from exhaustion. "There's no question now. From here, Santiago is ours for the taking."

Marty looked around at the exhausted soldiers. They were spread out all along the crest of the hill, some resting where they had collapsed, others tending to the wounded or reinforcing their positions. The aftermath of the battle was plain—more than a thousand American casualties and countless Spanish lives lost. The hill was strewn with the remnants of the bloody fight, yet amid it all, Marty saw something that filled her with pride. Black soldiers from the Tenth Cavalry and white soldiers from the Lightning Cavalry worked together, laughing, helping one another like true comrades.

Later that morning, the camp began to stir as word spread that General Shafter had prepared a message for Santiago. General Wheeler approached, holding a letter in his hand.

"Colonel Pickett," Wheeler began, handing the letter to him, "General Shafter wants you to personally deliver this message to the Spanish commander."

Nelson unfolded the paper, glancing over the contents. Marty stepped closer as Nelson read the note aloud:

"I shall be obliged, unless you surrender, to shell Santiago de Cuba. Please inform the citizens of foreign countries, and all women and children, that they should leave the city before 10 o'clock tomorrow morning.

Very respectfully, your obedient servant,

William R. Shafter, Major-General, U.S.A."

Nelson nodded grimly as he refolded the letter. "Understood. I'll deliver it under a flag of truce."

"I want to go with you," Marty said immediately.

Nelson turned to her, shaking his head. "No. Absolutely not."

"Why not?" she pressed. "You'll be under a flag of truce. It's not like it's an attack."

Nelson sighed, clearly frustrated. "It's not that simple. I don't think it's a good idea to bring you along."

Before Nelson could say more, General Wheeler spoke up. "Miss McGuire, would you really want to go if you had the chance?"

"Of course I would," Marty said without hesitation.

Wheeler looked at Nelson with a thoughtful expression. "I think you ought to let her go with you, Colonel."

Nelson blinked, caught off guard. "Uncle Joe, you can't be serious."

"I am," Wheeler said firmly. "If Miss McGuire goes with you, it'll show the Spanish that we aren't playing any tricks. It's a gesture of good faith. And besides," he added with a slight smile, "she speaks Spanish. You might need her help as an interpreter."

Nelson looked at Marty, then back at Wheeler, his resolve slowly wavering. He let out a long breath, clearly outnumbered. "Fine," he said at last, turning back to Marty. "You win. But you stay close to me."

Marty nodded, her heart racing with excitement and nerves. She knew the risks, but this was a chance she couldn't pass up.

As Nelson tucked the letter into his coat, he glanced at her with a faint smile. I guess I'm outnumbered," he muttered.

Marty grinned in return, knowing she had earned her place by his side.

NELSON CALLED FOR HORSES, and within minutes, he and Marty were riding down the hill toward Santiago, both carrying white flags. Their pace was slow, deliberate, the truce flags fluttering in the breeze. They rode in silence, eyes fixed on the city ahead.

As they neared the outskirts, two Spanish riders came out to meet them, dust trailing behind them as they closed the distance. The men reined in their horses sharply, their expressions guarded. One of the riders called out in Spanish, his voice terse.

"Are either of you armed?" Marty translated quickly, her voice steady despite the knot in her stomach.

Nelson nodded to her. "Tell them no. And tell them we have a message from General Shafter to General Linares."

Marty relayed the message, her Spanish fluid and calm. After a brief exchange, the Spanish officers turned and motioned for them to follow.

As they rode into Santiago, Marty looked around. There was a great difference between what she was seeing here and what was on the hill behind them. Behind them were the bodies and wounded soldiers of this morning's battle. Even those who hadn't been wounded were showing the results of the fight. Here, though, there had been no battle. All the soldiers were fresh and unbloodied. And yet, the Americans were asking the Spanish to surrender.

Nelson and Marty were led to the old church where her trial had been, its facade cracked but still standing strong. Inside, the air was thick with tension. General Toral, acting commander in the absence of General Linares, who had been wounded in the battle, stood at the altar, his eyes hard and cold. Marty recognized him instantly—the man who had overseen her court-martial.

"I see you managed to survive the sentence our court imposed on you," General Toral said, his voice low and gravelly.

"Yes," Marty replied, meeting his gaze without flinching.

Toral rubbed a hand over his graying hair, his expression softening for a brief moment. "I'm glad," he admitted, surprising her. "I didn't feel right sentencing a woman to die, but I had to follow my duty. Honor has been served."

"I doubt Colonel Diaz would have shared your sentiment," Marty said, the memory of the cruel colonel still fresh in her mind.

"Colonel Diaz is dead. He was killed in this morning's battle."

Nelson, standing at Marty's side, stepped forward and handed Toral the letter. "We bring a message from General Shafter."

Toral took the letter and unfolded it, reading the English words silently. The lines on his face deepened as he stroked his chin, considering the ultimatum.

After a tense moment, he finally spoke. "This city will not surrender," Toral said, his voice firm. "I will inform the foreign consuls and citizens of your message, but Santiago will fight to the end."

As they turned to leave, Marty's eyes were drawn to the altar. It had been transformed into a makeshift operating table. There, a thin, pale man lay under the dim light, his body stripped to a breechclout. His frail figure reminded her, for a dizzying moment, of Christ on the cross. Marty could believe that he had just been taken down from the cross. The impression was brief, but so intense that it illuminated all the horrors of war, and Marty recalled Nelson's words. *There is no glory in war*, he had said. For a moment, everything stopped. Now, after their great victory on San Juan Hill, she understood those words more than ever. What was the victory worth to the dead on both sides? What did triumph mean when so many had been lost?

Nelson placed a hand on her shoulder, snapping her from her reverie. Without a word, they mounted their horses and rode back to the American lines, the white flags still fluttering weakly in the wind.

THE FOLLOWING DAY, refugees began pouring out of the city, but by the deadline the next morning, the Spanish army was still entrenched in and around Santiago. True to his word, General Shafter ordered the bombardment to begin. The thunder of cannons echoed across the hills as American naval ships moved into position, their eight-inch guns raining fire onto the city. The American army, entrenched on San Juan Hill, unleashed a barrage from the other side. For two relentless weeks, the skies over Santiago were filled with smoke and death.

Every day, the Spanish took casualties. Every day, their food supplies dwindled. Santiago was trapped, slowly strangled by the might of the American forces.

Finally, on Sunday, July 17th, the Spanish resistance crumbled. The formal surrender ceremony was held, the defiant city now silent in the face of inevitable defeat. Marty stood by, her notebook in hand, recording the moment, her mind still haunted by the image of the man on the altar and the cost of victory.

The Surrender of Santiago

By Marty McGuire, Special Correspondent

Santiago de Cuba, July 17, 1898—In a scene of both dignity and solemnity, the Spanish forces in Santiago formally surrendered to the United States

Army. General William R. Shafter, accompanied by the distinguished officers of his staff, including Colonel Nelson Pickett and a troop from the renowned Lightning Cavalry, rode to a broad field near the city. There, they were met by General José Toral, who was accompanied by one hundred of his remaining Spanish soldiers, their faces a reflection of the hard-fought struggle they had endured.

In a moment that will be remembered with honor by both sides, General Shafter performed a magnanimous gesture, presenting General Toral with the sword and spurs of the late General Vara del Rey, a valiant Spanish officer who fell at El Caney. This act, noble in its intent, was a fitting tribute to the bravery of the Spanish defenders.

Following this, the Spanish troops presented arms for the final time, as the flag that had flown over Santiago for 382 years was slowly lowered and furled. It was a moment heavy with history as the banner of Spain, which had long symbolized their reign over the island, came down for the last time. In respect, the American soldiers also presented arms, acknowledging the gravity of the occasion.

After the flag was lowered, the combined forces rode into the heart of Santiago. The Spanish army, now disarmed, surrendered their weapons to an armory, marking the official end of the Spanish military presence in the city.

By midday, the plaza in Santiago was filled with thousands of spectators who had gathered to witness the raising of the American flag over the governor's palace. At precisely noon, as the stars and stripes ascended, a salute of twenty-one guns echoed through the air, and the band struck up the strains of Hail Columbia. *It was a moment of triumph for the American forces and the beginning of a new chapter for Cuba.*

An unexpected bonus resulted from the surrender of Santiago, a bonus that not only pacified the city, but effectively ended the entire war. During the final arrangements, General Toral asked General Shafter if the surrender included his entire command. General Shafter, who had negotiated only for Santiago, was surprised by the question, and he asked Marty to repeat it.

"He wants to know if your demand for surrender includes his entire command?" Marty said again.

General Shafter, having believed the surrender negotiations were solely for Santiago, looked perplexed. "Ask him what he means by that," he instructed.

Marty relayed the question to General Toral, whose reply came swiftly. "I have 11,500 men here in Santiago," he explained. "But in addition, I command 7,000 troops stationed in Guantánamo, 3,500 at San Luis, and another 1,500 encamped thirty miles from here."

Shafter's eyes widened slightly, the significance of the moment not lost on him. Until now, the American forces had focused primarily on securing Santiago, with its strategic location and harbor under Spanish control. But here was Toral, offering up the surrender of not just the city but the entirety of the Spanish forces under his command in eastern Cuba.

"Certainly," Shafter replied quickly, realizing the opportunity before him. "The surrender includes everyone under your command, General."

There was no argument from Toral, only a nod of

acceptance. "Very well," he said without argument. "I shall arrange for their arms to be turned over to you."

The magnitude of this agreement was profound. General Toral's forces had been among the last remaining Spanish troops in Cuba. With the surrender of Santiago and now Guantánamo, San Luis, and the outlying camps, the Spanish military presence in the eastern half of the island had effectively collapsed. This single act of surrender, negotiated almost in passing, dealt a death blow to Spain's ability to wage war in Cuba.

What had begun as a local surrender quickly became a turning point in the war. The collapse of Spanish resistance in eastern Cuba, combined with the American naval victory at Santiago's harbor, sealed Spain's fate. Within weeks, the Spanish government would sue for peace, bringing the war to a close.

Marty, standing beside Nelson, could see the weight of the moment settling over both generals. The war, which had raged for months, was nearing its end—not through continued bloodshed but through an act of quiet surrender.

With decisive victories in Puerto Rico and the Philippines, the Spanish-American War reached its conclusion. In Puerto Rico, the US forces swiftly overcame the Spanish defenders, with General Nelson Miles leading a successful invasion. The island, though only a short campaign, would soon fall under American control. Thousands of miles away, in the Philippines, Admiral George Dewey had shattered the Spanish fleet in Manila Bay at the very start of the war, and US troops under General Wesley Merritt secured the final surrender of Spanish forces in the region. These victories on distant shores signaled the collapse of Spain's once-mighty empire and marked the rise of the United States as a global power.

AT A DINNER HELD to celebrate the victory, Colonel Theodore Roosevelt handed a letter to Marty. It was from John Hay, the US ambassador to England.

"It's a splendid little war," Hay had written, "begun with the highest motives, carried on with magnificent intelligence and spirit, favored by that fortune which loves the brave."

Marty read the words aloud to the gathered officers. When she finished, Roosevelt leaned back in his chair, a thoughtful expression on his face.

"I'll tell you this," Roosevelt said, his voice carrying across the table. "It may have been a 'splendid little war,' as Hay calls it, but it has forever changed the history of the world. The United States is now a world power, with territories spread across the globe—from Puerto Rico to the Philippines."

Marty looked up from the letter, her eyes searching Roosevelt's face. "Colonel Roosevelt, do you really believe the United States will take Spain's place in Cuba?"

Roosevelt smiled but shook his head. "Annex Cuba? There are some who think we should, but I believe the right thing to do is grant Cuba her freedom. She's earned it, and I believe Cuba will stand as a new, independent nation in our hemisphere. A hundred years from now, she'll still be a strong ally."

Nelson, who had been listening quietly, raised an eyebrow. "A lot can happen in a hundred years, Colonel. It's a long time to predict alliances."

Roosevelt nodded, polishing his glasses thoughtfully. "Perhaps so," he admitted, "but I like to think that the values of freedom and democracy will guide us both." He glanced at Nelson and Marty, a glint of humor returning to his eyes. "I suppose that's a question for your grandchildren to answer."

Marty blushed as Roosevelt's meaning sank in, and Nelson smiled. "It's a little early to be talking about grandchildren, don't you think?" he said, chuckling.

"Grandchildren are the natural result of children," Roosevelt replied matter-of-factly. "And children, well, they're the natural result of marriage. You two are planning to get married, aren't you? Or has Father Damien gone to all that trouble to get his church in order for nothing?"

Nelson shifted in his chair, caught off guard. "Well, I…we hadn't planned to get married here in Cuba. We were thinking of waiting until we got back to New York."

"Why wait?" General Shafter chimed in, his booming voice joining the conversation as he stepped into the circle. "If Father Damien has prepared his church, I see no reason why you can't get married right here."

"Indeed," General Wheeler added with a smile. "There are plenty of places to stay until you return to the States. And besides, a wedding would be a fine way to lift morale."

Roosevelt grinned broadly. "Imagine it—a wedding amid the closing days of a war! It'll remind the men what they've been fighting for."

Nelson turned to Marty, a new light in his eyes. Taking her hands in his, he smiled warmly. "What do you think?" he asked softly. "Would you be willing to marry me here? I know it's probably not what you had in mind, but—"

Marty, smiling, placed her fingers gently on his lips to silence him. "Silly," she whispered, her eyes shining. "I had this in mind from the moment I set foot on the *Conqueror*."

Nelson blinked in surprise. "You mean…you knew all along?"

Before he could finish his thought, Marty leaned forward and kissed him, unbothered by the presence of generals and officers around them. It was a kiss that carried with it all the emotion, the shared dangers, and the unspoken promises of their journey together.

Nelson made no move to break away, returning the kiss with the same passion. In that moment, it didn't matter where they were—whether in Cuba, New York, or anywhere else. What mattered was that they had found each other amid the chaos of war, and now they had a lifetime ahead to share together.

As the conversation around them resumed, Marty leaned against Nelson's shoulder, feeling the warmth of his presence. The war was over. The future was uncertain, but together, they would face whatever came next, just as they had faced everything so far.

The world had changed, but for Nelson and Marty, it was only the beginning.

A Look At:

Trail to Brimstone

In the unforgiving Wild West, a man's reputation can be as deadly as his aim.

Dane Calder is known for one thing: never missing his mark. As a seasoned bounty hunter, he's set his sights on the notorious Cottrell gang, infamous for their ruthless crimes across the frontier. With a lucrative bounty on their heads, Dane plans to offer them a simple choice—surrender to justice or meet their fates in a gun blazing showdown.

Tracking the dwindling outlaws through rugged terrain, Dane faces deceptive tactics that test even his seasoned abilities. And as each confrontation blurs the line between hunter and hunted and he closes in on the gang's elusive leader, a final showdown looms that will not only test his skill but also force him to make a choice that will define his legacy in the annals of the West.

In a land where bullets speak louder than words, can Dane Calder deliver a reckoning on the bloody trail to Brimstone?

AVAILABLE NOW

About the Author

Robert Vaughan sold his first book when he was nineteen. That was several years and nearly five-hundred books ago. Since then, he has written the novelization for the mini-series Andersonville, as well as wrote, produced, and appeared in the History Channel documentary Vietnam Homecoming.

Vaughan's books have hit the *NYT* bestseller list seven times. He has won the Spur Award, the Porgie Award in Best Paperback Original, the Western Fictioneers Lifetime Achievement Award, the Read-west President's Award for Excellence in Western Fiction, and is a member of the American Writers Hall of Fame and a Pulitzer Prize nominee.

He is also a retired army officer, helicopter pilot with three tours in Vietnam, who has received the Distinguished Flying Cross, the Purple Heart, The Bronze Star with three oak leaf clusters, the Air Medal for valor with 35 oak leaf clusters, the Army Commendation Medal, the Meritorious Service Medal, and the Vietnamese Cross of Gallantry.